"I Think You Want Me Only Because I Fight You."

"It's not true," he protested. "I don't care how you come to me. I lie in my bed at night and I dream of you coming into my bedroom, and you put your hand on me, and you want me. I want you fighting; I want you willing; I want you in every way there is, Kate. It doesn't matter to me. I just want to hear you say the word to me."

"I've said it," she keened helplessly, as his mouth burned against her skin. "Whatever word you've wanted to hear from me, I've said a hundred times."

Dear Reader,

When two people fall in love, the world is suddenly new and exciting, and it's that same excitement we bring to you in Silhouette Intimate Moments. These are stories with scope, with grandeur. These characters lead the lives we all dream of, and everything they do reflects the wonder of being in love.

Longer and more sensuous than most romances, Silhouette Intimate Moments novels take you away from everyday life and let you share the magic of love. Adventure, glamour, drama, even suspense—these are the passwords that let you into a world where love has a power beyond the ordinary, where the best authors in the field today create stories of love and commitment that will stay with you always.

In coming months look for novels by your favorite authors: Maura Seger, Parris Afton Bonds, Elizabeth Lowell and Erin St. Claire, to name just a few. And whenever you buy books, look for all the Silhouette Intimate Moments, love stories *for* today's women *by* today's women.

Leslie J. Wainger
Senior Editor
Silhouette Books

IMRL-7/85

The Male Chauvinist

Alexandra Sellers

Silhouette Intimate Moments

Published by Silhouette Books New York

America's Publisher of Contemporary Romance

For Sophia, for Veta
and
for the Goddess

SILHOUETTE BOOKS
300 E. 42nd St., New York, N.Y. 10017

Copyright © 1985 by Alexandra Sellers

Distributed by Pocket Books

ISBN: 0-373-07110-8

First Silhouette Books printing September 1985

10 9 8 7 6 5 4 3 2 1

America's Publisher of Contemporary Romance

Printed in the U.S.A.

Silhouette Books by Alexandra Sellers

The Real Man (IM #73)
The Male Chauvinist (IM #110)

ALEXANDRA SELLERS

used to make people read to her for hours. She wrote her first short story at ten, but as an adult got sidetracked and wasn't published until she was twenty-seven. She also loves travel; she wrote her first book in Israel and began this one in Greece.

The male and the female equally I sing.
—Walt Whitman

AUTHOR'S NOTE

The archaeological information in this book is, to the best of my knowledge, correct. All quotes, sources and facts I have cited regarding Atlantis, Crete, Santoríni and the Sanctuary site on Samothráki are also, to the best of my knowledge and belief, correct.

Neathera, its site, its history and its excavation are wholly imaginary. The opinions and deductions of the characters in this book with regard to Neathera and the above-mentioned islands and sites are entirely their own, and to the best of my knowledge have, unless otherwise stated in the text, not been proffered by anyone before.

The name Andreas, in Greece, is pronounced An-*dray*-as except when he is being directly addressed; then it becomes Andrea and is pronounced An-*dray*-ah.

Chapter 1
KÉRKYRA

THE SEA WAS CALM TODAY. TWO SANDY-HAIRED, naked children were digging a hole to China with bucket, spade and their bare hands. Kate had seen them before, sitting primly at a table in the taverna with their parents, and they had then been totally unremarkable. Now their unconscious delight in their nakedness, their abandonment, transformed them. They pressed their wet bodies into the sand, they sprawled, they ran, they fell laughing into the sea, quite unaware of any taboo prohibiting the joy they experienced from their bodies. There was no self-consciousness about them, no sly awareness of their bodies as wrong or sinful. Just innocent delight.

Which was perhaps not the only sign that the world was changing. Up and down the beach, women of all ages and shapes went topless, demanding and achieving a new freedom—or the illusion of one, Kate reminded herself cynically. Because on most of the beaches of

7

North America and England, these very same women would be protected—relatively decorously—by the now discarded tops of their brief bikinis.

As she would herself. And why was that? Why was her freedom being dictated like this by a simple question of geography? And since it was, could it be called freedom? Perhaps it wasn't a question of emancipation at all, but of fashion? Perhaps she and all the other topless women along the half-mile stretch of Mediterranean sand were simply succumbing to a different style of fetter?

It was something to think about. Maybe something to write about, when she could manage the objectivity. For she didn't want to believe that the freedom she felt in being able to swim or lie on the beach nearly naked and yet unmolested by strange men was only a conditioned response. For years she had felt hampered by the moral code that dictated the particular parts of her body that must remain covered in her particular society; she had felt it alien to herself. No inner voice had ever told her that certain parts of her body were shameful. She had always felt the arbitrariness of it, right from a child, exactly as she would feel now, if a missionary group from a distant planet had insisted that she wear coverings on her knees, or her ears, or her neck. And presumably all these other women, now relievedly stripping down to the one essential covering still demanded by society, felt the same?

So, if it was not instinctive in women, which could be proven a thousand ways here in Greece alone, by reference to the ancient Greek glorification of both male and female nudity, what had caused the taboo in the first place? Or who?

Well, monotheistic religion, for a start. Judaism, Christianity and Islam all seemed to have gone a little rabid on the subject of female modesty. But of course all the great monotheistic religions had more in common than the One God: they were all also fiercely male-supremacist.

Men. Would it always come down to men, in the end? Men, who, in the modern world, saw only certain areas of the body as sexual and therefore insisted—through the power of their ownership over women's bodies—on their right to keep their possessions hidden from public view?

Was that why women of every age and shape grasped this new freedom so determinedly? Because it was more than just the freedom to swim unhampered by an extra bit of cloth? It was women's staking out of a new territory of ownership over themselves, their own bodies.

Worth an essay, anyway, she thought. And how interesting—if predictable—it was, that men responded by desexualizing the breast. On this beach, anyway, the female breast was no longer an erogenous zone. The only men who looked more than once, even at those women who were obviously alone, were the old Greek men wandering up and down selling oranges, figs and cherries on the beach.

So while women saw this new trend as establishing ownership over their own bodies, men were simply abandoning the importance they had previously given the area called *breast,* and were satisfied that their ownership was still signified by that one area of the body still left covered. And presumably, if women began stripping completely, men would shift again, taking comfort in some other area of exclusivity, like cooking or sex—giving up territory in one area only to grab it in another, but always, ever, with the determination that their women would not be free.

If she stripped off the tiny piece of material that lay between her and total nudity now, Kate supposed, she would immediately be plagued by stares and advances from all the lone male cruisers. It would be a sign of some sort, some sort of signal that she had abandoned the right to privacy, that she had no current "owner." Yet if she moved one-half mile down the beach, to the so-called wild beach, the nudist beach of Corfu, she would attract no more attention than she did now here. Or, if she could go back five years in time, she might be arrested on this beach for having disposed of her bikini top. And not a few of the women now themselves going topless would be sniffing in outrage over her "behaviour." Five years in the future—well, the trend then might be a continuation towards total nudity, or it might have leaped backwards to conventional modesty; she might get arrested five years in the future, too.

And the same people might sniff in outrage. Not, as they thought, because she was indecent. But because she was operating outside of the current trend.

One of the problems for a feminist writer was in trying to separate the "feminist" issues from such phenomena as "place and time" and "trend." Because of course at the bottom everything was connected; in the past few years she had come to understand that you couldn't effectively separate an issue like women's ownership over their bodies from the larger ideas like human freedom—or collective blindness—or conditioned response.

Kate would have preferred not to separate them, but her first book had been seen as a feminist tract—not least because of the trend she herself had been caught up in while writing it—and now the magazines she contributed to still preferred her by-line to deliver a feminist viewpoint.

And she delivered, partly because she was not sure yet how the feminist viewpoint did connect with the other areas of human experience she was slowly allowing herself to investigate. And partly because there was no point in trying to pretend that a writer was "free."

She was aware that her second book, which had just been published, was in danger of being widely viewed as another feminist tract, though in her view it encompassed a great deal more than feminism. She had wanted, with that book, to shift the public perception of her, to finally cause people—the critics—to see her as not entirely inhabiting that now stereotyped area of thought known as "sex-role consciousness."

But although she could be certain of what she was putting into the book, it was not in her power to dictate how it would be read. Even very intelligent reviewers and readers were affected by their expectations.

And they were expecting a feminist diatribe from Katherine Fenton.

A man was coming along the beach towards her. He was wearing the determinedly invasive gaze that she particularly resented, especially after the trend of her thoughts during the past half hour. It was the gaze of a man assessing his chances, assessing her. In answer, she allowed her own eyes to glide over him, cool, dismissing, and then away, as though what she had seen was not worth going over twice. It was a look that worked, for the most part: there weren't many men so eager to court rejection that they would challenge the unspoken message in that look, and besides, there were plenty of very attractive women on the beach. If he had any sense he should realize he'd be better off approaching someone else.

But there were exceptions to every rule, and this looked like one of them, because the man was coming steadily on, pretty obviously making straight for her.

This time, with her eyes slitted against the sun, she

allowed herself to assess him. Wearing shorts and an open shirt, he was dark, hairy, thick-knit—everything she least liked in a man. He wasn't her type at all.

He was probably a Greek, and definitely a male chauvinist. Every line of his body, every movement, every assessing glance, bespoke the man who is sure of having been born into the ruling caste, as far as Kate could see, the man who is convinced of his own superiority, and constantly aware of his sexual power.

But as those last derogatory words slipped mechanically through her mind, they jarred. Part of the ruling caste he might consider himself, she realized, watching, and he might even be convinced of his own superiority. But there was no consciousness of his sexual power in this man. It was something else that she sensed in him, and she lay watching him with heightened interest. She wanted to pinpoint the quality she sensed in him, as she did most things in life, for the sense of satisfaction it gave her analytical side. . . .

He was making for her as directly as he could, weaving a path between the beach beds, the faded umbrellas and the brown bodies that lay at random in his path. His gaze sometimes dropped to flicker lazily over a woman here or there who offered her body up to the sun in a particularly abandoned pose, and there was something in his posture, in his attitude—that quality that she did not recognize. But though several of the women were alone, the man did not pause in his progress towards her.

Kate herself was lying in a fairly abandoned pose; she loved the sun, the way it beat into her body, and as the man came closer she dropped her head back and remained as she was, her legs lazily apart, her arms above her head, her whole body eager for the caress of the sun. Only her eyes changed, to squint at him in frank and curious challenge, as he moved across the golden sand and walked straight up under her umbrella and stood looking down at her, at her body naked and languid under the burning sun, looking at her as though he would like to drive her mad with sex.

"Miss Fenton?" he said abruptly, veiling the look with what seemed conscious effort. "My name is Constantinou."

Kate shot upright, propelled as much by the shock of the message in his eyes as by the sound of his name. "Constantinou?" she repeated, groping with one hand for her shirt and gazing at him open-mouthed while dismay rushed through her. "Andreas Constantinou?"

He nodded, and she felt a burst of irritation. Damn it all anyway, what a way to be forced to meet the man—three-quarters naked and covered with oil! What had he hunted her down here for? Nobody conducted business on a beach! But she must not let her irritation show. She needed him; he didn't need her. Kate forced her annoyance back, smiled pleasantly and offered her hand. "What a pleasure to meet you! How on earth did you know where to find me?"

When he released her oiled, sand-dusted hand, she slipped her arms into the old buttonless blue cotton shirt that matched her blue denim-look monokini, and instead of tying it underneath her breasts, as she usually did, she wrapped it across her stomach and folded her arms.

Amazing how much less vulnerable you felt with your body covered, in spite of everything. No wonder even the pagans had "girded their loins" before going into battle.

"My cousin Sophia called me last night from Athens to tell me to expect a call from you," Constantinou was saying. That was all part of the plan, but why hadn't he stayed home and waited for her to call? "And the owner of your hotel is a friend of mine who took the

trouble to point you out to me. I came in order to save
the time and trouble of further—"

"Well, thank you, but I—"

"Not your time and trouble, Miss Fenton. My own."
His speech was accented, his voice strong and certain,
and he was smiling a little—a cool smile, but she had
the uncomfortable, edgy feeling that the dark look he
had greeted her with, and which she was still involuntarily remembering, was only a blink away, behind the
veil. "I am not giving permission this year, to you or to
anyone else, to visit the Samothrákian dig. I am sorry if
your long trip has been wasted, but we did tell you so
when we replied to your letters."

Kate made an involuntary grimace. She'd been hoping that he was too busy and preoccupied to connect his
cousin Sophia's writer friend in Athens with the person
who had written from Toronto two months ago and
been so unceremoniously rebuffed. Well, it was a
setback, but Kate wasn't finished yet. She had met a lot
of people in her work who were initially hostile to the
idea of her research.

"I promise you I'm not interested in jumping the gun
on any archaeological announcements you're planning
to make," she began. Andreas Constantinou was an
expert in Bronze Age Greece, and his latest dig, about
to start in earnest on the remote island of Samothráki,
was apparently already a subject of interest in the
archaeological world. But Kate's interest wasn't really
archaeology. Archaeology to her was only secondary;
he could keep all the glory for himself in any discoveries about his Bronze Age inhabitants of Samothráki.
She wished she could make that clear enough for him to
be able to accept it. "I'm truly only interested in getting
a firsthand look at something that may uncover—"

"The status of women in prehistory," he finished for
her, proving that he remembered not only her name

from the letters, but also the subject matter of the book she was working on.

"Yes," she said urgently. "You understand I'm hoping to show that in prehistory—in particular in pregeometric period Greece—women were equal, or even considered the superior sex. There's written evidence, of course, in Herodotus and elsewhere, that in some areas women's equality came down even to historic times, but what I want to show is broader than that. I want to look at prehistorical evidence for women in the priesthood, and as monarchs and deities—examine the cults of Athena and Demeter for clues to their precursors in the prehistoric world. I'm hoping that you'll—"

Constantinou interrupted her again. "I know all this, Miss Fenton. I wish you luck with your theory. But unless you wish to wait a year or so until my preliminary findings are published, you must write your book without any information or help from me. Only what I've already published on previous sites—this might be of help to you; this of course you are welcome to use."

She was stunned at his adamance. "But *why*? I mean—you know I'm not an archaeologist. You know exactly what I'm looking for, and it's undoubtedly only secondary to your own search. . . ."

The tail of her shirt was wet with seawater, and the wind was making it uncomfortably clammy against her hips. Absently Kate unwrapped her arms, pulled the shirttails up and tied them in their more accustomed place, against her brown midriff. "Look, if you're worried about what I may publish, I've signed guarantees before; I can give you the right to vet my book before publication."

"I'm sorry," he said finally, as if that were the end of it. Unless he had some incredible secret to protect, this was the most pigheaded person she'd met up with in a long, long time. Kate felt fury, the old, familiar fury against irrationality, turn over in her stomach. "Look," she said reasonably. "I don't know who you think I am, but I promise you, I am not a sensation-seeker, Mr. Constantinou. I am a serious writer. I've written two books on—"

"I know who you are, Miss Fenton," he interrupted again. "I have been at pains to tell you so, so that I would not insult you." She began to feel a real dislike for this indifferent man, whose feet had sunk into the sand a couple of inches so that he was now at eye level with her. Good. She had more confidence when dealing on a level. "But you must understand that a hundred others just like you also write me, and for the moment we turn them all away. We even see them come from thousands of miles away, like you, after we have explained to them, that we do not allow—"

"But why not?" she demanded, interrupting in her turn, partly because she was smarting under that "hundred others just like you," and partly to show him that sauce for the goose was sauce for the gander. "Believe me, in my work I've interviewed many scientists just like you, and not one of them has ever complained that I've significantly anticipated anything they were going to publish themselves. In fact, if anything, they've been happy for me to provide a forum for their views, which they felt didn't in any way hamper their later expansion of their own themes in . . ."

This time he didn't interrupt. Kate stopped because he was standing there shaking his head. "I'm sorry. No," he said again, as though she were being unwarrantably importunate. Kate cursed under her breath, wanting to stop this, wanting to tell him he could take his dig and his theories and put them somewhere uncomfortable, knowing she could get along without Andreas Constantinou, who was, after all, only one

Bronze Age expert among many. But she couldn't do it. Even while she was telling herself to shut up and let it go, she heard herself saying, "All right, look. Can I just come and interview you for a couple of hours? Maybe you could—"

He was shaking his head again, in that infuriatingly chauvinist way, so that she felt like a little girl being refused a treat by a firm but tolerant father. Kate closed her eyes, because masculine patronization made her see red every time.

"We are talking to no one; I'm sorry. We allow only fellow archaeologists to visit." And if he didn't stop using that damned royal *we*, she was going to slug him.

Well, since she was going to have to concede defeat, Kate could afford to be rude. She laughed at him and said, "What *are* you protecting? The lost treasure of Atlantis?"

Andreas Constantinou went very, very still, and his black eyes were suddenly riveted on her. He reminded her of a cat who watches for movement from a mouse he is not sure is alive or dead.

Then, in a voice calculated to convince her that she had said something childishly stupid, he said, "Where did you get that idea?"

But he said it one beat too late, and Kate had had her innings getting information out of hostile sources for her first book. She knew the signs by now.

"Just a rumour I picked up," she lied offhandedly; and now the mouse watched back.

"It's impossible," he muttered, more to himself than to her. He shook his head. "No one could be so stupid."

Kate grinned. "Your workers, you mean? Maybe it wasn't stupidity. Maybe they were paid well for the tip."

Suddenly he was very much *there*, all his personality

focused on her. A kind of raw energy emanated from
him, the sort of energy that she had felt in that
unexpected moment when he had first stood looking
down at her. Kate felt the full force of a high-burn
vitality that would blaze through life, leaving its mark
on everything it touched. It was a way of meeting life
that Kate recognized, from long ago and far away, and
inside her some distant, nearly dead fire, grey after
years of suffocation, puffed, extraordinarily, into flame.

She discovered that she wanted to hit him.

But the cat had decided the mouse was dead, after
all. Constantinou smiled slowly. "Tip?" he said.
"Don't be ridiculous. Do you really imagine there
could be any basis for thinking I had found Atlantis? I
am not afraid of any such 'tip' leaking out from the
team. What I fear, what any archaeologist fears, is the
sort of wild rumour that will convince a credulous
public that he has found some famous or rich ancient
site, and bring them flocking, press and sensation-
seekers all over the place. Not to mention those thieves
who supply the world black market in antiquities."

"Oh," Kate said softly, blinking at him, reserving
judgement on whether that were the truth or just dust
in her eyes.

He stared at her from black eyes for a silent moment.
"You're a dangerous woman," he said after a moment.
Kate felt a little thrill of anticipation. It would be quite
an experience to lock horns with this man. "Did you
make it up, or is there really such a rumour?"

She didn't answer. She didn't because the look was
back in his eyes as he gazed at her, and when she
opened her mouth to speak, she found she was sucking
air in in a little involuntary gasp.

"Will you please stop that!" she demanded unthink-
ingly, because he had caught her on the raw.

"Stop what?"

She told him coldly, "Stop mentally undressing me. I don't like it." And when he laughed she knew she had let herself in for it. What was she thinking of, to be challenging him so openly? No man ever admitted to that kind of sexist preoccupation, and all he had to do to make her feel small now was let her know that she was rating her attractions too highly. She had learned long ago never to leave herself open to that kind of mockery.

Yet she knew, and men knew, that a woman's sexual attraction had nothing to do with it. Undressing a woman with your eyes was just one more form of deliberate degradation.

There was also the fact that he hadn't actually taken his eyes off her face when she'd challenged him. It wasn't her body that the man was imagining naked; it was her soul. The look was shocking, because he had been seeing her the way she would look while he was making love to her, and because for one moment she had wanted to experience the unknown pleasures that the look promised.

But Andreas Constantinou was laughing for another reason. "But I don't have to," he pointed out with a look of lazy purpose in his eyes, as for the first time his glance took in her body.

It took her a moment to understand what he meant, and then she was very conscious of the tiny, stylish monokini she wore: two little triangles of mock denim, front and back, joined across the hips with fabric no wider than a bootlace; and above it, after a long stretch of brown, oiled skin, the soft folds of the denim shirt tied under her breasts, the small upstanding collar accentuating the deep V that was open to the knot.

Some people would certainly say she was more undressed than dressed; but Kate made no instinctive move to cover herself or to let down the shirt again.

Her instincts were all the other way. She straightened a little, and set her hands on her hips and looked at him, and suddenly she felt the sexual provocation in her own actions. It was as though she were wordlessly challenging him to make good on his promise. She took a small, surprised, laughing breath. This wasn't like her.

Suddenly Kate Fenton snapped to attention. For God's sake, was she getting weak in the head? He wasn't even her type; he wasn't her type *at all*. She couldn't stand the sex-before-anything mentality, for a start. And she didn't like all that intensity.

And besides, she had a job to do.

She said, "Are you going to give me an interview, Mr. Constantinou?"

Without wishing it, she found her gaze locked with his again. "What exactly is it you're offering?" he asked, surprised and intent.

She drew back, angry, fierce, not stopping to think how her question, following on that sudden thrill of provocation, might legitimately have been misconstrued. "How dare you!" she demanded. "Who do you think you are?"

He was burning her up with that look, and she recognized for the first time that the look was involuntary, not deliberate, but she did not know what the discovery meant. It seemed irrelevant to her.

Constantinou was shrugging, reining the look in. "Good day, Miss Fenton," he said, turning away. Irrationally, she felt the rebuff as a personal one. She felt as though he had slapped her both professionally and sexually, and even though she told herself that was ridiculous, she felt her quick anger coming to her rescue.

She was furious, but fury was not an emotion she'd had much practice in dealing with lately. Like so many other women, she had had it drummed into her through much of her childhood that female anger was inappropriate, unattractive. Hotheaded little Katie Fenton hadn't been supposed to *feel* anger.

So here she was, her nails digging into her palms, wanting nothing so much as to fling herself at that damned back moving away from her and claw it to ribbons. She didn't, of course. Instead she took refuge in a childish taunt. "Going back to Atlantis?" she called. "Going to keep all that lost treasure for yourself?"

He stopped and turned and narrowed his eyes at her. Now, she realized, *he* was angry, and he was probably a lot better at expressing it than she was. With the air of someone who was about to make her feel intellectually insignificant, he said, "There are many things more valuable to an archaeologist, Miss Fenton, than buried treasure, believe me."

And that was no more than the truth, Kate knew. But this time, she knew as if she'd been told, it was also something less than the truth. She had a sudden, overwhelming feeling of discovery.

Well, I've really hit it this time, she was telling herself silently, grinning at Constantinou in a way she couldn't control. This is the kind of luck destined to make me think I should have been an investigative reporter. He shouldn't have turned back, he shouldn't have answered, because he's given himself away. This guy thinks—Andreas Constantinou, an archaeologist respected by all his colleagues—really, truly thinks he's found the lost continent of Atlantis.

And he wants to keep it all to himself.

Chapter 2

ATHENS

IF HER YEARS AS A WRITER—OR, AS SHE WOULD have called herself, an observer of life—had taught Kate Fenton one thing, it was this: that somehow everything in life was connected. For that reason, she rarely refused to allow herself to be sidetracked from whatever project was at hand into any interesting byways that presented themselves during the course of her research. She was, in any case, more interested in observing than in writing, but, as often as not, what had initially appeared to be an unconnected digression proved to lead her straight back onto the main theme.

At the moment, it was difficult to conceive how an archaeologist's possible conviction that he had discovered the lost civilisation of Atlantis could have any bearing on the role of women in prehistory, but it was nevertheless far too compelling to ignore. Whatever Andreas Constantinou had found on Samothráki, the chances were that the eyes of the world were going to be riveted on him at some not-too-distant date; and Kate had the chance right now of firsthand observation.

Personally, she thought he must be mad. Or going the way of such men as Erich von Daniken, who drew extraordinary conclusions from doubtful facts; but for a man of Constantinou's apparent standing in the archaeological world, that would be the equivalent of madness. For a start, he was a Bronze Age specialist, and Atlantis was supposed to have existed thousands of years before the Bronze Age, if her memory served her correctly. And besides, the whole point about Atlantis was that it had sunk without a trace. Of course, there had been all kinds of speculation over the years that it hadn't sunk in any way except metaphorically. Could the man possibly be trying to prove . . .

"Where was Atlantis supposed to be?" she asked her friend Sophia over dinner the next night in Athens. There had been no point in remaining on Kérkyra, the beautiful island where both Sophia and her cousin had been raised, and where he still returned, as Sophia had explained, for a holiday every year. There had been no point, because as far as Andreas Constantinou was concerned, she had ceased to exist the moment he'd left her on the beach.

Sophia shrugged in the Greek fashion: pushing out her lower lip and chin. "*I* don't know," she said. "Wasn't it in the Atlantic Ocean? That's why it's called Atlantis, isn't it?"

"Or that's why the Atlantic is called the Atlantic," Kate agreed, spearing another succulent meatball with her fork and closing her eyes in appreciation as she chewed it. Sophia was the best cook she had ever met in her life, inside or outside a restaurant. "When I get home," she said absently, "Canadian food is going to taste like sawdust after this. Where did the legend come from?" She speared another meatball.

Sophia pushed her lower lip out again and grinned. She hadn't stopped grinning ever since Kate had described her meeting on the beach with Andreas. "*I* don't know," she said again. Sophia spoke fluent English but had an idiosyncratic pattern of emphasis. "From the Egyptians, maybe?"

"The Egyptians? God, I hope it's closer to home than that!" Kate responded, ripping her bread apart with her hands in the approved manner and soaking a bit in the olive oil and oregano that dressed the tomato and onion salad. Then she glared at it for a moment before popping it into her mouth. "Your cousin Andreas," she told Sophia darkly, "is a male chauvinist."

"He is?" She had heard the story the moment a still irate Kate had climbed off the plane in Athens, but she wasn't averse to hearing it again.

"He'd have had us making love right there on the beach if I'd let him." Kate had a well-known talent for exaggeration, and right now she was remembering that intense look and her shocked response to it as though it had only just happened. "Probably he thinks women are only good for one thing. I'll bet he wouldn't give me an interview because he hates to admit the possibility that there was ever a time when women were equal. He probably doesn't think women have brains. I'll show him brains!"

She chomped a large piece of onion, and her eyes instantly began to water. Everything in Greece seemed to have ten times the flavour of its counterpart at home, and she wasn't entirely acclimatised yet.

"If a man likes to think about taking a woman to bed," Sophia asked mildly, "does it mean he doesn't respect her brain?" She was known in her circle for her intelligence, but she was currently being pursued by someone from outside the circle. She obviously did not care for the inference. Kate grinned across at her ruefully.

"I guess not, but I know a male chauvinist when I see one. And this is one male chauvinist I'm gonna make sit up and take notice! Before I'm through with him, he's going to wish . . . What's that? Yogurt and honey? Omigod, Sophia, I'm going to get so fat!"

"How can you get fat on yogurt and honey? It's so natural."

"Eat two quarts of it, that's how. Are you going to come to the library with me while I plot your cousin's downfall?"

Sophia laughed her hoarse smoker's laugh. "I'm not going to miss it, that's for sure!"

Sophia had been a godsend. She had gone from being merely a name in an address book when Kate arrived in Athens—a friend of a friend whom Kate had promised to look up—to a good friend, in less time than Kate would have thought possible. She had black hair, black eyes and a voluptuous figure that were almost the exact opposite of Kate's own fragile bones and chic, permed, red-gold crop; and a ready sense of humour and a quick temper, traits which Kate shared. She was also a marvelous, easygoing hostess with a string of friends that seemed never-ending, and within a week she had invited Kate to move into her spare room and make the apartment her Athens headquarters.

Kate knew she had struck gold in Sophia. Whatever country you were in, friendships like this didn't grow on trees. It wasn't till she heard Sophia say casually, "Andreas Constantinou? He's my cousin; we grew up together on Kérkyra," that she'd realized the gold was diamond-studded.

Now, having encountered the difficulty of doing research in a foreign language, and Sophia, who as chance would have it was a professional interpreter, having volunteered her help, Kate sat at a desk taking notes and thanked her stars one more time for her luck as Sophia translated a passage from an encyclopedia.

"Plato!" she exclaimed, as Sophia made her way through the first few sentences. "Is *that* who it was!"

"It was the Egyptians, too," Sophia said, reading along a little way. "They told Solon, who was related to Plato's great-grandfather, when he visited Egypt. He told it to Critias, Plato's grandfather, who told Plato."

Kate laughed at her friend's air of triumph. "I see you only quote the source material," she joked. Not many people, she supposed, would have remembered Plato's source.

"Aristotle discounted the story," Sophia went on, not having lifted her nose from the book. "He called it a poetic fiction."

"Aristotle," Kate said dismissingly, "was left-brain obsessed."

Now that she knew what she was looking for, she found several books on the subject in an English bookstore, at astronomical prices. Among them were English translations of Plato's *Timaeus* and *Critias*, where, after a great deal of eye-straining reading of the tiny type, she found the accounts of Atlantis.

"Damn!" she exploded mildly one night, from her corner of Sophia's sitting room, where she had sat curled up for an hour, reading, and oblivious to the heated discussion that had waxed and waned around her head in excited Greek. "It *was* in the Atlantic!" She must have been mistaken about that panicked look after all. Perhaps it had been nothing more than what Andreas Constantinou had said: fear that someone should start a rumour that he was on to actual treasure or some famous site.

But he would be especially afraid if the rumour were

true. Maybe it wasn't the word *Atlantis* that had got him going, but the word *treasure*?

"Pio?" called Sophia, her interest diverted from the conversation of the half dozen of her friends who regularly gathered here for food and conversation.

"The Egyptians told Solon told Plato that the damned island was beyond the Pillars of Hercules," Kate explained. The Pillars of Hercules were the tips of Morocco and Gibraltar, which separated the Mediterranean Sea from the Atlantic. "It couldn't have been anywhere near Samothráki."

At her obvious disappointment, Sophia laughed.

"Ti légei?" asked Ilias curiously, looking at Sophia with raised eyebrows, and the conversation died as everyone fixed their attention on Kate.

"Légei," Sophia began—which Kate knew meant "she says"—and there followed a spate of rapid Greek, in which the only words Kate could decipher were "Atlantis" and *"thálasso,"* which meant "sea."

At the end of it there was good-natured laughter and a few comments. "What are they saying?" Kate asked in her turn. None of Sophia's friends spoke more than a few words of English at most, but Sophia's translations were as rapid-fire as the comments, and somehow the time lapse between speech and comprehension was hardly noticeable.

"Takkis says that if you want an island, there are many beautiful ones in the Aegean which have *not* sunk," Sophia translated, and Kate grinned.

"And what did Veta say?" Veta was beautiful, blond and slow-moving, with a very deceptive air of lazy calm about her.

"She says that maybe they made a mistake."

"Who? The Egyptians? Plato?"

Sophia shrugged. Kate smiled across the room at

Veta. Greek women were so beautiful, seemed so much more real than North American women. Sophia and Veta could get more guiltlessly angry than any women Kate had ever met. Greek men might be the worst male chauvinists in the Western world, and Greek women the most put upon of their sex, but at least they weren't afraid of their own anger.

But Veta wasn't angry now, and if it had occurred to Veta that Plato's account could be wrong in some respects while still retaining a basic element of truth, it could have occurred to Andreas Constantinou, too.

"You're right," Kate told her. "You're absolutely right."

"*Sostí eísai,*" translated Sophia.

She didn't really need Andreas Constantinou in order to research her book. He wasn't the only Bronze Age specialist in Greece, by any means. It was only a question of proving something, of getting some revenge, at first. She had hoped to dazzle the man with a bit of whirlwind research, perhaps shake him up a bit.

But on this subject, it seemed, there was no such thing as whirlwind research; and Kate kept telling herself she was going to drop the whole thing, because the man wasn't worth it. But if the man wasn't, the myth was, and before she quite realized it, Kate had succumbed to the grip of the fascinating legend of Atlantis.

As countless others had done in the 2,500 years since Plato, and quite possibly before him. The idea of a lost civilisation, and that civilisation the highest, the best, all that the family of man consciously and unconsciously visualizes when we use the word "civilisation"—the possibility that a truly enlightened civilisation had once actually existed in the world—had a power over her imagination that she could not control. In the days and weeks that followed her encounter with the archaeologist, Kate read, and visited museums, and asked questions, and read some more.

"I'm getting good practice with my English," Sophia laughed when Kate apologized for bringing yet another passage to her for translation.

"Lucky for you you don't read ancient Greek," Kate told her with a grin, for the ancient tongue of Plato and Saint Paul bears little resemblance to the language we know as Greek today. "I think you'd feel you were getting too much of a good thing!"

Fortunately, most of the archaeologists and modern theorists who had been gripped by the Atlantis legend either had been English or had been translated into English, because there were a good few of them.

In the modern era, as early as 1909, someone had suggested, as Veta had, that Plato was wrong in his placement of Atlantis in both time and space, but substantially right in other respects. He suggested that Crete and the advanced Minoan civilisation, which had been destroyed in an instant in the fifteenth century B.C., had formed the basis of the legend, and *that* would put Atlantis squarely on the Mediterranean side of the Pillars of Hercules. Kate could feel her blood heat up with excitement as the trail got warmer and warmer, wondering if Andreas Constantinou had read the same books not so long ago himself.

But nowhere in the annals of Atlantology did she find any connection with the northerly island of Samothráki, or any suggestion that the island had suffered any sort of natural catastrophe, even in myth. The only mention made of the island was in an account of phenomena contemporary with the Cretan disaster on neighbouring islands, in which Samothráki was said to have experienced flooding and unnaturally high tides at the time that the great palaces of the Minoan civilisation had been destroyed.

So Kate turned her attention to the Samothráki end. If the thread did not lead from Atlantis to Samothráki, perhaps it led from Samothráki to Atlantis.

This time the research was easy. The remote, unspoiled island of Samothráki was archaeologically famous for only one thing: the mysterious Cult of the Great Gods, whose beginnings were shrouded in prehistory, but which in historical times had had such adherents as Philip II of Macedon and his son, Alexander the Great, and which had not died out until as late as the fourth century A.D.

Kate's heart thumped harder and harder as she read the account of the ancient religion, and at last she closed the book and sat staring off into space. It was incredible, it was absolutely incredible the way her digressions were constantly leading her back to the main road. Every time she turned around, she found further evidence that everything in life was deeply connected.

Because the Supreme Being in the Religion of the Great Gods had been the Mother Goddess.

If Samothráki had any connection with the lost island of Atlantis, then Atlantis had been a matriarchal society.

One way or the other, she couldn't let Andreas Constantinou get away from her now.

She titled the article "Atlantis: Longing for a Matriarchy," and she made a good case in it for the sense of longing and loss universally aroused by the Atlantean legend being attributable to the loss of the matriarchal orientation of the universe. She wrote that men had an intuitive, instinctive need to worship the power of woman to create and nurture life; that when that power had been debased and put under masculine control, humanity had lost its proper orientation; and that the myth of Atlantis was a parable of that loss, harbouring an unknown quantity of historical fact.

She said that the loss of female equality, even supremacy, had paved the way for the Western loss of a proper respect for and connection with nature and human nature; for the modern loss of attention to mankind's rich heritage of myth, mysteries and dreams; for the undue attention paid in the West to reason, logic and the scientific method; and the consequent withering of intuition and the spirit. She said that the loss of the matriarchal society, in fact, had paved the way for the left brain's overthrow of the right in the Western world—since Greece had been the cradle of Western civilisation—and the consequent imbalance and undue emphasis on outward-based activity, individualism and militarism.

Throughout the article, she used Atlantis only in its mythical connotation, as a representative of the prehistoric cultures from which there was certain evidence that indicated there was either equality between the sexes or "matriocracy"—"the Mothers rule"—a word Kate coined herself.

At the end of the article she turned to the possibility of Atlantis as fact. Giving a brief précis of Plato's account of the civilisation, she commented, "Over the centuries, except for the wackos among us, not many have given credence to the possibility of a factual Atlantis—especially among scientists and scholars. From Aristotle on down through history, with a few exceptions, Atlantis has been labelled 'invention,' 'fable,' 'a plaisanterie.'

"But perhaps the myth of Atlantis is about to be exploded. At this moment, on the tiny northern Aegean Island of Samothráki, in great secrecy, an archaeologist named Andreas Constantinou is excavating a recently discovered late Bronze Age site that may have some connection with the legend of Atlantis."

Then she brought in the evidence of the Religion of the Great Gods, with its unknown origins and unknown language, and ended up, "Whether the settlement on Samothráki was an outpost of the Atlantean empire which effectively died when Atlantis did, or whether it is merely another Bronze Age settlement, further discoveries about the origins of the Religion of the Great Gods and the Mother Goddess are sure to cast some very interesting light on the status of women in prehistory."

Before she sent it off to the editor of the magazine that had contracted to print excerpts like this from her book in progress, some demon prompted her to send a copy to Andreas Constantinou at the University of Athens, with a note inviting him to comment before publication. Kate did not expect any response, though she did hope that if they ever met again, he might be somewhat more respectful. But having made the invitation, scholarly courtesy dictated that she give him a reasonable length of time in which to reply before submitting the article.

"Two weeks," she told Sophia. "That's all he gets."

"The mail sometimes isn't very fast in Greece," Sophia pointed out worriedly. "He won't be at the university now; he'll be at the dig. They always start at the dig on July first."

"Three weeks, then," Kate conceded guiltily. She had almost forgotten that her new friend and her new adversary were related, but now she could see that Sophia was worrying on her cousin's behalf.

But she needn't have worried. Only six days later, late one evening when the two women were alone and Sophia was reading Kate's fortune in the cards, Sophia got a phone call. That wasn't at all unusual in itself; Kate had got used to midnight phone calls and visits in Athens, where life went on well into the night. What was unusual was that after the conventional *"Ne, ne . . . ya su, Andrea! . . . Ne"* sort of thing that Kate was used to hearing, Sophia's voice changed. *"Ne,"* she said again, and her eyes were suddenly on Kate, and her heavy brows came together over her worried eyes. Then she looked startled and called, *"Oríste, oríste!"* into the phone, tapping the hook as though there'd been a disconnect.

Then, with an air of helplessness, she hung up the receiver and turned to Kate. "That was my cousin Andreas," she told Kate unnecessarily. "He's in Alexandroúpolis. He asked me if you were still here. He sounded very angry. Then he hung up."

Across the spread of playing cards on the dining table, Kate looked at her. "Where's Alexándroúpolis?" she asked.

"It's near Samothráki, on the mainland," Sophia said, still looking bewildered. "It's where you catch the ferry to Samothráki." She paused. "Or the plane to Athens."

Kate grinned at her, feeling the grip of nervous anticipation. "Which do you think?"

Sophia looked at the cards spread out in front of her. "I think he's coming here," she said. "I think . . ." She nodded to herself in confirmation. "I think he's the dark-haired man in the cards. The one who is so angry." She looked up at Kate, and her next words wiped all trace of the nervous grin from Kate's face.

"The man who casts his shadow over your whole life," said Sophia unhappily.

Chapter 3

ATHENS

Sophia got ready for work the next morning with the air of someone abandoning a condemned man to his fate. The usual flurry of her early-morning activity was subdued, and once or twice she stopped in the middle of her preparations to dash into the kitchen, where Kate was finishing her first cup of coffee for the day. "I'm sorry," she said guiltily, "but I have to go to work."

Both times Kate laughed and waved her hand. "Don't worry about me," she said, but it was a calm she didn't quite feel. There was something about the thought of an impending confrontation with Andreas Constantinou that was making her blood pound.

Sophia waited as long as she could and then some, but it was obvious Andreas wasn't going to arrive before she was going to have to leave. "I'll take a taxi," she said, biting her lip and looking at her watch again. "I can wait a little longer."

"You know perfectly well it's impossible to get a taxi in Athens during rush hour," Kate told her, opening the door for her. "It'll take you longer to find a cab than it will to take a bus."

"But—"

"Please, Sophia, I'll be all right. Don't make yourself late because of me. What's he going to do? He may be angry about the article, but other than asking me not to publish it, what can he do?"

Sophia still looked doubtful. "Ye-es . . ." she said, and then, "You don't mind if I leave you? They'll be angry if I'm late again. I'm late too much." She started down the building corridor towards the elevator, looking backwards. Then she was struck by a sudden happy thought. "You don't have to let him in, Kate! He has to ring the bell downstairs; you could ignore it!"

"*Adio,*" said Kate, by way of an answer. "I can hold my own against a male chauvinist any old day."

"I don't think he is, you know." Sophia pushed the button to summon the elevator. "Maybe . . . but maybe in North America it's different."

"Maybe." The elevator arrived, and with one last look Sophia stepped inside. Kate shut the apartment door and leaned against it, laughing a little. Maybe, nothing! She had never *seen* so many male chauvinists before in her life as she had in the few short weeks she had been in Greece. Men who never lifted a finger to help Sophia in the kitchen, men who, after she had cooked a gigantic meal, would take all the available chairs around the table without even a thought as to where their hostess was going to sit. Kate had watched Takkis and Ari actually dig in and start eating while Sophia was still in the other room collecting a chair for herself.

It was a way of life here. Not only did men relegate women to second place, but also all the chivalric ritual of the English-speaking world—the door opening, the chair holding, the politeness, all the little things by which men in the West had for years disguised women's second-class citizenship—were totally lacking here in Greece. Here, women stood while men sat. Women stood back while men pushed ahead. Men took the best of everything as if by right, and not even a pretense of respect for womanhood was there to sugar-coat the pill.

Kate hadn't so far decided whether that was a better or worse state of affairs than what she had grown up with, but it was obvious that, in all this, a Greek male wouldn't have to be very civilised to look better than most of his compatriots.

So she was taking the information that Andreas Constantinou wasn't a male chauvinist with a grain of salt. She had seen him.

And she was about to see him again, she reflected half an hour later, as the apartment buzzer rang.

It was hot, and Kate wiped sweat from her forehead as she stood in the apartment foyer waiting for the knock to sound on the door. She did not mind confrontation, she had teethed on it, but as always her heart was pounding in anticipation. Not for the first time she wondered what had possessed her to so unnecessarily take on Andreas Constantinou.

When the hard knock sounded, the adrenaline shot through her system, making all her nerve ends jangle, and with a quick intake of breath to sustain her, Kate opened the door.

Andreas Constantinou stood with his arms linked over his chest and the light of battle in his eyes, and for the first moment of staring at each other, nobody moved.

Then, "Woman," he said, "why don't you leave me alone?"

It wasn't at all what she had expected, and Kate fell back as the dark burly figure stepped determinedly forward into the apartment.

"What do you want from me?" he demanded, taking the handle from her and closing the door, and then turning to face her in the suddenly claustrophobic space of Sophia's small foyer. "I already told you, by letter and in person, that I cannot allow you to come on the site, or give you the interview you wish me to give you. You are a friend of my cousin Sophia; I understand you are a woman with a respected reputation. Why do you threaten me? What will you gain from information extorted from me by force?"

Kate's jaw fell open under the unexpectedness of this attack. "What do you . . . I haven't threatened you!"

He laughed without mirth. "For a woman who takes such pride in her reputation, you are very close to losing it. Are you an expert on Bronze Age Greece?"

She imagined he was pulling intellectual rank. "No, I'm not, as you well know," she said stonily. She turned and stalked down the hallway towards the kitchen. Constantinou followed.

"Then what can you gain through forcing cooperation from me in this way? I could fill your head with enough misinformation to destroy your reputation forever. Or, at the least, to cause you to spend weeks on useless research."

Kate was doing a slow burn. "I have not used any force on you, Mr. Constantinou," she said levelly, putting the table between them as she faced him. "I don't know what you're talking about."

He was wearing casual, worn jeans and an open-neck shirt; his hands were empty. Now he reached around into a back pocket and pulled out a sheaf of typing paper folded lengthways. She recognized her Atlantis article. Constantinou held it in the air at eye level.

"What do you call this?" His accent was thicker than she had heard it before, and she realized suddenly that it was because he was angry. He dropped the pages onto the table between them, making a little *thwack*, and the anger gave his movements a controlled economy that triggered her own angry, nervous tension.

"I call it the documentation of a very interesting possibility. What did you imagine it was?" Her voice was full of such blatant intellectual contempt that if he had used it on her, it would have set her teeth on edge.

He only grinned dangerously at her. "If you want to theorize about myths, it does not concern me. For the parts concerning me, however, I *imagined* it was a very stupid, insupportable comment from a woman who not only should but obviously does know better," he said. "I *imagined* that it was an attempt to blackmail me."

"*Blackmail?*" she gasped, outraged. "Who the hell do you think you are? I've never blackmailed anybo—"

"What do you call it, when you try to force me to give you time and information I do not want to give you by threatening to publish a stupid, dangerous paragraph that will bring every idiot in the English-speaking world to overrun my dig before I have time even to make a judgement on what we will find? What do you call this?" He made a noise of angry contempt. "Now I understand why so many scientists let you publish their findings in your books."

Kate stared at him, aghast. "What on earth do you mean?" she demanded. She had only wanted to prove something to him, just why she couldn't imagine now. But surely he didn't think she . . .

Suddenly Constantinou's anger burst the dam. "You plotting little fool!" he shouted at her. "Don't play the games with *me*!" His accent and grammar had both gone out the window. He was furious. He bent towards her, one hand flat on the table, the other thick forefinger stabbing violently at the sheaf of papers lying there. "This is going to destroy my dig! You know it! This makes me fence the area before I even know what the area is! This makes me spend money on guards twenty-four hours a day when my grant is not big enough even to hire the staff that I need! Already I have volunteers and students where I need professional staff!"

"Stop shouting at me!" Kate shouted at him. "I didn't know all this!" She felt stricken, not least because she should have given anyone cause to think her so unscrupulous. Of course she wouldn't publish her damn speculation if it meant all that. "I won't—" she began.

"Of course you know it!" he overrode her. "I told you already what will happen to us, so if you don't know it, I think you are very unintelligent as well."

"Don't you call me unintelligent!" she warned, fury gaining the upper hand. All her life she had been smarter than most of the people around her, and a lot of men had hated that, and tried to convince her otherwise. Masculine denigration of her brain power drove her mad, every time. "Don't you call *me* stupid!"

"Stupid!" he repeated, pressing his advantage. "You are a stupid woman. You know nothing, only what you want, what other people must give to you!"

"Shut up!" she shouted, in a voice that would have done even Veta proud. "If you don't shut up right now, I swear I'll write sixteen articles about you!" Kate was not stopping to wonder at the propriety of engaging in a shouting match with an almost total stranger. She was suddenly drunk on her own fury. "I'll publish your name in every magazine in North America! You may think I'm stupid, but my publishers don't! I can make you *news* so fast it'll make your head spin! I'll have them crawling over you like cockroaches!" It wasn't true, of course. She didn't have that sort of power, but her anger had entirely got the better of her. "I'm a writer, and believe me, I will have the last word!"

"Writer!" he snorted. "You are a dreamer; you are

only a sensation-seeker! A writer cares about facts! What do you care about facts? Nothing!"

Constantinou gripped the pages of her article in a fist that shook with fury, lifted up his other hand and tore them across, once, twice. "This is what your editor should do with such tripe." His voice was calm now, icy with contempt, as though, having transferred his rage to his hands, he was free to stop expressing it with his voice. He threw the little bundle of torn pages at her, and she gasped as they struck her chest and showered into the air around her.

It chilled her as perhaps nothing else could have. Kate stood motionless as the bits of her essay floated down around her to the floor. Then she said, in a flat, frozen voice, "It's all very well to say 'Publish and be damned,' Mr. Constantinou, but I remind you that if I publish, *you'll* be damned."

He stared at her in mute hostility; then very deliberately he pulled out a chair and sat down. "You are right," he said. "It is useless to reason with a blackmailer. So. What is your price, Miss Fenton?"

She had never hated anyone as much as she hated Andreas Constantinou in that moment. Kate slipped her hands into her pants pocket and stood looking down at him, enjoying the height that forced him to look up at her. "For not publishing those paragraphs about you?" she asked in a businesslike voice. She rocked slowly back and forth on her heels.

"That's right."

"Well, that's easy," she said, with a deceptive, unfriendly smile. "I want to work with your team on the Samothrákian dig."

She spoke as the idea formed in her head, and felt almost as shocked as he looked when she heard her own voice. She wasn't even sure why she was saying it. "I want to be by your side every minute of the day, Mr.

Constantinou. I want to hear your theories, your observations; I want to be with you when you examine every find, important and unimportant."

"It is out of the question. I have no more budget."

"I'm not asking you to put me on the payroll," she informed him coldly. My God, someday he would pay for this. He would be sorry. "I will not be working for you, but for myself. This is research. I finance my own research."

He was no longer amazed, only disgusted. "For how long?" he asked expressionlessly.

She must be out of her mind. Why was she doing this? She was only confirming him in the lowest opinion he could possibly have of her. Even as a banner-carrying feminist, she couldn't spare much effort for making a male chauvinist see the light. And yet . . . and yet, it was just what she wanted, being handed to her on a platter . . . the chance to spend a few weeks right on the site of a prehistoric dig, looking at the evidence for herself, before it got interpreted through someone else's vision. And she could hardly hope to find a better situation than a brand-new dig with a man of the calibre of Andreas Constantinou.

She at least knew that his estimation of her was wrong. She knew that, whatever was found on Samothráki, she would not publish what he himself did not want her to publish. All she wanted was the experience, the chance to judge for herself.

And serve him right if he hated it. Every minute of it. For, whatever he said, Kate was convinced that if she had been a man, she would have been granted permission from the first.

"For a month," she said. "Starting as soon as possible."

"And when will you publish the ideas you steal from me?"

Kate gritted her teeth. "I'll publish nothing that you don't wish me to publish, at any time. You know what it is I'm interested in. But I won't present any of your finds or conclusions, Mr. Constantinou, without your permission."

"You will never get permission to print one word of what I find," he told her. "So if you are going to steal my work, I think I prefer to have the crazy tourists."

"I have told you before, I can sign a guarantee that would give you the right of approval before I publish anything concerning you. My publisher couldn't publish until you had signed a release." She was struck by a sudden thought. "Within reason, of course," she amended.

"And how do I know that you will hold to your side of the bargain, after you have had your month of picking my brain?"

"You would have to trust me," she said, before she thought.

He threw back his dark head and laughed. *"Oreia!"* he laughed. *"Poly oreia!* I have to trust you!" He laughed loud and long, while Kate stood with her hands clenched inside her pockets. At last he sobered. "This is excellent, Miss Fenton! At least you will provide amusement. My friends tell me I have an enjoyment of the ridiculous."

He did not say she was ridiculous; he only implied it with his eyes and his voice. And while she stood wondering how the hell she had managed to get herself so totally misjudged, he clapped his hands together with a satisfied finality.

"Yes, all right. Today I return to Alexandroúpolis; I must not be away for long. So. You will come, when? Tomorrow? Thursday? Next week?"

"I . . . um, I'll have to think." My God, what was

she going to tell Sophia? What was *he* going to tell
Sophia? "When are you leaving? Are you going to wait
for Sophia to come home for lunch?" God, if he was,
she was going to have to leave. She couldn't sit in the
apartment with him till two o'clock. The thought of
going out into the midday heat of Athens appalled her.
Even the back of a taxi was hell in this weather.

"I will go to my office at the university," he said, as
though he did not care to put up with her company any
more than she with his. "Only, I had a bad flight.
Before I go I need a cup of coffee."

Kate deliberately sat herself down at the table, but if
he had expected her to cater to his need, he didn't show
it. He stood up and walked around her to the stove,
apparently not noticing when she involuntarily drew
away from him as he passed. Taking the small alumi-
num dipper from the sink, he spooned in sugar and
coffee. "Do you want coffee, too? I make *metrio*."

Metrio meant equal parts of dark coffee and sugar,
boiled up into the thick strong liquid most people call
Turkish coffee, but which Kate had learned very quickly to call Greek coffee here. Centuries of Turkish
occupation of Greece as well as the latter-day dispute
over Cyprus had left their residue of anti-Turk bitter-
ness in this country, and only ignorant tourists ordered
"Turkish" coffee anywhere in the land of Homer.

She was amazed he was civilised enough to offer her
coffee after what they had just been through, but if she
still felt shaky with reaction, he seemed to have recovered completely.

"No, thank you," she said. "I'm drinking Nescafe."
In Greece and other Mediterranean countries, Kate
had discovered, the generic term for instant coffee was
the brand name.

Shrugging, he set the tiny pot on the stove to boil.

His movements were deft and economical, and she imagined that an archaeologist would get used to roughing it, to not having a woman around to cater to his needs.

As though he had read her mind, he came and sat back down at the table. "I have been thinking," he told her. "If you insist on working with me at the site, you must come as my assistant. My students and volunteers work where they are told; it would look very strange if a volunteer could do whatever she wished." He smiled a little. "It will be a luxury to me to have an assistant," he told her. "You must work hard. Everybody on the site works hard. You understand, if you don't work, they will know something is wrong about you. Do you want them to know that you blackmail me, or do you want to be thought one of the crew?"

Well, he certainly knew what a sore spot was. For a fleeting moment Kate wondered who would make whom pay, but the small warning shudder was lost in a wave of determination and a vision of Andreas Constantinou eating crow. "I . . ." she began.

"You understand, if they know you are a blackmailer, no one will speak to you, eat with you. They are all dedicated, you understand. They are students and professional archaeologists who devote their whole life to discovering the past."

"Of course I expect to work," she said, wishing she didn't feel as though she'd been goaded into saying that, because it was the truth. Kate was a worker; it wouldn't have occurred to her to sit around while everyone else was hard at work. "But couldn't you tell them the truth? That I'm a writer researching a book?"

The coffee came to a boil on the stove, and Constantinou jumped up to snatch it from the heat before it could froth over. With the little pot in one hand he moved unerringly to a cupboard and found himself one of Sophia's tiny coffee cups. He poured and sat down.

"There is enough for two," he said, "if you changed your mind."

The Nescafe was cold in front of her, and the frothy chocolate-coloured liquid looked very attractive. Kate got up and poured herself a cup. When she realized she had in some nameless way lost points by drinking something he had made, it was too late to change her mind.

"They would treat a writer even worse than a blackmailer," he said calmly. "A writer is dangerous on an archaeological site. Every comment must be watched in case you write something that brings the sightseers."

Why did she feel, having won the war, that she was losing all the battles? Something was nagging at her, but she couldn't put her finger on it.

"The best thing would be," Constantinou was saying, "if they think you are my lover. Then no one will ask questions."

For no good reason she shivered a little. "Let's stick with assistant, shall we?" she told him.

He shrugged. "Anyway, they will think it. They know I can't have an assistant; I can't afford it. They will know you aren't paid. So, why else are you there, waiting on me, hanging around? They will think you are a woman with nothing better to do than to follow your man around. . . . They will think you hope to get me into marriage."

"Not when they see how much I hate you," she promised him, gritting her teeth. God, what a chauvinist bastard! The thought that she had ever felt even a flicker of sexual interest in him nearly made her sick.

He shrugged. "But you are already not a young woman anymore. Women of your age must take whom they can get. Besides, they will think you treat me coldly to disguise our real relationship and protect your reputation."

"Women of my age," Kate began coldly, "have learned enough good sense to keep well away from marriage. If they're lucky. If you're trying to keep me away with these tactics, Mr. Constantinou, forget it."

He finished his coffee with a leisurely air. "You have been married before, Miss Fenton?"

"I have been married before," she agreed flatly. "And I know better than to try it again."

And then it struck her why she was such an easy target for Andreas Constantinou, why he was getting under her skin. He reminded her of Peter. He was like Peter. And that also explained why she was so irrationally determined to make him pay.

Because Peter had been the male chauvinist pig of all time. And she had never had the satisfaction of making him pay for what he'd done to her.

Chapter 4

SAMOTHRÁKI

ATHENS AIRPORT WAS WILD. OTHER THAN HAVING ONCE been caught in an airline strike, Kate had never seen anything like it. People were jammed six deep round every available counter and check-in point in sight, in lines extending well into the centre of the departures concourse, where they merged with a swirling, amorphous amoeba of humanity that was constantly dividing and regrouping.

At first she couldn't understand what was wrong. Then, with an incredulous laugh, she understood: It was mid-July. Tourist season in Greece was in full force.

And she had her ticket still to buy, and she had cut it rather fine. Getting a firmer grip on her duffel bag, Kate took a fix on a sign over a booth in the centre of the room that read *Same Day Departures* in English, and made for it, in as direct a line as possible. It was a bit like having one's canoe overturned in rushing water, she discovered: it was best not to try to fight the current, but to allow it to carry her towards her destination at a tangent.

At the outer edge of the crowd around the window, she checked her watch. A bare half hour till her flight left, and it was the last flight of the day to Alexandroúpolis. If she missed it, she missed tomorrow's ferry to Samothráki, and if she missed that, she missed Andreas Constantinou waiting for her on the dock.

Silently, Kate surveyed the crowd in front of her. She had two choices—miss her flight or push in ahead of most of the people here. Kate glanced to right and left. At home, of course, it wasn't the done thing. People who came late either waited politely at the end of the line in the sure knowledge that someone's brisk efficiency would solve their problem or politely approached the counter through the ranks, explaining and asking permission all along the way.

But Kate did not speak Greek, and there *was* no line. Just a horde of people shoving each other with unbelievable ferocity and shouting and waving tickets or money in the air, as though here, *this* was the done thing. Already she was no longer on the edge of the crowd—some law of nature had propelled her inside the mass so that her bag was in danger of being torn from her, along with her right arm, and her body was jammed nook and cranny against several others.

"Go for it," she muttered to herself, torn between amusement and dismay, and suddenly there was little Katie Fenton pushing and shoving with the best of them, with one goal in her head—the ticket window— and no thought at all for the niceties of polite behaviour.

Elbows were a handy weapon, she discovered, after having taken a couple in the ribs and losing her place in the siege. A person just couldn't help wincing away from a well-placed elbow, and that wincing left room for a leg or an arm that could, if you were adroit enough, quickly be followed by the rest of the body.

After six minutes she was only two bodies distant from the window, and it was directly in front of her. The harassed Olympiaki agent was shouting to be heard by the man at the window, who was expertly protecting his position with elbows spread out on the counter on both sides of the little gap in the glass through which communication and tickets passed. Kate placed her feet apart and braced her legs against the press of the crowd. With a little luck, when that man left, she might establish a beachhead as second in line, but she didn't make the mistake of letting her attention waver for a moment.

An elbow caught her in the ribs on the left and a short, squat, grey-haired man was already following up his advantage. Kate was light-headed with the effects of breaking so many social rules at once and getting away with it. It was as though she had suddenly discovered an ability to fly. *"Parakalo!"* she shouted indignantly at the man, as though she had not gained her position exactly the way he was trying to; and threw a block with her left shoulder whose effectiveness patently infuriated him.

He shouted at her, a barrage of Greek that she couldn't understand except for the last two words. *"Misi ora!"* he repeated more loudly, in the time-honoured way of attempting to make a foreigner understand: Say it louder.

Misi ora meant half an hour, Sophia's random Greek lessons had made that much stick, but Kate was unmoved. *"Kai ego misi ora!"* she shouted back at him, which might or might not mean "And me, half an hour!" and determinedly kept her place.

Luck was with her. When the customer at the window at last abandoned his post, he moved off left, battling almost as hard to get out of the crowd as he had to get in; and the man directly in front of her, obviously a seasoned campaigner, took his place at the window with a mere tactical body blow to what looked like a Danish tourist on his left.

And Kate was sucked into place right in behind him. "My God," muttered the slim blond student helplessly, in a strong accent. "How do you get a ticket here? It's impossible."

"You have to shove," Kate informed him kindly, as though she'd been born to it herself. But she wasn't letting him in front, whether he had been there first or not. He might lose her position for both of them if he weren't ruthless enough. "Wedge yourself in behind me, quickly."

"Wedge," he repeated, as though he didn't know the word, but he was quick to catch the idea, narrowly easing out the little man who had already lost to Kate, by the judicious use of his knapsack. The little man protested vehemently.

By the time she got to the window Kate was giggling weakly. This was truly bizarre. She felt as though she had stepped into a scene from *La Dolce Vita*.

"*Milate Anglika?*" she asked the ticket agent, spreading out her elbows in her turn and counting on the Dane to guard her rear. Of course the woman spoke English, all Olympiaki personnel spoke English, but Kate considered it the height of rudeness to approach someone in their own country with the automatic assumption that they spoke your language. Especially when that language was English. Decades of thoughtless tourist arrogance was something Kate did not want to be associated with, ever.

The agent wiped a tired hand over her wet forehead, pushing her thick hair aside. *"Ne,"* she said, giving the odd little twist of her head that looked like no but that meant yes in Greece. "Yes, what is your destination?"

Eleven minutes, and she still had to go to another window to *pay* for the ticket. Kate reached for the voucher the agent was tearing off for her and said to the blond student, who seemed to have caught on and was glued to her now, "I'll stand back to the right. Move in quickly."

"All right," he agreed, sounding bemused. "This is very crazy, yes?"

He wasn't quite ruthless enough, but at least he managed to maintain second place in line as a very irate woman snaffled the window position. Kate left him to his fate- and concentrated on getting back out of a crowd where no one wanted to shift an inch for fear of losing ground. As she passed the short grey-haired man she distinctly felt four rabbit punches to the ribs as he vented his annoyance on her. Kate had an advanced sense of the ridiculous anyway, and she felt a crazy amusement flood her brain. Turning back briefly as she struggled with humour, exhilaration and a zinging elation for which she had no explanation other than a system overload of adrenaline, Kate surprised herself and completed her social downfall by dealing the man a hard little kick in the ankle. Then the crowd finally opened and she almost fell out of the edge of it.

The *Pay* window was a breeze, because only those who had mastered the reservations window could pay for a ticket. Pondering, not for the first time, on the ludicrousness of such a system, Kate would now be forced to make her way back to the *first* window and hand in her receipt—over the heads of the crowd this time, since a person who had already paid was no threat to the status quo at the window—and receive in return her ticket.

Weakly she looked at the receipt. "It's a madhouse at the other window," she told the agent, as though he could perhaps not see for himself. "My flight leaves in fifteen minutes. Couldn't you just reach me the ticket from the other agent's desk?"

After some pause for consideration he let her off the hook of this latter-day Athenian ritual, and a minute later Kate was heading for the check-in counter at a jog trot.

She boarded the last airplane bus with four minutes to spare, her lack of checked baggage having worked greatly to her advantage, and fell into her aisle seat in the aircraft at last, giddy with the sudden release from tension and the leftover adrenaline zinging through her muscles and nerves.

The doors shut. A stewardess spoke briefly in Greek, and then translated. "Ladies and gentlemen, we regret to inform you that the plane has a small mechanical fault. There will be a delay of approximately twenty minutes. Thank you."

Andreas Constantinou wasn't the only one with a strong sense of the ridiculous. Subsiding weakly into her seat, Kate began to laugh.

The island was alone in the sea, a mountain that rose out of the mist of morning, green, purple and golden, and seemed to beckon her with a promise of silence and secrets. Kate stood on the deck of the island ferry, the wind ruffling her hair, and dreamed of pagan rites and religious enlightenment. Had they found it here, the ancient Greeks? Had they discovered some truth about the transformation of the human into the divine, or had they merely dabbled in warm oils and ritualized incantations and mysterious music?

Philip II of Macedon had been an initiate here, and he had gone from monarch of a backward northern province to King of all Greece. Alexander had come here as an initiate, and by the time he was thirty he had conquered all the known world. He had been an enlightened conqueror. His subject states had retained their integrity, their laws and religion, for the most part; he had not forced his foreign way of life on them. Had he learned that tolerance here, in the Religion of the Great Gods, where women, men, Greeks, foreigners, free and slave alike had, according to her research, been eligible for initiation? Where hundreds, perhaps a thousand, years be-fore Christ, there had been no discrimination on the basis of sex, creed, colour, race or political status? Or even, since Alexander's own sexuality was pretty well established historically, on sexual preference?

Long way we've come since then, Kate told herself cynically. Was there even one religion in the world today that could say the same? Never mind one political system.

Had they found it, then? Had they known all about it, whatever it was that the world had lost; had they been on the track that nations and religions had been unable to find for so long now? Or had the Religion of the Great Gods been just as filled with hypocrisy as modern ones?

The ferry had been approaching Samothráki from the north, but now it turned towards the western end of the island, where, she knew, the port city of Kamario-tissa was situated.

Andreas Constantinou would be waiting for her there, unless in the past two days he had decided to ignore or found some way to circumvent the problem she posed for him. She wished she were coming as a

friend, instead of an enemy. She wished he had agreed
to let her come when she'd asked.

She wished she had never tacked those stupid paragraphs onto the end of an otherwise good article. If she
hadn't cut them out, no doubt her editor would have,
but Constantinou couldn't be expected to know that. A
magazine article had to have an innate integrity; it
couldn't just jump on its horse and gallop off in all
directions like that.

It had served to fool the archaeologist, and allowed
her to impose on him, but it didn't guarantee polite
relationships with the people she was about to meet and
would spend the next month with.

Kate wasn't fooling herself: his team would be about
as likely to believe she was his lover as Kate was to fly
from the ferry to the island right now. Men like
Andreas Constantinou weren't capable of hiding their
rage when they'd been crossed, especially by a woman.
He would be constitutionally incapable of even being
civil to her, and the rest of them, if they had the normal
amount of loyalty for the boss, would follow suit.

She probably wouldn't feel like sticking it out for a
whole month—not unless what they were finding was
something no girl should miss. Not unless it was really
worth the price.

All her instincts told her it would be worth the price.

Suddenly she was as eager for adventure as a child
who still lives in a world where even the scent of the air
on a summer morning promises mystery and excitement. It had been a long time since little Katie Fenton
had picked up that scent on the wind, so long she had
forgotten its intensity, almost its existence. But it was
there now, filling her nostrils with a kind of crazy
cat-glee and a sense of life's limitless opportunities.

She began to strain over the boat rails, taking in as
much as she could of the island and the port town,

trying to pick out the figure of Andreas Constantinou in
the scene before her, of fishing boats and huge nets,
trucks, packing cases, produce and people. Greek
people. As far as she could tell, she was the only
foreigner on the ferry, so it was a fair guess that the
island wasn't a tourist haunt.

There he was. Though she had met him only twice,
he was easy enough to pick out: a workman's body,
among workmen; dark-haired and dark-eyed, amid a
dark race; and yet he was easy to pick out, standing
there, hands jammed into khaki pockets, his head flung
back, staring at the island ferry that bore her—staring
as though he would like to bomb it out of the water
before it touched the dock.

Kate abruptly turned away from the railing and
moved back into the lounge, against the flow of people
coming out. Her duffel bag was where she had left it,
and she unzipped a side pocket and pulled out her
hairbrush. She stood by the table, looking out the
window as the departing passengers brushed by her,
pulling the brush methodically through her thick hair,
staring at nothing.

She didn't want to meet Andreas Constantinou
again. She had the upper hand; she should have felt in
control, but somehow she didn't want to go out there
and face him, and she didn't know why.

Unless of course it was because the moment she
stepped off this boat she became exactly what the man
had said she was. Or because she was afraid of what
might be in store for anyone Andreas Constantinou
thought was a blackmailer.

All she wanted was the experience! She didn't want
to jump the gun on him; she had no intention of
preempting his own publication. She just wanted to be
on a Bronze Age dig while the discoveries were being
made! Why was he being so pigheaded about it? Why—

"This boat only makes one stop. You are at your destination," said a voice behind her, and Kate whirled to face Andreas Constantinou across half the length of the lounge. After a moment she realized that they were staring at each other.

He seemed to have no tension in his body; for such a muscular man he stood surprisingly loosely, his arms at his sides, his feet a little apart. Then it struck her that he was in the posture of a street fighter. It was as though at any second they would begin to circle. He was sizing her up, looking for her weak spots, as she was his. That the weak spots they were looking for were psychological ones made no difference; the atmosphere was as tense and shimmering around them as if each held a knife.

She felt the prod of his mind through his black eyes, and she put up a block like Krupp plate. Whatever he was looking for, he must not find it. She felt the determination to win grip her, bringing with it a strange physical excitement she had not felt for years: a kind of lust for battle, a shivering of her muscles and nerves that went with a determination to win against the odds.

Suddenly she was little Katie Fenton again, standing on a street corner in torn, dirty clothes, waiting to go in with tooth and claw against the advantage of brawn.

She clamped down on the laughter in her throat, but she could not suppress the fighter's grin as goose bumps shivered down her arms and back and she felt her nipples tighten into attention. She hadn't felt so alive for twenty years.

Andreas Constantinou straightened his shoulders almost imperceptibly, as though he were shaking himself awake, and moved along the aisle towards her. "Shall I help you with your bags?" he asked, extending a hand.

It wasn't a workman's hand. It was strong and callused, but lean, as though a pianist had taken to work in the fields, and when she placed the handle of her duffel bag across his palm she found herself watching the strong curl of his fingers around it with stopped breath. If their battle had been physical instead of mental, that hand might now be gripping her wrist with just such firm strength. Kate's wrist was slim, delicate-looking; she would feel the pressure of his fingers right to her bones.

Then she looked into Andreas Constantinou's eyes and knew that he, as much as she, wished their battle were a physical one.

"Thank you," was all she said. "Where do we go from here?"

Andreas Constantinou laughed.

The social sophistication of Kate Fenton was all veneer. Although no one now would know it to look at her, she had spent the first ten years of her life fighting. Born to a woman whose husband had already left her, the youngest of four children, Katie had never known the ease and security that her older sisters and brother had known, nor their terrible understanding of their fall from grace. Their early childhood had been a normal middle-class experience; Katie had understood hunger the day she had been weaned. They had remembered a playroom, a park, a backyard; Katie's only playground had been a grey and dirty city street, with friends as ragged and unkempt as herself to play with.

In the rough neighbourhood where Katie had grown up, her brother and sisters had been afraid. But to Katie it had been home, a place she knew and understood. Katie knew when to fight and when to run; she had absorbed that instinctive knowledge at a time when other children were learning what red and green traffic lights meant. Katie knew how to use her wily leanness, her teeth and knees and nails, against those bigger than she was; she had learned that her small size and her technique were successful only if she got in quick and got out quicker, and ran while her opponent was still groaning.

By the time she was eight she had a vocabulary that made Lenny Bruce look like a piker. At nine, she ran her own little gang, whose specialty was robbing fruit stalls, but only when they were hungry. At nine and a half she was starting to case out the five-and-dime. At ten . . .

At ten this promising career was nipped in the bud. At ten, an uncle and aunt in a distant city had written Katie's mother offering to "take one of the children off your hands," and making no bones that the one they wanted was the youngest and (they thought) most malleable. They had sent her mother a plane ticket and five hundred dollars. The plane ticket was for Katie. The five hundred had smelled, just a bit, like conscience money.

Her mother had cried over the letter, but Katie hadn't blinked. Five hundred dollars was a lot of money. People with money like that probably didn't have to steal food oftener than once or twice a month! Probably they didn't even have to hide the television set when the welfare woman came to visit, or so her sister led her to believe. They *might* even have a car, though Katie wasn't getting her hopes up. And she frankly didn't believe the envious suggestions that she might have a room all to herself to sleep in.

But it had been worth thinking about, that was for sure. Her mother had said, "To hell with them; we'll keep the money and send the ticket back," but she had looked at Katie, and she and all the others had known that if Katie decided to go, there'd be no stopping her.

Katie had decided to go, and Katie had bitterly regretted her decision every single day of the next ten years. Her uncle was a doctor, middle class and arrogant, though it would be many years before she learned to use the words "male chauvinist" to describe what he was. Her aunt was stiff and a prig, and it would be even longer before she got as far as "anal-oriented."

Between them, they had decided to "make something" of Katie, and by "something" they had meant a nice, middle-class, upwardly mobile "little lady," with the right politics (right), right religion (money), right turn of phrase (indirect) and the right subordination of herself.

And, of course, she must be very, very *feminine*.

The wild, unruly street brat was coaxed, coerced and mentally beaten into submission, into the role of the pretty little niece who made her people proud. Every instinct she had grown up with was subverted, whether it was the instinct to scratch when she was itchy or curse when she was riled. She could no longer fight when she felt threatened; but in any case she was too busy keeping her knees together now that she was no longer allowed to wear jeans. She could *never* answer back, no matter how wrong the adults in her life were, and although she was not forbidden to laugh, no one ever joined in at home.

Her wild red hair, which in the old days she had chopped off with the shears just above shoulder level, had grown long and been duly screwed back into tight thick braids that made her feel more confined than any other single feature of her new life.

To Katie, fighting was like breathing. After ten years she felt that unless she was fighting, she wasn't alive.

Being deprived of all her means of self-expression, all the experiences that told her she was alive, had felt like slow murder.

And slow it had been, because Katie had rebelled against it for years. If her uncle and aunt had beaten her physically, if they had fought her on her own ground, she might have been able to hold out. She might never have given in. But their methods had been all psychological, and that was a warfare Katie had no experience in at all. They had nagged, and carped, and made her feel guilty and bad about all that was best in her. They had deprived her of affection and approval and rights, and most of all, they had belittled her constantly in the effort to "keep her in line."

So the aggressive self-esteem that had been Katie's protection in the streets had been slowly stripped away, until she felt all the force of what had been beneath it: a deep sense of her own worthlessness in the world and a painful understanding that she was one of the refuse of humanity, one about whom nobody cared. She had rebelled against that only briefly, but once she had touched those depths her aunt and uncle had the upper hand and they knew it. After that it was only a matter of time before, mercifully, Katie's spirit had lain down and died.

For the first time in her life, she had begun to seek approval, and the way to gain approval from her uncle and aunt had been extremely well marked. Katie was a bright girl who caught on quickly. By the time she had finished high school there was almost no trace left of the wild, bright child whose great strengths had been a strong originality and an unimaginably generous heart.

She had studied English Lit in university; it was a nice, ladylike field of study, and teaching was a good occupation for a girl. It was just sheer good luck for

Kate that she loved the printed word. She had briefly thought of studying journalism and trying for a career on a newspaper, but of course that wouldn't have done, and English Lit had really been *much* more suitable.

And at the end of her first year, she had met Peter, and her doom was complete.

Chapter 5

SAMOTHRÁKI

ANDREAS CONSTANTINOU STOWED HER BAG IN THE BACK of a battered, rusting, green Jeep that looked as though it had first seen service bringing the Greek army back into Athens after the Germans pulled out. Swinging into the passenger seat, Kate was grateful that she had worn blue jeans and an old T-shirt, because the upholstery was split and none too clean, and there was a jumble of rubbish at her feet.

"Wait here," he said. "I have a shipment to pick up."

He walked off in the direction of the ferry, from which cars, people and supplies were still being unloaded, and Kate settled down to watch the passing scene. This was Greece, and she had already learned that little was done on time, and almost nobody rushed. She might have a long wait.

He was back within twenty minutes, which wasn't bad, but she would have had time for a quick coffee in one of the *cafenions* nearby, and a more comfortable wait. It didn't much matter, but Kate was determined to remind herself at every possible opportunity what a male chauvinist Andreas Constantinou was. Because she certainly didn't want to allow herself to get sexually interested in him. He was too dangerous for that.

He stowed two well-sealed cardboard boxes in the rear seat beside her duffel bag and fitted himself compactly into the driver's seat without saying a word, and that was all right with Kate. If she had imagined *his* awareness of *her*—and she had spent the last twenty minutes telling herself that was the case—she wouldn't have to worry about possible involvement. If he wasn't interested, that would be a terrific advantage.

The Jeep rattled and bucked over the potholes as Constantinou made a tight U-turn and drove along the pavement skirting the water to the nearest street that ran at right angles to it.

It was hot, but there was a stiff wind blowing, which was surprisingly cooling. Kate had heard of the *meltemi,* but she had always thought it was a hot, dry wind, not something that made you wish you had a light jacket.

"Where is Kamariotissa?" she asked after a moment, when the short street of houses they had driven along had suddenly given way to countryside.

"You must have blinked," Constantinou told her, over the sound of a badly grinding gear change.

Laughing, Kate turned in her seat. "You mean, that was it?" She looked back down the street behind them. "Is it really that small?"

"Kamariotissa has a population of about two hundred sixty-eight," he said. "Other villages on the island are larger, of course."

"Of course," she agreed dryly. After a moment, "How large?"

"Well, Khora still has between one and two thousand, but of course people are leaving Samothráki every day. The population here, as in most rural areas in Greece, is shrinking."

The mountain cluster that composed the major part of the island was ahead of them as he piloted the Jeep along a well-paved highway through fields of golden grass and groves of olive trees. The sun was high in a hazy blue sky, and the air was fresh and clear and beautiful. Slowly the curving road was leading them up the slopes of the mountain.

"Where is the dig?" she asked.

"Do you know the island at all?"

"I bought a map on the ferry; I've been having a look at it."

"We're on a hill between Lákoma and Prophétes Elías, a little closer to Lákoma," he explained. "The site is high, but with a clear run down to the sea."

"What made you choose the location?"

Constantinou shifted gears as the road became steeper. "I was looking for somewhere well above sea level, but with all the advantages that Bronze Age incomers would look for in a site. Aerial photographs of the island showed some interesting shapes under a farmer's field just above Lákoma."

"Why?"

"Pardon me?"

"Why were you looking for something well above sea level? Didn't Bronze Age people sometimes build very close to sea level?"

The archaeologist took his eyes off the road to look at her. "Sometimes," he said. "In this instance I had reason to believe they would not have done so."

Kate smiled and nodded as though completely satisfied. It was obvious she wouldn't get anything more from him right now, but she filed it away as something to find out.

Lakoma was a tiny, poor village with badly paved streets where they had to leave the highway and make their way over a rutted dirt track that shook the innards of both the Jeep and Kate and, presumably, of the man beside her. Then they left even that, and followed what looked like nothing more than a Jeep track over a farmer's field. A herd of grazing goats got frightened by their passing but, instead of running away from them, for some reason determined on getting to the other side of the track before the Jeep passed. Constantinou, already proceeding at a speed not much faster than a walk, braked and waited until the kids were reunited with their mothers and everyone was travelling away from the Jeep.

Kate took a deep breath and sighed. "It really is peaceful here," she said. "This island is really unspoilt, isn't it?"

"It doesn't have the beaches to attract tourists, and not much in the way of archaeology, either."

"No beaches?" she asked, surprised. "The whole northern side seemed to be one long beach as we came in."

"The beaches on Samothráki are stony," he returned. "There is a beautiful area at Vatos, on the south coast, but it's accessible only by sea. Unless someone puts a great deal of money into the island, these people are safe from tourism for a long time to come, not that they necessarily want to be. Of course, the Greek people come here for holidays. From Alexandroúpolis, Thessaloníki, Kaválla. There are some islands which mostly only Greeks vacation on. This is one of them."

"How do they feel about your dig? The islanders, I mean."

"Strangers bring money, and this is a poor island."

With a last roar from the motor, the Jeep topped a

rise, and suddenly the quiet farmer's field was quiet no more. Spread out in front of them over the hilltop was a collection of tents and shacks, and a huge spread of uncovered earth, where people were digging and moving about.

Andreas braked suddenly, before they reached the site. "I forgot to mention," he said, "I have told them you are a friend of my cousin Sophia's with time and money on your hands, and that you have offered to act as my secretary for a month."

Kate's mouth opened in indignation. "Your secretary!" she repeated, but she wasn't surprised. "Damn it, I don't want to spend my time typing and looking after you! Talk about typical male chauvinism! Couldn't you have thought of something better than that?"

He was unperturbed, naturally. "I didn't know what skills you have," he pointed out. "We need a photographer, too; now the site directors have to take the pictures, but I didn't know if you can use a camera. Also we need an artist-illustrator, but how shall I know if you can paint? But you are a writer; I thought you must be able to type." He released the brake and put his foot on the gas, because some people in the camp had already noticed their presence on the outskirts of the site.

"You mean, I'm a *woman*! That's why you thought I could type, right?" she muttered angrily. "Would it surprise you to learn, Mr. Constantinou, that I have my own secretary?"

He glanced at her in dismay, and she felt a ripple of satisfaction. Why she wanted to impress this man with her importance she couldn't have said, but he seemed to be bringing out all the worst of her early-lib side. She couldn't stand people who tried to impress you or threw their importance around, man or woman, but she had done a lot of it ten years ago, after leaving Peter, when her ego had been so bruised and the chip on her shoulder enormous.

"You mean, you can't type?" Constantinou was asking, and she stifled a laugh, not only at the look on his face—he would look a pretty fool, she imagined, if his cousin's friend turned out to be no help at all—but also at the thought of any girl having got her education while living with Aunt Pet and Uncle Sid and *not knowing how to type*.

It was on her lips to deny this skill when she suddenly relented. She didn't care what she did, as long as she was on the site, and she scarcely cared what people thought of her, except that Andreas Constantinou seemed to catch her on the raw. Besides, wouldn't she have a better chance to find out what was going on if she was typing for the man? He must be mad not to have thought of it himself. There would have to be times when she'd be left alone in his office, too. In fact, all things considered, this couldn't have worked out better.

She grinned. "Yes, of course I can type," she told him. "Though I have lived through an era when it was fashionable, if you were a woman, to pretend you couldn't."

Why she made the joke, she couldn't have said. She could hardly expect him to appreciate it. But Constantinou smiled back. "Of course," he returned. "With men, this has always been fashionable. Even now, I see professors at the university who insist that though they can "keyboard" a computer, they can't type."

Kate laughed. "Can *you* type?" she asked, irresistibly.

"Of course not," the archaeologist said, roaring into the compound in a swirl of dust and pulling to a stop between a tent and a small tumbledown building that might once have been a farmhouse. She laughed with him, eyeing him speculatively, but there was no chance for more conversation. The truck was surrounded by people.

"Did the bags come?" a young woman who looked no older than eighteen was demanding, in an unmistakably American accent. "Andrea, did they send the plastic bags?"

"What about my camera attachment? Have you got that?" a male voice asked urgently from behind the truck, and Kate turned to see a young man unashamedly rooting through her duffel bag. When he felt a likely-looking shape, he pulled out her portable hair dryer, attached to which happened to be a pair of delicate bikini briefs in lemon-yellow cotton and lace. The young blond stared at Kate as if seeing her for the first time, and slowly went beet red. While the others around the Jeep laughed lightly, he stuffed everything back in her bag and zipped it up. He babbled an apology.

"All right, everybody," Andreas Constantinou said loudly, cutting him off. "Only the plastic bags have arrived, I'm sorry to say. Nothing else. . . ."

A huge groan went up. "What about the soap? How can we do without the soap?" "Where's the *film*? Andrea, I've scarcely got one day's supply. . . ." Kate heard complaints from all sides. It seemed as though Andreas Constantinou had a dedicated group working with him.

"But as you can see," Constantinou continued calmly, "Demetrius has not returned with me. He is still in Alexandroúpolis, and probably will come with all your orders on tomorrow's ferry. So, let me introduce Miss Fenton to you, and then Sarah can take her plastic bags. Miss Fenton will be my secretary, as I told you. She will be coordinating all your field notes for me, among other things. Miss Fenton, there is no point in my telling you everyone's name now; you would not remember. But you will meet them all, I assure you."

The girl named Sarah was ecstatically pulling at the cardboard boxes, and calling, "Yiorgo, Yiorgo, can you give me a hand?" Everybody else chorused their hellos to Kate, and one or two of them shook her hand as she followed Constantinou out of the Jeep and into the little tumbledown house.

Inside, it had been transformed into an office. Although it had originally had a dirt floor, an obviously new wooden floor had been expertly laid, making the small entrance door seem even smaller with the necessity to step up six inches just inside the threshold. In the far wall a window seemed to have been enlarged, giving a view of the entire site, and sideways in front of the new glass was a large trestle table covered with papers and a lamp, obviously being put to use as a desk. There was a battered green filing cabinet that looked about the same vintage as, the Jeep, another smaller table facing the first one and other bits of furniture, papers and books. Along the wall beside the door were stacked a few boxes filled with plastic bags and bits of labelled pottery and other unrecognizable items. Above these, on the wall, were pinned several photographs, among them a large shot of a hilltop, presumably the aerial view of this site that had convinced Andreas Constantinou to dig here. On the back wall, behind his desk, was a huge map of the site, divided into tiny squares and covered with pins and markings. Kate began to breathe in the excitement of a working project where the expectations are high.

"Later, later!" Constantinou was shouting over the babble, which had followed them into the room. "Everybody out! *Exo, exo!*"

With the exception of one tall blonde, the room

emptied. "Miss Fenton—Kate," Constantinou said, "this is Rebecca Seigel, my assistant director. She is from the University of Pennsylvania. I think it will be a good idea if she shows you around the site—if you don't mind, Rebecca?"

Rebecca was tall, and slightly horsey, and although not exactly pretty, she had a friendly, open face. Until she smiled at Kate, that was. Then all the openness disappeared, and most of the friendliness. "Yes, of course. Will you come with me, Miss Fenton?" she said, opening the door and going out without waiting for an answer.

"Is she just jealous, or does she know I'm a spy?" Kate couldn't resist hissing at Andreas, who was already deep in a notebook. He looked up.

"Jealous," he said, without missing a beat. "All my women are terribly jealous. They fight out on the back dirt every evening to decide who shall have the privilege of sharing my bed at night."

"All right, all right, she's your assistant director; you had to tell her," Kate said in a voice that was unsteady with laughter, tacitly acknowledging the hit. "Do you mind telling me how much she knows? Is she going to hate me, or just guard her tongue?"

Andreas picked up a pen. "I have told her that you have no 'security clearance' and should be treated as outside labour. No more. I would like you, please, not to explain to her or anyone about the blackmail."

"No," agreed Kate quietly, feeling, after that friendly banter, as though she'd been slapped. She turned away from the bright sunlight streaming in around Constantinou through the window and headed for the door.

"Ready?" asked Rebecca Seigel, looking up from a conversation with the young girl named Sarah, who was holding up a plastic bag for her inspection. "Check the other box, Sarah. Anyway, we can use them if we have to."

They fell into step beside one another as Sarah headed off to one of the tents. At ten-thirty in the morning the sun was beating down on their heads as mercilessly as if they'd been in the desert. Kate bent her head back and squinted up at the blazing ball in the unending stretch of blue. "Yes," said Rebecca, as though she'd spoken. "One thing you must remember here at Neathera is to wear a hat at all times. We usually wear one even indoors, because if you take it off when you go in, it's too easy to forget it when you go out again. Of course, you'll be working inside, but at first, anyway, you won't have a full day's work to do. So if you're wandering out here, watching the diggers or running errands for them, be sure tó wear a hat. Have you got one?"

"In my bag," Kate said, and they turned towards the Jeep. She pulled out a white cotton beach hat with a narrow brim that fitted well down on her head and was emblazoned on the front with "I've been to Corfu." Rebecca leaned to read it.

"Oh, Corfu! That's Andreas's home island." Corfu was the foreigner's name for the island the Greeks called Kérkyra. "Have you really been there? Did you meet Andreas there?"

"Yes, and yes," admitted Kate. "What's that big tent there?"

"That's the cooktent. Because we're so far from the villages, and there really isn't a restaurant in either Lakoma or Prophetes Elias that could handle the business anyway, we feed everybody on site. It's expensive, but it saves a lot of man-hours, and besides, it means we don't have to pay the volunteers a meal allowance." She led the way inside a tent that was filled with tables and chairs in one half and cooking equipment in the other. "That probably sounds mercenary, but we're really tight for cash *and* time."

"Really?" Kate said interestedly. "Why are you tight for ti—"

"Do you want some coffee before we start out?" Rebecca went on as though she hadn't heard. "This machine is always full, because there are so many Americans in the team." She filled two mugs and led the way to a table. "In the morning, when everyone arrives, we serve coffee and rolls; that's between five-thirty and six, so you won't have to bother with breakfast wherever you're staying. Then at—"

Kate opened her eyes very wide. "Five-thirty?" she repeated faintly.

"In these hot climates we have to get started early, because we can't work in the afternoon," Rebecca told her kindly. "You'll get used to it. You'll probably even start to enjoy it. Then, at nine, we serve a big breakfast —eggs and toast and meat and fresh tomatoes, something like that. Then another meal at one, the main meal of the day, and after that everybody has siesta for two hours. It really helps if you actually sleep. Are you sleeping here, or do you have a room somewhere?"

"Oh, I—I don't know yet."

"Well, you can usually borrow someone's bed. Some of the volunteers use the time to write up their field reports. Then we start again at four and usually work till six or seven. Then we have a light meal. Usually some of us go into Kamariotissa for another meal at night, but nothing else is served here—except for coffee, of course—till early breakfast. Finished?"

This last was in reference to the coffee, and at Kate's nod Rebecca set her own cup down and stood up. "Right," she said. "Let's get you familiarised with the site. The cooktent, you'll notice, is set at a distance from the others. That's to prevent a kitchen fire from burning up all our paperwork, if we should have one. None of these tents are for accommodation; they're all work tents. The volunteers and labourers sleep down there." She pointed down the hill to a number of large canvas tents that stood at the bottom of the hill some distance from the site. "Let me show you the site before anything else. . . ."

The orientation tour of the site that had been dubbed Neathera was thorough and even friendly, and it left Kate amazed. The site itself was divided into large squares by a grid system, marked by stakes and white string. One side of the hill was designated the "back dirt," where the soil from the site was dumped—but not before it had been thoroughly sifted, and every tiniest find photographed, salvaged, cleaned, labelled and its position drawn on a detailed map. The earth was painstakingly scraped off each five-metre square in two-centimetre depths, and each newly uncovered layer had to be mapped.

"You can't just dig down till you find what you're looking for, I suppose?" Kate commented, for to her the work seemed almost unbearably painstaking.

"Are you kidding?" Rebecca laughed, horrified. "That's like asking a doctor if he's ever amputated a limb just for practice. But of course, in the early days of archaeology it's what happened all too often. Schliemann, who discovered Troy, was so keen to get to the level he wanted that he cut right through the Trojan War period and excavated a level a thousand years earlier. He wasn't in the Troy of Helen and Hector at all.

"The thing you have to remember about archaeology is that the archaeologist destroys his evidence as he goes. So we have to map it with complete accuracy, and

photograph it in situ before it's moved. . . . Well, it's
quite a process, as you saw. And even though what
we're interested in may be two or three or even ten
layers down, we have to—we want to—chart those
other layers as we come to them."

"But isn't it a problem, when you're so pressed for
time?"

Rebecca cast her a look. "Oh, well, we aren't the
first to have unimaginative backers, and we won't be
the last. These are the lab tents here; this is where all
the finds are brought for photographing, washing,
labelling, cataloguing, etcetera. Demetrius is the lab
director; he's in Alexandroúpolis today. Anybody
home?" She raised her voice as she lifted the tent flap.

"*Ya su,* Rebecca," called a female voice, and they
walked in to find a middle-aged, dark-haired woman
bending over a basin of water, using a brush on a tiny
shard of pottery. She glanced up at Kate in surprise, set
down her work and stood up. "Hello," she said curiously.

This was about the tenth face Kate had seen with just
that closed, possessive look in the eyes, and she had
finally decided that it wasn't anything to do with a
supposed relationship between herself and Andreas
Constantinou. It was her mere *presence* here on the site
that made everybody jealous and wary! Kate had seen
the look before, always among people who had to work
closely together on a project, and who were dedicated
to the work. There came a time when the group became
a unit and began to resent outsiders.

This group had been together barely two weeks,
and so far as Kate knew, nothing of significance
had yet been found. So perhaps they were united by
a secret purpose or by the personality of Andreas
Constantinou. Or both, perhaps. He would tell

them the secret and swear them to silence, and they would feel honoured to be chosen by him. . . .

If they didn't accept *her* as one of them, as another person chosen by Constantinou, did that mean somebody knew he hadn't chosen her?

"Agapi is our ceramics specialist and one of our site assistants. Agapi, this is Kate, Andrea's volunteer secretary."

"Oh, yes, he told me." Agapi offered her a muddy hand without apologizing, and as she took it Kate thought amusedly that she must be muddy so often she no longer noticed the fact. "How are you enjoying the work?"

"I haven't begun it yet. I've only just arrived."

"Ah! I see! What day is it, then?"

"Friday."

"Is the ferry in? Did Demetrius bring me the soap?"

"Sorry, Agapi, he didn't come back today. He must have needed more time. He'll be in on tomorrow's ferry."

"Yes, I see. Kate, is it? Andreas won't have enough work to fill all your time. Are you an artist, by any chance? Do you draw at all?"

"I'm sorry, not at all."

"What a pity. We'll need someone to illustrate soon, and we haven't got the budget for it. Well, we're all right so far. . . ." She turned away from them, back to her bucket, and it seemed as if they were instantly forgotten.

"Bye, Agapi, see you at lunch," said Rebecca.

"Yes . . . he'll have to let some of the labourers go, after one or two weeks. This pottery is . . . We're going to need an illustrator. Tell him for me, Rebecca."

"He knows, Agapi. Bye."

When they came out again the sun seemed percepti-

bly hotter, but here on the hilltop the *meltemi* was still
blowing. Kate was very glad of her hat.

"It's a quarter to one," Rebecca said, looking at her
watch. "Lunch is at one. Why don't I take you back to
Andreas? He could probably use the time to get you
oriented in the office."

"Fine," said Kate.

For the first time she wondered whether Andreas
really intended to let her do any secretarial work for
him. It must surely have occurred to him, as it had to
her, that she would be uniquely situated for spying, if
that was her intent? She would be sorry if he didn't let
her work; she was already being infected by the determination and dedication of the archaeological team.
She certainly couldn't spend a month kicking her heels
while everyone around her worked like slaves. Perhaps
if Constantinou didn't want her services, she would
tackle the illustrations after all. One presumably didn't
have to be an *artist,* just a good copyist.

"All through?" asked Andreas, looking up from his
paperwork as they entered the admin hut again. "Is it
lunchtime?"

"Not quite, Andrea, but I want to get back on site
before they knock off, all right? I've brought Kate back
to you in case there was anything you wanted to go over
with her."

A quick look passed between Rebecca and Andreas,
one which Kate was not meant to intercept. But she
caught it, and it told her very plainly that her delivery
to Andreas Constantinou was quite deliberate. They
did not want her wandering loose on the site. With an
impassive face, Andreas tossed down his pen, saying,
"Yes, of course, come and sit down, Kate."

Rebecca went out and closed the door as Kate
crossed the short distance to the chair he indicated. She
was angry; she hated the feeling of not being trusted.

Even though she had brought it upon herself, that look they had exchanged rankled.

She pulled off her hat and wiped her forehead as she sank into the chair. She was more tired than she'd realised, after walking in the sun for two hours. "It's hot in here," she murmured. "How do you stand it?"

"You get used to it," Andreas said.

He was actually quite attractive, in his own way. Kate preferred a tall, thin, intellectual and sensitive kind of man. Someone who might not be overtly sexy, as Andreas was, but who knew how to treat a woman as an equal. The kind of man who, when the romance was over, didn't go away with hard feelings. In fact, Kate was still good friends with two: a philosophy professor she had met while teaching a summer course in women's studies, and a fellow writer she had bumped into in her publisher's office. Both times the agreement had been more or less mutual that it was over, but she couldn't see that kind of thing happening with Andreas Constantinou. Either he'd leave a woman long before she was ready for the split, and it would be bad for her, or he'd try to refuse to let her leave when she wanted to, and it would be bad for him.

Kate looked into Andreas's dark eyes and thought of what it would feel like to have this man holding you, begging you not to go, and then, in spite of the heat, she shivered.

And he suddenly demanded, "Is your name Mrs. or Miss Fenton?"

"Oh—well, Ms., really. Everybody uses Ms. at home. But aren't you going to call me Kate? It'll seem—"

"Yes," he said impatiently. "I meant, is it your husband's name, Fenton?"

"My *husband's* name? No, of course not! It's my own, I took my own name back after the divorce."

"Oh," he said.

"Why?"

He shrugged. "I was wondering; that is all."

She demanded suddenly, "Are you checking up on me, or something? What's going on? What are you hoping to find?"

Andreas shook his head. "Nothing's going on. I know who you are. I know what you want. You are scarcely here under false pretences. This is honest blackmail, isn't it." He said it like that, as a statement, but she was hardly reassured.

"Then why do you want to know about my name?"

He looked at her. "I was wondering why your husband let you go," he said simply.

Kate jumped as the shock went through her. Lord, she was so right about this man. He was one to leave alone. "Let you go," indeed, as though she were a piece of property without a will of her own.

"He had no choice in the matter," she said in a hard voice.

Andreas shook his head. "A man has a choice," he said. "If a woman once loved a man, he has always a choice, a way to keep her loving him."

"And what way would you use?" she demanded sarcastically. She was angry; his chauvinism always made her angry. And yet, if Peter had changed, if he had been willing to let her grow . . . "Put her in a cage and starve her into submission?"

"You think that would make a woman love a man?" asked Andreas Constantinou in surprise. "Then perhaps that would be the way with you. A man who wants to keep a woman loving him must learn what it is she wants and thinks he cannot give her, and then he must give it to her."

"And does that hold true for women who want to

keep their men?" she couldn't help asking, knowing what his answer would be.

Andreas shrugged. "Unfortunately, many men are not in love with a woman, but only with her beauty or her youth. You know this. Later, if her man wants youth and beauty, sadly, the woman cannot give it to him. He must go to someone younger, whom he still cannot love."

"You seem to be speaking from experience," Kate observed sweetly. "What age are you working on these days?"

He shook his head. "I am one of the lucky ones," he said softly. "I do not love what I find beautiful; I find beautiful what I love."

"So all your wife has to do to keep you is give you what you want. And does she?"

"I am not married. Before I marry, I will be sure that I want what my wife can give me."

"Or sure your wife can give you what you want?" she pursued, wondering why she was driven to keep this strange conversation going. It was beginning to have a sexual undercurrent, or perhaps it had always had one, and she ought to be changing the subject. But she was suddenly torn with a need to know what Andreas Constantinou wanted in a woman.

And he was suddenly smiling as if that was exactly what he wanted her to want to know. A drop of perspiration trickled between her breasts, and in the silence a gong sounded.

"Lunch," said Andreas Constantinou.

She spent her siesta on the cot in the back room of the admin hut, because after a meal like that in such heat, there was nothing to do *but* sleep. She awoke at four, feeling refreshed and ready for work, and for the first time understood the wonderful logic in the Mediterranean way of life.

Andreas was out on the dig, but he had left a pile of notes beside the typewriter on the smaller desk in the office, and a note asking her to type them. Kate glanced through the first few pages and then laughed. If she was going to be a spy on this dig, she was going to need either a translator or a crash course in archaeology. Where was "30 centimetres below datum," for example? Or "the NW quadrant of 61s2"? She might read exactly where the treasure of Atlantis was buried in these notes and she still wouldn't be able to find it! But she wouldn't, of course. There would be nothing in the least exciting in these notes, because Andreas Constantinou wouldn't have trusted her to type them if there were. Kate sighed and settled to work. Ah, well, she had to earn her keep somehow.

The worst of the heat was over, and she was conscious of a sudden envy of those working outside. Through the window she could see them on the dig: the volunteers and labourers in their respective squares of the grid; Andreas and Rebecca moving about, sometimes working at one area, sometimes at another, or, when called, moving to view something interesting, perhaps, but invisible to Kate at this distance.

Samothráki seemed to be cooler and was certainly a lot more pleasant than Athens, and she found working in the hot dry air of the office quite easy. By the time Andreas Constantinou returned to the admin hut, she had finished typing and was, from force of habit, proofreading the pages. It was nearly seven o'clock and the sun was low in the sky.

"Finished?" asked Andreas, glancing over the pages of his field report with evident approval. "Excellent." He pulled on his shirt, which he had stripped off while he worked, and began closing drawers and doors in the room preparatory to leaving. "Rebecca is driving some of the volunteers down to the beach for a swim. It's the only chance they get for a bath. Do you want to go along, or would you prefer to go home?"

He closed the door behind them, and they crossed the compound towards the cooktent. "Where is my home?" Kate asked.

"Ah! I didn't tell you? I have booked you in at the hotel in Kamariotissa; I'll drive you back. You'll have a private bathroom, of course; you can clean up there if you prefer."

She had had a long day; she was tired. "Yes, I think so, please."

"Was it an interesting day?" she asked as, having eaten and listened to a lot of excitable archaeological chatter, they finally clambered into the Jeep for the trip home. It was nearly dark now, and the lights were on in the compound, to the accompaniment of the site generator, which had been running on and off all day and had started again with a roar not long before.

"Interesting enough. We are finding some interesting pottery, only small shards so far, but enough to make us optimistic. Unfortunately, still no sign of walls or a floor."

"Is that important?" she said, hoping that the question sounded like what it was—genuine interest—and not as though she were spying.

"It's very important to find the floor; it will tell us, first of all, whether we have a single or multiple occupation site on our hands."

She knew that was a reference to different layers on a site, reflecting different eras or different civilisations inhabiting the same site. "I guess it's more exciting when there have been many different periods on the one site," she suggested.

"In general, yes," Andreas agreed. The darkness had become complete suddenly, and now the only source of illumination was the Jeep's headlights, which pierced the night ahead of them as they rolled down the mountainside. "In this particular instance, however, it would suit my purposes to find that we had only one or two layers of occupation on the site."

"Is that because of the pressure of time?"

He glanced over at her in the reflected glow from the headlights. "Time, yes, but other reasons, also. It would suit my time pressures if we found evidence of the Bronze Age people I hope to find immediately, and it would suit my theory if they were the first to inhabit the site. Therefore I hope for only a few layers."

Kate wrinkled her brow. "What's the danger of finding what you're looking for because you're looking for it?"

He laughed as though she had struck home. "Too great," he admitted. "Much too great. We are always dealing with the human element in archaeology, and possibly in the other sciences as well. That is why modern archaeology often attempts, where it is feasible, to leave some of the evidence untouched, for the benefit of future archaeologists."

That impressed her. "Really?" she said. "Are you going to do that?"

"We are unfortunately working against time. I will leave the northeast section untouched, if the finds elsewhere are sufficiently compelling to substantiate or disprove my theory."

"What *is* your theory?"

The lights of Kamariotissa appeared beyond and slightly below them, curving around the harbour in the black, attractive and peaceful. Constantinou changed gears. "My theory is that there were incomers to the island in about 1450 B.C."

"That's the Bronze Age, right?"

"Bronze Age, yes."

"Were there other people here when they came?"

"There have already been prehistoric discoveries on Samothráki, yes, which are evidence of a different people than the ones I believe came here later on. There is no reason yet to postulate that they did not coexist, if I am right."

"And where did your people come from?"

They had turned off the well-paved highway onto a somewhat older road which Kate recognized as the way they had taken through Kamariotissa. They were almost home, then. She felt a small sense of disappointment. She enjoyed talking to Andreas; she didn't want it to be over so soon.

"That remains to be seen, doesn't it?" He smiled at her, so that she almost didn't notice the fact that he was avoiding giving her an answer.

"This is the road to your hotel. There is only one hotel in Kamariotissa, so if you get lost, you need only ask for '*toh ksenothokheio*,' and someone will point it out to you."

"Toe what?"

Andreas repeated the word, and Kate sighed. "Another five-syllable word. Greek seems a very difficult language, for a foreigner."

He looked interested. "Are you trying to learn Greek?"

"Sophia was giving me lessons. I like to try to learn at least something of the language when I'm in a country."

"*Katalavéneis óti léo tóra?*" he asked.

She repressed the pleasure she felt at the fact that he was using the personal, and not the formal, *you*.

"*Ne, katalavéno, allá then eínai thískolo, Andrea.*"

"*Vérveia.*" There followed a long series of syllables of which she understood not a word, and she laughed.

"You see? I didn't get any of that."

Andreas smiled at her. "Just as well," he said, pulling the Jeep over to the side of the road, where bright lights proclaimed a small modern hotel. He shut off the engine and turned to reach for her duffel bag in the backseat, his movement bringing him not much closer to her, but opening his body to her, so that her cheek was near his chest, instead of his shoulder, and it was like an intimacy, in the softly lighted darkness.

Kate clambered out of her side of the Jeep, wondering, like a teenager, if it were possible that she could be feeling such a physical excitement in a vacuum, or whether half of it emanated from him, as she imagined. If so, would he make a move or not?

He followed her across the road and into the cool marble lobby of the hotel, where she was suddenly made aware of their dust and general dishevelment, compared to several attractive women wearing white and impeccably made up, who were sitting in the lounge with their escorts, laughing and chatting. Their sophistication proclaimed them as Athenians, she was sure. Even a few short weeks was enough for Kate to have learned the vast difference between villagers and those who came from the capital.

But the receptionist who was handing Andreas a key seemed unperturbed, and presumably in a town this size—on an island this size—everybody knew about the dig, and no one was shocked by their dust or their old clothes. Andreas, she noted in this new environment, following him down a corridor, looked like a manual labourer, with his heavy protective boots, and his sturdy and beautifully muscled brown legs and arms, and that thick black hair and its coating of dust. . . .

He was fitting the key in a lock, and he opened the door and went in—a typically Greek male, she noted at once. A North American man would have stood back to let her go in first. The thought flashed through her mind that she would then have called him "typically chauvinist," and brought face to face with her own conditioned responses like this, she had a moment of thinking, Men can't win. None of us can win, as long as we define the world so arbitrarily. But as such small bursts of enlightenment will, it disappeared under the pressure of the necessity to see the world as one has always seen it.

Andreas had set her duffel bag down on a chair, and now he caught sight of himself in the mirror above the dressing table. Ruefully he rubbed his hand over his dust-covered hair. "I should have gone swimming with Rebecca and the others," he said, smiling.

"Don't you have a shower where you're staying?" she asked.

"At the moment I am sleeping in the admin hut," he responded. "We are going to fix up an open-air shower on the site, but we have been too busy to spare the labourers."

"Would you like to shower here? I don't mind."

It was said before she thought, but she had ample time to recognize her stupidity in the long, long pause which followed. "I'll go and have a drink," she babbled then. "Just let me get my wallet. . . ."

He was smiling with one corner of his mouth, an

expression she couldn't read, though it might have held disappointment. "You are very tired after your first day," Andreas suggested slowly, crossing the room to the door. "You need the shower yourself, yes? I can go to the beach; it isn't late."

And he was gone on the word.

Chapter 6

SAMOTHRÁKI

WHEN THE DOOR CLOSED BEHIND HIM, KATE LET OUT HER tension in a rush of breath. Of course it was a relief not to have had to deal with any sexual overtures from the man, but Kate knew as surely as she was standing there that tonight's avoidance of the issue was only a postponement. She almost wished Andreas Constantinou had made a pass so that she could have made it clear once and for all that, though she was adult enough to recognize the humming sexual awareness between them, she had no intention of getting involved with him.

Oh, well, maybe *he* had no interest in getting involved, either. Maybe she was worrying over nothing. Kate sighed in honest physical exhaustion and began to strip where she was. Her clothes and skin were covered with dust, and her muscles were feeling stiff. It was a hot night, and the hotel had no air conditioning, but she was going to take a hot bath anyway.

She was naked and bending over the bath taps when a knock sounded on the door, and she dashed into the bedroom and made a grab for her duffel bag. *"Miso lepto!"* she called in the direction of the door. Most people in Samothráki didn't speak English, she knew, and a chambermaid certainly would not.

When she located her bathrobe she pulled it quickly around herself and opened the door, still tying the belt.

"I forgot to tell you," said Andreas Constantinou, "about renting a scooter."

She stepped back automatically, and he came into the room and shut the door behind him. "Just down this street, I meant to point it out to you when we passed, there is a shop that rents motor scooters. It's not very expensive; six or seven hundred drachmas a day, I think. It's a good way for you to get around the island, because no one from the dig is staying here in Kamariotissa. You have to get to the dig every morning yourself."

"Yes," she muttered. "Thank you. I'll do that tomorrow morning."

"It's just down on the right, before you make the turn onto the Khora road."

"Yes, all right." He turned to go. "Why is no one else staying here?"

Constantinou turned back and looked at her, and there was a flicker of warning in her head that told her she would have been better to let him go. "Because it's more expensive than the tents, and we don't have to worry about transportation." He paused. "I have interrupted your bath, but I was afraid you were expecting me to pick you up tomorrow morning."

"Yes," she said for the third time. Why couldn't she stand in the same room with the man without feeling her legs turn to jelly? He wasn't—he definitely wasn't—

her type at all. Yet the wanting him to touch her was nearly unbearable.

She had seen a statue in one of the museums not long ago; a votive statue of a god, a tiny figure with an enormous phallus thrusting up from between his legs. You couldn't look at the statue and not think of sex. Sex as a colossal power, a driving life force.

That was how she felt with Andreas Constantinou in the room. She was aware of sex—her sex, his sex, sex as a great primal force of nature. And she discovered that that kind of awareness—of sex as a life force—eroded everything else: reason, social conditioning, concentration. She was staring at him, her hands still gripping the belt of her bathrobe; and in spite of everything she had just been telling herself, she was glad that the fabric of the robe was thin enough that she could be sure he saw the outline of her nipples through it, glad that its loose neckline showed the thrusting curve of her breasts, primitively, shockingly glad that the length of her forward leg was fully outlined, and that where her thigh met her body the silky cloth clung to the obvious curl of thick, springing hair.

When she realized where she was looking, she snatched her gaze away from his khaki-covered loins, and then their eyes locked, and Kate was suddenly very aware of the invitation he must be reading into her attitude. She was being about as subtle as a cat in mating season. And yet she was quite sure she did not want sex with this man; she just couldn't control the effect he seemed to have on her.

"You'd better go," she said, at exactly the same moment that Andreas Constantinou said, "Or you might have been expecting that I would not leave you tonight," and reached for her.

His long hands first gripped her arms at the elbows,

and then one hand was against the small of her back.
Kate made a tiny grunting moan and arched back over
the pressure of his palm, for the heat of him stirred her
unbearably. She heard a sound like a crack of thunder
and felt her own wild relief about to swamp her, and
she knew that the storm was going to break. And at all
costs she must prevent it.

"Please," she whispered, turning her face to avoid
the kiss that every nerve ending ached to feel. "Please
don't." Her brain was clamouring with a belated panic.
She had never had any doubt of being able to control
herself; she had turned down men before when she'd
felt a strong sexual desire, because they were already
attached to someone, or because she was, or because
things weren't right otherwise. If you didn't know how
to say no to your own physical desires now and then,
Kate felt, you were a poor excuse for a human.

Right now she didn't feel like a poor excuse for a
human, though. She felt like the ultimate design break-
through. She felt as though she had finally discovered
the purpose of the human race, the reason for existence: to love and be loved, in every possible way.

Andreas Constantinou lifted one hand to her cheek,
turning her face back to his as though he enjoyed her
evasion of his mouth, as though . . . as though resistance were a front she put up in order to increase the
excitement and the pleasure for them both. She heard a
small noise like a laugh in his throat, and above her his
eyes slitted with lazy pleasure as he held her face and
lowered his mouth towards hers.

She turned her face again, into the unyielding pressure of his hand, and he forced it back, and there shot
through her a stab of mingled pleasure and excitement
so startlingly profound she gasped. His arm around her
was irresistibly strong, holding her securely into the
curve of his body, and his palm against her cheek was

gentle but firm, and she realized with a sudden feeling of vertigo that Andreas Constantinou was stronger than she was, and that she could fight with all her strength, and still he would win.

The knowledge did not frighten her. It thrilled her immeasurably. She had to close her eyes against it, for fear that he would read in the mere quiver of her lashes how desperately she wanted to feed his appetite with resistance.

Kate jerked her head to the other side, and a tingling excitement filled her to bursting. She was breathless. "Stop," she whispered, not knowing whether she meant it or not, and Andreas Constantinou smiled deep into her eyes. Then, as his dark gaze locked with hers, his smile slipped away till his face was filled with a passionate intent that made her own passion thrum in her breast and her body; and then he held her face and bent to kiss her.

She was virtually powerless under his hands; she realized now that he could have kissed her at any time in the past few minutes. He had waited because of the pleasure it gave them; he had *allowed* her to evade his mouth, but now he would allow it no longer, and her heartbeat was painful in her breast.

The touch of his mouth against hers was honey and fire, and she moaned as his hand slipped away from her cheek and trailed its gentle heat down to her breast, enclosing it with sweet flame. He stirred her like no other lover, and if she gave in to their desire, she would never be sorry.

But he had left her free, as though he knew she would not struggle anymore; and the primitive instinct that ruled her now prompted her to teach him that she was not so easily won over. Kate lifted her hands to push against his chest and drew her lips away.

She felt his arm tighten around her back, and now

when he looked into her eyes he was not smiling. "Don't fight me," he said hoarsely. "I want you." But she knew that the battle was as potently erotic to him as it was to her. His free hand came up to the back of her head, and when he kissed her he bent her backwards over his arm, and her body was forced against his.

Now his kiss was deep and thrusting, and no longer gentle, and in the moment that she knew that he had won the battle that it had been foreordained he would win, the moment when her desire became too much for games, a certain programming fell into place in her brain, and coursing through her suddenly was the horror of feeling a traitor to her sex.

What is this? she thought wildly. Some sort of rape fantasy? And then, immediately on the heels of that thought, I said no to this man, and he ignored me.

She began to strain away in earnest, and her legs bumped up against something, and suddenly she was falling backwards through space, and the softness of the bed was under her back, and Andreas Constantinou was on top of her, and he was not soft.

And in spite of herself, the thrust of him against her stomach made her ache with yearning. She wished suddenly that she hadn't remembered the feminist view of sex; she wished she hadn't remembered till afterwards, because something told her that one night of lovemaking with this man would be worth anything. . . .

"Will you stop this?" she demanded feebly. "What do you think you're doing?"

Andreas Constantinou laughed. He said, "I don't think you are so naive," and he took her pushing hand in a lazy grip and locked it helplessly against the bed near her head. She smelled the mingled scent of dust, and work sweat, and the indefinable perfume of male sexual arousal, and it went to her head like a drug. The collar of his khaki workshirt was frayed and worn, and open at the throat, where the dust of the dig clung lightly to the black hairs curling on his chest. She had a sudden memory of that afternoon on the site, when in the heat this man had stripped off his shirt, and his chest and back, glistening with sweat, had been alive with working muscle. She had stopped and watched unconsciously, but knowing then, as she knew it now, just how those muscles would work under the skin as he moved above her during the act of sex.

She said, "I am not in the least naive, and I have no intention of making love with you, so will you please get off me?"

His grin became quizzical; his eyebrows moved in an amused frown. "What?" he said.

"Let go of me." Her voice was a croak, her chest was heaving, but that was nothing compared to the turmoil in her brain. How could she, a modern woman, be stirred by a man ignoring her protests? How could she be lying here wishing with all her heart that he would ignore what she said now and make love to her as wildly as she knew he could? It made no sense, no sense at all, unless she was a screaming masochist.

Suddenly she wished he did not speak any English at all. She wished that whatever she said were unintelligible to him, so that he would read the only signs he knew—the evidence of her body, which could not lie. She wished she could make all the mandatory protests that a woman being taken for the first time must make, and that he, not understanding, would take it all for love cries and make love to her anyway, teaching her with his body that the rules did not matter. She suddenly, passionately, desperately wanted him to make love to her while she cried "No, no, no" and was given the pleasure in spite of herself.

There was nothing to help her understand why she

wished it, but everything she had learned in the past ten years was there to tell her that her desire was a betrayal of feminism and womanhood and herself. And she knew that he would have done just what she wished, two minutes ago; but now it was impossible, because now she could not allow it to happen.

"What is it?" asked Andreas Constantinou in concern. "What is the matter?"

Her passion had been slowly draining away; now the residue left her in a rush, and she felt cold and bored. "Let me up, please," she said, and there was no mistaking that uninterested, matter-of-fact tone.

He let her go and stood up. "What has happened?" he demanded, staring down at her, and Kate rolled to a sitting position and let her head droop for a moment as he watched. Then, pulling her robe around her, she said tiredly, "Nothing's happened, Andrea; you're just not my type, that's all."

She was prepared for snide male hostility, but not for angry indignation. *"Type?"* he blazed at her, and she swung her amazed gaze up to his. "Not your *type*? What are you talking about?" As always, when he was angry, his accent became more pronounced. "We are a man and a woman; we were going to make love because we want each other. What is *type*? I am not a piece of meat; I am a man! What is your type? My hair isn't the right colour? My body maybe not the right shape for you? What is your type?"

My God, he sounded just like the women in her consciousness-raising group ten years ago. She had always thought that men were so used to depersonalizing women that their own depersonalization was accepted as a matter of course.

"I'm sorry," she said. "You're right. But you . . . I just do not want to go to bed with you."

He waited. Then he said, "I want to understand.

Tonight, when I thought you wanted me to make love to you, I was mistaken? You didn't want it? You don't want me to touch you?"

She stared up at him, willing her mouth to open on the lie. "Andrea, I . . . uh . . . it isn't that simple," she managed at last.

For some unfathomable reason all the angry tension seemed to leave him at her words, and he was left looking down at her, his eyes lazily narrowed, a half smile hovering around his lips. "No, I see that, for you, it isn't simple. For me, it is very simple," he said.

She understood. He would leave her alone now, and really, it was better this way. For all she would regret the lost lovemaking, she would have regretted the destruction of her entire value system even more. "Yes," she said gratefully, only the faintest tinge of the might-have-been colouring her voice. "Yes, it's better if we just forget all this, Andrea."

Andreas Constantinou reached down and stroked her face from temple to chin. "Good night, Kate," he said. He strode to the door and opened it. "It's all right. Don't worry. I understand you."

Kate lay in the bath, soaking and thinking. Sometimes she did her best thinking like this, up to her chin in hot water. Right now she was thinking about Andreas's parting shot. What had he meant by it? Did he mean he was going to ignore what she said? That would be chauvinistic all right. Nothing could be more arrogant than a man pursuing a woman who had told him plainly that she didn't want him.

In a sudden access of honesty, Kate shook herself aware. She shouldn't be attaching general rules to specific incidents like this. The fact was, she *hadn't* told Andreas plainly that she didn't want him. It must have been obvious to him that she was attracted to him.

Until she had changed her mind they had both been playing a game, a game they had found exciting.

The fact was, she *did* want him. And if she were honest with herself, really honest, wasn't the feeling she was now trying to suppress a tiny thrill of excitement at the possibility that Andreas Constantinou was *not* going to take her at her word?

What a horrible thought. What on earth did it mean? Did she have a sexual "Uncle Tom" mentality after all? Did she want some big strong man to take the decision out of her hands, just like some 1950s virgin?

Kate took a deep breath and swirled the water aimlessly around her. She didn't know the answer. And if she didn't know, how could she expect Andreas—or any man—to know? She had a sudden recollection of her moment of understanding earlier. A man was damned if he did and damned if he didn't, wasn't he?

Why did we never notice—or never admit, she thought suddenly—that men are caught in as much of a bind as we are? How could we expect to break out of the mould if we didn't admit that men were forced into a mould just as uncomfortable, just as unsuitable? We ought to have done it *together*; surely we ought to have declared war on our joint conditioned responses, instead of on *men*? And then perhaps the revolution would have succeeded.

Worth an article, anyway, she thought, filing away, as she often did, thoughts which were too uncomfortable to swallow in one sitting. It was the first time she had consciously admitted to herself that the women's revolution had failed. Of course, everyone knew that it was *over*; it was fashionable to talk about it as a thing of the past—but how many examined the gains and losses, even now?

When women ran the world, if they ever had, would

it really have been any better? Would it really be better if they ran it now? As long as you had a slave class and a master class, could it possibly matter who was in which group?

Now there was a question that could blow not only her feminist reputation, but also the entire subtext of her new book. For the first time, Kate began to see the complexity of the need that had driven her to get onto a dig and observe the evidence firsthand, before it had been translated by someone else's conditioned responses. If women *had* once run the world, had it been different, had it been better run? Or had it been just as unbalanced, but in a different way? In order for the world to work, didn't women and men have to run it *together*?

Well, perhaps, but none of that explained or excused her bizarre reaction to Andreas Constantinou tonight, did it? At worst, it was masochistic, and at best, immature, for surely the game she had been playing had been that feminist's anathema, the please-take-the-responsibility-for-my-decision game?

And what about Andreas's motives? He was angry at her for being here, for having forced her way in; he surely considered her an enemy. Wasn't this just an obvious case of sex as punishment, sex to reestablish his masculine superiority after she had got the better of him?

Kate cringed with embarrassment. Thank God she had stopped him in time. She couldn't have borne his mocking triumph if he had succeeded.

She didn't want to think about it anymore. There was no point in punishing herself by going over and over it. Besides, she had other, more profitable trains of thought to pursue. Kate bent her knee and squooshed water out of her sponge over her thigh. It was too hot for a hot bath, but she could feel the ache in her muscles soaking away. She had been scrambling over the dig very energetically during Rebecca's tour.

It had been an interesting day at the dig, not least because of an unguarded comment Rebecca Seigel had made during the chatter over supper. Kate had been sitting with the supervisors, the professional archaeologists, an arrangement which had happened naturally because she had entered with Andreas and because of the age factor. And after a while Rebecca had forgotten her presence.

Andreas, it seemed, was going to a place called Akrotíri to visit an archaeologist there, and it had something to do with the dig here. That was all she knew, and she wouldn't have noticed even that much, if it hadn't been for the sudden silence that had fallen over the table and the fact that Rebecca had obviously been annoyed with herself for letting this plan of Andreas's out of the bag, as though either the visit itself, or any connection between Akrotíri and Samothráki, must be kept secret.

Kate had kept the sudden leap of interest she'd felt to herself, and Rebecca and several others, including Andreas, had breathed well-concealed relief. She had stored that information, too, in the back of her head, and it had lain dormant since, waiting for the first moment of relaxation to push itself forward.

With a sudden burst of impatient energy, Kate sat forward and pulled the plug, then stood up and reached for the towel. In her bedroom she rooted around in her bag for the pocket encyclopedia of archaeological sites she had purchased at the English bookstore in Athens. Her fingers left wet marks on the newsprint pages, and impatiently she dried them.

Akrotíri: Théra. Arch: S. Marinatos. O: 1967. A late–Bronze Age site buried under several metres of volcanic lava. It was evidently a highly advanced civilisation with an advanced architecture: some of the buildings are three stories high. Trade connections with Knossos. Catastrophe overtook the island in approximately 1450 B.C. (the date is in dispute), when the volcano erupted and half the island sank into the ocean. Marinatos postulates that it was this eruption and a subsequent tidal wave of enormous proportions that caused the downfall of the neighbouring Minoan kingdom of Crete. The site is open to visitors. . . .

Kate turned the book facedown on the table and pulled out her map of Greece. Théra, Théra, where the devil was Théra? She knew she had heard the name before, only recently. There were so many islands making up Greece, and the map eschewed such niceties as a legend. You either had to know where the place was before you started or else go over the map with a fine-tooth— There! Théra! In the tiniest red print, under the name Santoríni. Which meant, she had learned, that the island had two names, as so many places in this country did. Lésvos was also Mytílene; Kérkyra was otherwise known as Corfu; Thessaloníki was called Saloníki by the Greeks . . . and Théra was Santoríni, and Andreas Constantinou was going to visit it in a few days.

Kate turned to root through her duffel bag for the rest of the books she had brought with her from Athens. There must be one with a fuller explanation of Santoríni's disaster in it. . . . She found it, and read avidly, and then sat back to absorb the information and think.

As the guidebook mentioned, the great Bronze Age

Minoan Empire on Crete had been destroyed, literally overnight. Life had mysteriously, for no apparent reason, simply ceased in all but one of the great palaces on the island kingdom. Up until 1939, this disaster had been halfheartedly explained by archaeologists and historians as being due to a peasant uprising at the largest palace at Knossos, or by a "passive renunciation of power" to the invading Mycenaeans. Then, in 1939, the young archaeoleogist Spyridon Marinatos, excavating at the palace of Malia on Crete, and observing stone walls that seemed to have been pushed forward and sucked back by the sea, had postulated that the destruction of the Minoan kingdom had been caused by a great tidal wave, following violent volcanic activity on the neighbouring island of Santoríni.

It had been an extremely provocative theory, in 1939. And there had been no archaeological excavation on Santoríni to support it. There was not to be, for another thirty years. Thanks to the Second World War, and then the civil war that followed in Greece, and then other obstacles like lack of funding, Spyridon Marinatos had not begun excavations on Santoríni until the late sixties.

He had begun near a village called Akrotíri, and the dig had confirmed his amazing theory to the satisfaction of all save the most immovable. There had been a civilisation on Santoríni, too, in the Bronze Age, and it was now covered with several metres of volcanic ash. The island had literally blown up and sunk into the ocean, and like Krakatoa three millennia later, had caused disaster for all its neighbors, but most horribly for the great kingdom of the Minoans, with its advanced art and architecture, and its great palaces, and the Minotaur of Greek legend.

Spyridon Marinatos had done what every archaeologist must hope to do: he had cast new light on an entire period of history, had brought historical order out of the chaos of conflicting theory.

But there was one theory that his discovery had not changed; in fact, it might have enhanced it: the theory that the island of Crete during the Minoan era was the historical basis for the legend of Atlantis. For now, with the tidal wave theory, it could be seen that the disaster had been all the things the legend said it was: lightning swift, unexpected and totally destructive. An overnight disaster.

Kate sat back and stared at the wall without seeing it.

In the past few days, she had pretty well discarded her theory of an Atlantean connection with Andreas Constantinou and the dig on Samothráki. Yet in a few days Andreas Constantinou was going to visit the site of a civilisation that had coexisted with the one some people thought had been Atlantis. Which had been destroyed at the same time, literally in the same night.

What connection could those civilisations have with the remote little island in the northern Aegean?

What was the connection between Atlantis and Nea-thera?

Chapter 7

SAMOTHRÁKI

KATE PILOTED THE BRIGHT YELLOW MOTORBIKE ALONG THE highway in the rich, warm light of sunrise as the wind caressed her face and hair. She took a deep breath and smiled to herself in the pleasure of another morning breaking like the first morning. She would have been hard-pressed to remember another period in her life that she had enjoyed as much as she was enjoying these days on Samothráki. She awoke early with a sense of joy and purpose; she worked hard all day; she fell asleep at night with a wonderful, tired abandon she hadn't enjoyed since her first year at university.

Kate was an all-or-nothing woman. She loved the sense of being totally involved in some project or cause; she was never more alive than when something completely absorbed her.

The dig at Neathera had begun to absorb her completely. Although she had always been a night person, she had no trouble these days getting up at five in the morning, with the sun, in order to make this pleasant, twenty-minute trek by motor scooter up to the dig for first breakfast. She found these early-morning rides peaceful and soothing as she made her solitary way along a cool, obliquely lighted highway towards the sun-kissed peak of Mount Fengari.

She rarely met other drivers on the road, but there was an old man who rode his donkey down the mountain towards Kamariotissa at that hour, she had found, and a young goatherd whose flock never got used to the noise of her passing, and several others who recognized her each day and gave her that special salute that belongs to those who are in on the secret of being awake together while the rest of the world sleeps.

Below her, as she climbed the mountain, the wheat fields of Samothráki gradually caught the rays of the sun slanting out from behind the peak, and were transformed, golden against the deep blue of the sea. She could not remember ever feeling such a sense of peace as she felt seeing that rural scenery spread out above and below her.

As she rounded a wide curve in the smooth road, Kate saw a familiar sight and throttled down, then smiled and waved. She always drove slowly past the goats, to reduce the noise of her engine, and she always looked out for her favourite, a little kid who was white before and black behind, and who bleated louder and more appealingly than any of the others, and always with a look of indignant terror on its face that made her laugh, every time.

She slowed down while passing through the village of Lákoma, too, because even here in this remote pastoral landscape not everyone got up at the crack of dawn. Then, as she hit the dirt track that led to the dig, the peace and the morning and the sense of purpose all combined in her breast to fill her with a sense of utter well-being, and she battled her way over the steep,

rough track on the little bike with the grin of challenge
on her face, slamming her feet against the earth to
guide the bike over the ruts.

Breakfast with the team, even, was something to
look forward to. Most of them knew her only as a new
worker, and the ranks had quickly parted to include
her. That closed, secretive look she had seen on so
many faces her first day was only for outsiders, and
Kate was no longer an outsider. The volunteers in any
case knew not much more than she did, she had found;
certainly they did not have access to the "secret" of the
dig. And the professional archaeologists were used to
keeping close about that secret. So Kate was in no way
the pariah she had feared she would be, and she
enjoyed the camaraderie of the dig, starting every
morning over coffee and rolls.

This morning, as she brought the bike to a halt
outside the admin hut and knocked the kickstand into
place with one practised motion, she saw Andreas
Constantinou sitting at his desk, watching her through
the open door.

"*Ya su*, Andrea," she called happily. His presence
was a large factor in the sense of well-being she was
experiencing here, she knew. He kept her alert; the air
always seemed to crackle when he was around. She felt
a mental challenge from him, a kind of stimulus that
put her on top of her form. It was like the old days, her
street fighter days. She felt ready for anything; she was
alive in every pore.

"*Ya su*," he called as she shut off the bike and
pocketed the key. "Ready for breakfast?"

She nodded, stepping inside the admin hut to drop
into her chair, then reaching into her handbag for her
brush. The ride was exhilarating, but it always left her
smart curls in wild disorder. "Anything new and excit-

ing happening?" she asked, running the brush through the tangles without mercy.

Andreas smiled. "Agapi says some pottery found last night is very primitive in the firing, and means we're at an early occupation period, at last."

Kate was delighted. "You mean, we're finally there? We're into the level you're interested in?" She stood up and tossed the brush back into her bag.

Andreas shrugged, dropping his pen and standing up. "That depends on the dating. The civilisation I'm interested in may be this one, or it may be the people who inhabited this site immediately prior to what we're excavating now. I think my theory will be proven or disproven—to my satisfaction—in the next two weeks."

She laughed in her excitement. "So we're really getting close?"

Suddenly he was standing right beside her, and she had no time to move. "I don't know," he said softly. He reached out and stroked her arm from shoulder to elbow. "Sometimes I think so; sometimes I'm not so sure. Are we getting close, Kate?"

She shivered at the unexpectedness of it. He was always doing this to her, catching her at odd moments when she least expected it, so that she was totally off her guard and hard put to disguise her reaction to his nearness, his touch.

"Andrea," she protested after a moment. "Please." His hand on her bare arm was a more potent arousal than most men's kisses, and now it stopped its stroking motion and he gripped the flesh of her arm and pulled her irresistibly towards him. She put a hand against his chest and tried to ward off the kiss that was coming.

"Kate," he said, his lips within a whisper of hers. "Don't pull away from me. We need this, yes? We are going crazy in here, working together so closely and not touching, never once, the whole day. And every time I touch you, you pull away from me. Kate . . ." He moved his lips, if possible, closer, and his voice was hypnotic. "I want to kiss you, Kate; I want to—"

His mouth sealed hers with the touch that her body ached for, and in spite of her best intentions, she sank against him, feeling her body melt into his. He was right; this was what she wanted, what she had always wanted. She had managed to resist him for days, and now—

A warning bell rang in her brain, reminding her that the first battle was the hardest; all the others would get progressively easier for him now, until she woke up one morning with Andreas beside her in bed, having lost the battles and the war and become involved yet again with an exciting, dangerous man who would think he owned her, body and soul.

Kate pulled back out of his arms. "Please don't do that again," she said, and the effort it cost her to sound cool and unaffected by that kiss was almost more than she could afford. She turned blindly for the door, desperate to escape his nearness and regain some sanity. "I'm going for breakfast," she said. "Coming?" She didn't wait for an answer, but went out into the blinding sunshine, knowing that he followed her, feeling his presence beside her as sharply as a touch.

They entered the cooktent to the babble of forty voices and a fair amount of cigarette smoke. To Kate's amazement, nearly everyone on the site, Greek and American, smoked. The Greeks were very heavy smokers, particularly the hired labour, the professional diggers brought in from the mainland for the season, but Kate had seen that among Sophia's friends. It was the Americans who surprised her. Andreas and Agapi were among the very few on the site who did not smoke. Rebecca had told her that smoking was an occupational hazard for archaeologists.

"I like to dig in Israel and Greece," she had said laughingly. "I *never* feel guilty about smoking in a Greek restaurant. They haven't heard the word yet, or if they have, they have too many other things to worry about first. Like me."

Everyone called hello as Kate and Andreas poured themselves coffee and wandered down to one of the tables. Sarah, the redheaded American student, jumped up and came over. "Andrea," she began in a low voice, drawing his attention while the others at the table smiled ruefully among themselves. Sarah was only eighteen, and she had a king-size crush on Andreas Constantinou that she couldn't hide. She was constantly asking him questions, bringing bits of pottery to him or calling him over to the square where she dug harder and longer than anyone else in the hopes of being the one to find "the find"—the first real clue to the civilisation being dug, the thing that would justify Andreas to his backers and indebt him to her forever.

This morning, it seemed, she might just have done that. As Kate delicately let Andreas's attention go, she was claimed from her other side.

"Hi, Kate!" she was greeted by an excitable girl with a strong American accent, whose name she could not remember. "Have you heard what Sarah's found, the lucky devil?"

Kate smiled and looked teasingly around all the fresh, glowing young faces, and felt a moment of envy of the girls. She had never experienced this youthful enthusiasm in a career. Any joy she had felt in her talents had been crushed early; it had been years before she had learned what she could really do. "Not the walls . . ." she said, as though she were thinking hard. She knew that it was the pottery, of course, but it was a surprise to learn that it was Sarah who had uncovered it. So she had made the big find after all. No wonder she had claimed Andreas's attention just now with such a self-confident air.

For one surprising, swiftly suppressed, jealous moment, Kate found herself wondering how much a thing like this would count with Andreas Constantinou. Would he see Sarah in a new light now? Sarah was young yet, but she was extremely highly motivated, determined to graduate at the top of her class and be a successful archaeologist. She sometimes helped Agapi in the lab, work she had begged because ceramics was her major interest, and Kate had heard Agapi say that she was being given more responsibility than was usual for her age and position. Add to that her obvious hero worship of Andreas, and it might be a combination that he found irresistible.

"Not the walls," agreed the young woman, whom Kate finally placed as Marian. Marian waited expectantly for another guess, but then could not hold it in. "Pottery!" she announced as Kate slipped over into the vacant seat beside her. She felt, rather than saw, Sarah move round to take the seat beside Andreas, but she had already forgotten that moment of unreasoning jealousy. She had turned down Andreas once, and she knew she should keep away from him when she could, as now, without making it obvious. She would be relieved if he turned that high-burn sexual focus onto someone else and left her alone. "About a hundred fragments, all in one place, so when Agapi's put it together, it looks as though we'll have almost a whole jug."

The lack of any significant pottery finds so far had been a real disappointment at Neathera. The surface debris had had the regular amount of pottery shards in it, all of them latter-day, and, disappointingly, many of the shards so far found at the deeper levels had been of the same period—late nineteenth century and after—as though the refuse of the later civilisation had worked its way down through the soil. It was disappointing for everyone, and there were those who were beginning to feel that the site had nothing to offer.

Kate took a gulp of hot coffee. "That's wonderful, isn't it?" She grinned hugely, and although she already knew the answer, it was second nature to her to ask the same question over again of different people. "What period? What did she find?"

Marian took a deep breath. "Agapi says primitive Bronze Age. With a slipped design. It looks like leaves, maybe barley. Baked in a very primitive kiln that didn't get to very high temperatures, but still, kilned. Local clay, so they may not have had trade connections."

And they certainly weren't cultured Atlanteans, either, by the sound of it. But Kate was on the verge of giving up on her theory that Samothráki had a connection with Atlantis, so she wasn't disappointed. And it was extremely exciting to know that they were pretty well guaranteed a Bronze Age site at the bottom of it all.

"Isn't that unusual in itself?" Kate asked. She had been doing her homework on Samothráki for the past few days. "Wasn't this on an established trade route?"

"That's what we're here to find out, isn't it?" asked one of the young men sitting at the other end of the table. "But I sure hope Sarah isn't going to have *all* the luck."

If they had lost some of their intense motivation in the disappointment of the past few days, they would be digging again with a real purpose after this morning; she could hear that in his voice.

"When did it happen? Not this morning?"

"She uncovered it last night; she and Agapi and

Andreas stayed late to get it photographed and charted in situ so we could take it out and examine it. Sarah was pretty sure when she saw it, and she called Agapi right away. Agapi was certain, just looking at it."

"How did we miss all this last night?" Kate asked jealously, and by the laughter round the table, it was obvious everyone else had asked the same thing.

"People were already going in for supper when she called Agapi. We didn't find out until Sarah got back to the sleeping tent, and by then it was too late to see anything."

And they had spent the night in a state of excited anticipation, obviously, and the excitement had carried over into this morning.

It would carry them through the day, too, Kate thought, and probably as many others as were needed before another significant find was made.

But the next significant find was not that long in coming. Late the same morning, just before lunch, a rustle of excitement ran through the dig, in the wake of a young man who almost ran from the square where he and several others were working, to the admin hut, to call Andreas to the site. That had everyone downing tools at speed and clambering out of their own squares, or coming from the various tents, to encircle the five-by-five-metre square hole in the ground that had been the work for the past three weeks of a man named Bill and his team of two Greek labourers and two American students.

"A wall," one of the young Americans was telling them excitedly. "We've found a wall!"

The circle of people was parting automatically to let Andreas through as he and Kate arrived. Everyone held their breath as Andreas jumped lightly down into the hole. "It's under the damned baulk, Andrea!" Bill was saying excitedly, squatting down in one corner of the hole to point out what looked to Kate like no more than the front edge of a few stacked stones sticking out of the wall of earth that marked the side of the almost mathematically square excavation. "Costa here ran into these stones at the bottom, and I told him to go into the baulk a couple of inches higher up, and it was so thin it just fell away and exposed all this."

Yet when she looked closer, couldn't her eye detect a kind of human intent in that arrangement, rather than the randomness of nature? Hadn't someone put smaller stones in between larger ones, balanced them for a human purpose?

And how long ago? How many thousands of years ago had a man and a woman carried those stones to this spot and piled them up and stood back sweating to admire their handiwork and their new home? Had they held hands and smiled into each other's eyes? Had they done it alone, or had the whole village, the whole tribe, worked together, helping, encouraging them?

Kate felt a strange, unexpected excitement constricting her chest. She had never felt anything quite like it before, but then she had never been in on anything quite like this project before. Her heart was beating in heavy, quick thuds through her body, and she felt the sun on her head and wished she had remembered to grab her hat as she'd left the admin hut. But she wasn't leaving now; she wasn't going to miss a moment of this.

"I think it runs on a slant under the baulk," Bill was saying to his fascinated audience, managing to sound scientific and reasoned in spite of his obvious excitement. "See how only the one edge comes into the trench here? If we'd been over even an inch we'd have missed it entirely." He was hovering over the bent backs of Andreas and Rebecca, who were conferring as they squatted in the corner, touching and examining the arrangement of rock and stone.

At last they stood up. "We'll dig down this baulk," Andreas announced, indicating the north-south baulk in which the stone wall was buried. "And let's take a line on the angle we think we've got . . ." Followed by Rebecca, he got a hand up out of the hole and strode over the narrow baulk of undug earth that crisscrossed the site in a grid pattern between all the dug and undug squares. "And see if it runs as far as this." He stood over the hole that neighboured the first on the south, a hole that was somewhat more shallowly dug than the other, and Kate could see that, depending on where the wall had begun and how big the house had been, it might run under the east-west baulk, too, and into this hole.

Everyone was volunteering for the honour of digging down the baulk, but Rebecca said quietly that Bill's team would do it, and that was that. At last, talking and exclaiming over this latest find, the rest of the workers drifted off and went back to their own squares and jobs.

Kate did the same. Though she would have preferred to stay out on the site, watching Andreas and Rebecca, watching Bill's team dig down the baulk, she had got a lesson from watching Sarah over the past few days. Andreas already had one female fan trailing him around like a puppy. And even though her real interest was that wall, Kate would wait to be called with the others when there was something to see. She didn't want anyone thinking that *she* couldn't keep away from Andreas Constantinou, either.

The next afternoon Kate did something she'd been meaning to do for several days—she visited the archaeological ruins of the Sanctuary of the Great Gods on the north coast of the island.

The site was in an open area on the slope of a hill that

looked down to a view of the sea. It was a location not unlike Neathera, except that here the hills were thickly forested, and the site itself was not so high up, nor so far from the sea.

If it had been a temple, it had been a very extensive one. Parts of it seemed to extend over three small hills, with building ruins labelled the Sacristy, the Anaktoron, the Rotunda, the Stoa, the Theatre and others of whose function the archaeologists seemed uncertain. There were different layers of civilisation, too, so that inside the circular wall of stones that was called the Rotunda of Arsinoë there were excavated remains of an earlier building's foundations down below.

Several pillars of the Hieron had been restored, and it looked like a minor copy of the Parthenon, which it probably had been, twenty-five hundred years ago when Athens had been the be-all and end-all of fashion. Kate wandered through the ruins with a guidebook in her hand, trying to separate the archaeologists' guesses from the facts, trying to imagine how it had looked, how it had really looked, feeling for a trace of the people who had lived and died here so long ago.

In the Anaktoron, the book told her, one received the first degree of initiation. The northern part of the building was closed off, the "holy of holies." Only those who had received the second degree of initiation were allowed in. Interestingly enough, the ritual for receiving the second degree of initiation, according to some archaeologists, had been, in the fourth century *before* Christ, the confessing of your sins at a marble block outside the Hieron.

It was in this second degree of initiation that the Religion of the Great Gods—which Kate privately felt was a title given it by modern male archaeologists in order not to have to call it the religion of the Mother

Goddess, which it obviously had been—it was in this that the religion was unique. For no one had been forbidden to the second degree of initiation on the grounds of sex, or race, or social status.

Kate tried to imagine a world wherein every second Pope, every second Archbishop of Canterbury, was a woman, where worshippers were blessed by both "fathers" and "mothers." "Forgive me, Mother, for I have sinned," she said aloud, to try it out. "Hear, O Israel, the Lord thy Goddess, the Lord is One." She began to giggle. Even to her, it had a sudden feeling of blasphemy. And yet, why should it? Why should it? Why was the raising of woman to full equality something that felt shocking? Deliberately, she forced herself at the fence. "Our Mother, who art in Heaven . . ." "Blessed art Thou, O Lord our Goddess, Queen of the Universe, who hast not made me a man . . ." "God the Mother, God the Daughter . . ." "There is no Goddess but Allah, and Mohammed is Her prophet . . ."

After a while, it stopped feeling like blasphemy. It began to feel ridiculous. Did she believe God had a sex? Of course not. God was a force for good, perhaps, a spiritual force, the giver of life . . . but any sex attributed to that force was a reflection of humankind, surely, not of God.

In a world in which men are dominant, she thought, God had to become a male. That was the first requisite after the downfall of women—get rid of any worship of the feminine. Naturally.

The Giver of Life, she thought suddenly. That's what we call our masculine God, and that's ridiculous. A man does not give life without a woman, and a woman doesn't give life without a man. God could not possibly be entirely male.

The ancients had naturally thought of the female

principle as the life-giving one. That at least was logical. But what had allowed the moderns to revere the masculine—all three of the great monotheistic religions to choose exclusively the male element for worship?

It had been a powerful religion, the worship of the Mother. It had stood up against Christianity for four centuries.

But it had fallen in the end, and look at the role models religion provided women with now: Eve, the temptress, barely escaping the brand of evil incarnate. Or Mary, the eternal virgin, never succumbing to sex, yet somehow giving birth. . . .

In the middle of the Stoa, with the sun beating down on her head and the insects squeaking and chirruping on all sides, all alone with the universe, Kate stopped dead. A thought had just slammed into place in her brain, and it was mind-boggling.

Perhaps it had stood up even longer. Perhaps the religion of the Mother was still standing up, not against Christianity, but right inside it.

"Hail, Mary, full of grace," she said aloud, feeling as though she had been hit by a thunderclap. She might be *called* the Virgin, but she was *worshipped* as the *Mother*! Ninety-nine percent of the pictures Kate had ever seen of Mary showed her with a baby in her arms!

If men had tried to change what was valued in a woman—her virginity and value as a piece of property rather than her fertility and value as life-giver—they had succeeded. But perhaps they hadn't completely covered up their tracks.

There were many people today who said that the elevation of the prophet Jesus to Godhead had been necessary to provide the converts from polytheistic religions with the comfort of another God. Had the worship of Mary grown out of the need to provide the converts from the Mother Goddess religion with a feminine substitute?

"Mother of God," she said, and laughed aloud. Poor old humankind, jumbling through the bits and pieces of old and new religions and coming up with a pattern it insisted was the truth. Needing it to be the truth so badly, the *real* way to God, that entire populations could turn a blind eye to huge contradictions for centuries and centuries. Talk about the Emperor's new clothes! Mother of God! The Mother of God was the Mother Goddess! Who else could she be?

Kate spent an hour in the small but interesting museum on the site, wondering, as she wandered, whether the finds from Neathera would eventually be placed here, or whether they would go to Athens, or into a museum of their own. That would give Lákoma or Prophétes Elías a tourist attraction, she supposed, but probably only archaeologists and diehard scholars would be drawn, and that was a relief to Kate. She didn't like to think of the peace of this remote corner of the world being shattered by thrill-seekers.

She stood for a few moments in front of the statue called the Victory of Samothráki before she read the small printed notice and realized that this was only a copy. The real "Nike" was in Paris, in the Louvre, and here, where it had been made and found, the museum had to be satisfied with a cast, "a gift of the French government." Kate shook her head. Perhaps that was the additional price that had to be paid by a country that had already suffered five centuries of foreign occupation: the Turkish government hadn't cared enough about Greek history to preserve its archaeological finds, so foreigners had been allowed to come and dig almost at will, if they had enough money to pay for the privilege. And they had taken their finds out of

Greece, back to museums in their own countries. And since they had protected this cultural wealth from the Turks, the host countries were naturally reluctant, now that Greece was independent again, to part with the finds. But the Greek people were just as determined that their heritage be returned to them.

Kate, who had seen the part of the Parthenon from which Lord Elgin had stripped the famous "Elgin marbles" and carted them home to the British Museum, had felt the force of the irony then, as now, standing in front of the cast of this famous and beautiful statue.

Later, as she returned to the dig, Kate felt that the closer she got to Neathera, the more excitement she felt building up inside, partly at the knowledge that whatever was found by Andreas Constantinou, at least the site had never been excavated in modern times. Whatever he found would stay in Greece by law. Kate knew that nothing like the beautiful Nike statue would be discovered here, because the statue, like the later parts of the Sanctuary, dated from the classical and postclassical periods of Greek history. A Bronze Age site like Neathera could date a thousand years or more before the Sanctuary buildings.

But each age had had its own art, its own beauty, and although not many things appealed to the artistic sense as completely as did the beautiful marble sculpture of classical Greece, Kate and all the others were as excited about what might be uncovered at Neathera as they would have been if they hoped to find carved marble. In fact, more so, because even those who were not in on the archaeological secret of the dig felt in their bones that this dig might make history. Everybody felt that this dig had the potential to fill in some gaps in prehistory; it was a feeling that somehow permeated the air.

So when Kate rode up the dirt track and parked her bike beside the admin hut, she didn't go in. Instead, as though a magnet drew her, she walked across the site, in a zigzag pattern enforced by the grid of baulks and holes, heading for the square where the wall had been found. The siesta period wasn't over yet; she had the site to herself, and Kate stood on a baulk and looked down at the pattern of piled stones that was emerging from the dug earth in the distinctive shape of a wall, two feet wide and in a moderately straight line.

A wall, built by human hands and human hopes, and she was among the first to lay eyes on it in possibly three thousand years.

Kate turned, slipping her hands into the pockets of her loose shorts that she wore daily now because of the heat, and, lost in thought, stood looking out over the hillside and the long valley that led down to wheat fields and the sea. It was a beautiful location; even three thousand years ago people who woke up here each morning must have appreciated the freshness, the purity of the air. They must have known they were lucky. What God had they worshipped? Had they walked down the hill to a forest grove every morning to pour a libation or leave an offering for the Mother Goddess? Was it the religion of these villagers which, centuries later, had caused the building of the Sanctuary she had just visited? Kate turned and walked back along the baulks towards the admin hut. Whatever archaeology could dig up from the past, and whatever it could say about life and times and religion, there was one thing the world could never know about a prehistoric civilisation: the thoughts, the beliefs, the real people who had lived and died on a site.

By the time she reached the admin hut, rest time was over, and people were beginning to show from the sleep tents, the cooktent and other places where they had been resting or quietly working through the hot afternoon hours. Kate pushed open the door of the admin hut and entered to see Andreas Constantinou already bent over his desk, working. He looked up.

"I'm going to Akrotíri tomorrow," he said. "I want you to come with me."

Chapter 8

SANTORÍNI

ATHENS SMELLED LIKE NAIL POLISH REMOVER. KATE LAY in her familiar bed in Sophia's apartment and tried to ignore the strong smell of chemical pollution that was coming in through the balcony doors. Either she shut the doors and died of the heat, or she left the room open to the mercy of Athenian pollution, which was probably, she had decided, second to none.

After the peace of Samothráki, Athens was a shock to most of the senses. Kate wondered what it was that had awakened her. She could hear a dog barking, and a couple of men arguing in an apartment somewhere below. The traffic noises were incessant, even at this hour of the night. Kate tried to see her watch in the pale light streaming through the shutters. It might say three o'clock.

She tossed restlessly in the bed. In another hour the rooster across the way would start to crow, and if she weren't asleep by then, she could forget it for the rest of the night.

Perhaps it was worry that had woken her up; certainly now that she was awake she couldn't stop thinking. Why had Andreas brought her along on this trip? She had told him that she wanted to be at his elbow all the time, but he knew quite well that he could have left her on Samothráki. Of course, it was possible he intended to leave her right here in Athens. She had nothing but his word for it that he would pick her up here tomorrow.

Was she here because he hoped to break down her resistance while they were away together, or because he was afraid to leave her on the site for fear of what she might find out?

If he tried to break down her resistance, was she going to let him?

Kate kicked aside the sheet and found a new position. He was a threat to her; she'd be lying if she denied that. Andreas Constantinou was the first man since her husband who'd disturbed her on any level deeper than simple physical need. Andreas Constantinou, like Peter, got inside her, somehow got under her skin.

Was that why she'd felt reminded of Peter? Physically he was somewhat like Peter all right—Peter had been short and stocky, muscular . . . but after ten years, how good was she at remembering the essential personality of her husband?

She had met Peter at the end of her first year of university. Without a thought for freedom or independence, she had married him; and although she was a bit young, really that had been much more suitable, Aunt Pet had agreed, than Kate worrying about a career. Especially as Peter came from such a good family and was on his way to being a doctor, like her uncle.

And she had loved him so much. Peter had brought excitement and sparkle back into Kate's life after nearly a decade of drought. Peter had not minded if she raised her voice when she was annoyed, or laughed aloud, or acted like a hoyden—though she had almost forgotten how. And the night they had had their first real argument, a real shouting match, where for the first time in years she had actually been angry *aloud* and had even taken a swing at him—and Peter hadn't *minded*— had been the night she'd realized she was in love. It had been like being drunk, like going home again. And Peter had been so excited, as though he had loved her, too, had loved this glimpse of the real Kate Fenton. He had grabbed her and kissed her, and then pulled her down and made wild love to her, so that she was gasping and crying and telling him over and over that she loved him. . . .

The first year of married life had been magic. The second year, she had hardly seen him, because he'd been interning at the hospital. The third year the roof had fallen in.

He was her uncle and aunt all over again. The little disagreements she had been too besotted to notice in the first year, disagreements over her independence and self-fulfillment and expression, became small areas of contention in the second, ignored because there wasn't time in Peter's schedule to run them into full-scale battles. But in the third year Peter's character as a doctor and a man was shaped in cement. He wanted a wife, not a partner in life. And he no longer considered it sexy or amusing to fight with his wife. If she disagreed with him, he felt emasculated. He was a doctor. He was used to being right. Women kowtowed to him, whether they were nurses or patients, so why should he get less from his own wife?

This time Katie pulled in her horns without protest. The real work had been done for Peter by her uncle and aunt; this time she hardly noticed the loss of her freedom—or at least, she had forgotten that it was hers by right. She scarcely even felt dwarfed by the restrictions that hedged her in again. If she had thought about it, she might have said she had had a brief holiday—but she returned to the real business of life with hardly a whimper.

Halfway through that year, thank God, the women's movement came to her rescue. Kate Fenton, assisted by some college friends, had felt the "click," had had her consciousness raised, and at last, with a little return of her old spark, had told Peter where he got off.

There had followed the mother and father of all fights, which had lasted for weeks, and which not even Kate had enjoyed. Even in the most uneven of her street matches in the old days, she had never felt so brutalized. Peter had never touched her, of course, though the look in his eyes had been black hatred and murder. His brutality had been verbal, venomously verbal, and Katie had been hopelessly outmatched. Ten years of her uncle and aunt's training, and the last three of Peter's, had assured that that belittling tone of voice would shrivel her before she began.

At length, Peter had told her where *she* got off. Unless, of course, she gave up all notion of liberation and all that women's garbage and settled into being his wife. . . .

With a little help from her friends, Kate had had just enough stuffing left in her to agree that, yes, this was where she got off.

Peter had been surprised and furious, but the first taste of freedom had been enough for Kate. She was her own woman, and she was never going to change that again. The ten years since she had left Peter had been the best years of her life, and she could only see it getting better.

But not if she got mixed up with another male chauvinist who wanted to prove his masculine superiority on her.

The rooster across the way started crowing, a full half hour before his usual time. Swinging her feet over the edge of the bed, Kate gave in to the inevitable. Anyway, she might be cooler on her feet. As quietly as she could, she opened her bedroom door and slunk down the passage past Sophia's room to the kitchen. Coffee was a stupid thing to drink now, but she had to do something.

Silently pushing the door to, Kate flicked on the light and reached for the tiny coffeepot. Four-thirty, she noticed on her watch. The bird was half an hour late, not early. Oh, well, then, things weren't so bad. She'd had three hours' sleep; she could manage on that.

As the little pot came to the boil, the door squeaked open. Sophia's head poked into the room. "*Kaliméra!*" She grinned.

"*Kaliméra!*" returned Kate happily. This was much better. If Sophia was awake, the wait till dawn would be much more pleasant. "Did I wake you up?"

Sophia pushed out her chin and jerked her head upwards in the motion Kate was still having to consciously remember was the Greek for no. To her, it still meant, I don't know, or Who cares, or I'll think about it, depending on the circumstances.

"That's good," Kate said. "I'm making coffee; want some?"

Sophia pushed open the door and came in. She had cigarettes and a lighter in her hand, Kate noted with amusement, so they had both been hoping for company tonight. And no wonder, after the evening they had spent.

"How much sleep did you get?" she asked.

Sophia shrugged. "*I* couldn't sleep," she said.

"What, not at all?" Kate laughed. "Not even after the boring novel?"

Sophia shrugged again, lighting a cigarette. "Men," she said. "What good are they?" She drew in the smoke and blew it out again in a motion so obviously satisfactory it made Kate wish she smoked.

"Well, it's your own fault," Kate pointed out, getting a tin of milk out of the fridge. "You're the one insisting on a revenge that punishes you as much as him."

· "*I* don't care," she said. "He's the one who cares; he's sorry now."

"Yes, well, I cared, too," Kate said with a laugh. "The pair of you were driving me crazy. The air was sizzling every time you looked at each other. How are you ever going to manage to keep on seeing him, but still keep him at arm's length?"

Sophia began to laugh her croaking, attractively husky smoker's laugh, which turned abruptly into a cough, reminding Kate just in time why it was she didn't smoke. "You're crazy!" Sophia rasped over the cough. "What do you mean, driving you crazy?"

They had gone out to dinner in a foursome, Andreas, Sophia, Sophia's old flame Takkis, and Kate. Nowhere posh, just the neighbourhood souvlaki joint, which served excellent food in extremely casual surroundings. Takkis did not speak English, so Sophia had been at liberty to explain things to Kate under cover of a discussion in Greek between the men.

"We are from the same village," she told Kate. "When my husband left me, I went back there for a year, and he was there. We were always together; he didn't see any other woman after I came there. Only me. His friends all told him to marry me, it was perfect with us, but he didn't ask me. All of a sudden one day he has got engaged to a young girl in the village, someone he hardly said hello to. He loved me, but he married her."

"Good God," Kate said, shocked. "What did he do that for?"

"Because I was divorced; I had a child. Greek men don't marry divorced women, women with children. Never." Sophia's young daughter still lived in Corfu with her grandparents, while her mother earned a living in Athens and sent money home. "He was afraid."

"But he still comes to see you?"

"That was five years ago. He can't stand his wife. She's nothing but a villager; she's not educated. Now he knows he loves me, he should have married me. Now he's sorry for what he did." She laughed mirthlessly. "He says. But I know, if he had to do it again, he would do the same thing. Greek men don't think about anything except whether a woman is young and pretty when they marry. A woman to sleep with, it's a little different."

What a dreadful situation. "What happens now?"

"Now he thinks maybe he'll have both. He wants me to sleep with him, and he'll leave his wife on the island, and he'll have everything he wants."

Kate had shaken her head, looking across the table to where Takkis and Andreas were deep in friendly conversation, and with a sudden swell of bitter anger, both for Sophia's sake and her own, remembered Andreas saying, "Women of your age must take whom they can get." She had never met such deeply ingrained male chauvinism as in this country. Did he imagine now that he was doing Kate a favour by being attracted to her? Men. She snorted. And they imagined they were created in the image of God.

"What about you?" she asked. "Are you still in love with Takkis?"

Sophia had shrugged. "*I* don't know," she said, in a voice that meant yes.

"What are you going to do?"

"I'm not going to sleep with him. Now he can pay for being a coward. Now he can beg me; he's not getting anything. I'll make sure of that."

"A man loves a woman because she is young and beautiful," Andreas had told her, too, and she looked at Sophia and felt another rush of indignation. How dared Takkis do this to her? How dared anybody do such a thing? He'd made his choice; he'd eaten his cake—and now he was expecting Sophia to let him have it, as well. He was counting on her love, using it.

In fact, like so many men, he loved her just enough to make her essential to his happiness, without wanting *her* happiness.

I hope she makes you pay, Kate thought violently, looking at the man and feeling a sudden surge of protective warmth for Sophia. I hope she makes you pay royally.

For the rest of the evening, it was obvious that Takkis was indeed paying. Every time he looked at Sophia, the air seemed to go up in smoke. And he looked at her often; he sometimes spent minutes just gazing at her as she spoke and laughed and became the life of the party. It was obvious that the heat was getting to her, too; she was excitable, on the top of her form.

And every time their gazes locked, he was looking at her with a mute, desperate pleading in his eyes.

The heat had spread to Kate, too; no one could have sat near such open sexual heat without being affected by it. To make things worse, there was Andreas Constantinou sitting across from her, his hands and his mouth constantly within the range of her vision; his arms and throat left bare by his shirt; his glance flicking her lazily from time to time with such electricity that she shivered into goose bumps each time.

She couldn't remember ever experiencing anything like it. Every mouthful of food, every movement at the table, had had sexual significance.

They had parted with the men on the street, and then Sophia had come upstairs and gone to bed with a book, and hadn't slept a wink.

"Of course you were driving me crazy," Kate said now. "It's more than human nature can take, to sit through something like that. Why don't you sleep with the man just once, for goodness' sake, and put me out of my misery?" She was laughing; she wasn't serious, and Sophia knew it.

Sophia laughed. "Why don't *you* sleep with my cousin?" she demanded suddenly, catching Kate completely off guard. She jerked upright as if she'd been shot.

"What do you mean?"

"You don't want me to sleep with Takkis; you want Andreas, that's all! Even Takkis said so."

Kate gasped. "What?" she demanded in horror. "What did he say?"

Sophia crushed out her cigarette and lit a fresh one. "He said," she reported, grinning, "'The women at this table have hard hearts; they can say no even if it's driving them crazy!'"

"How did he know? Did Andreas tell him?" Kate demanded, and Sophia laughed delightedly.

"Nobody had to tell him! He only had to see you looking at each other. Andreas looked like he wanted to kill somebody, and you didn't sit still all night!"

Kate's horror had turned to helpless laughter. "Oh, my God, how embarrassing!" she groaned. "A public seduction, that's all I need." She took a long drink of her coffee and set down her cup.

"I told Andreas he could sleep on the couch if he wanted. Usually he has your bed when he's in Athens, but he said he's sleeping at the university tonight."

Kate's eyes widened. That would have been all she needed tonight—knowing Andreas Constantinou was sleeping in the next room. She began to laugh helplessly. "You wretch!" she accused. "You would have, wouldn't you?"

"If I can't sleep," Sophia pointed out, "why should anyone else? We could have played cards."

They laughed together like old friends and finished their coffee; and then, in spite of the caffeine, Kate began to yawn. "It's five o'clock," she remarked. "Are you going to try to get some sleep? I'm so tired suddenly, I think I could even ignore that rooster." She was right, perhaps because she had grown more used to the pastoral sound on Samothráki. She fell asleep almost instantly.

But she dreamed of Andreas.

"Are you going to visit Spyridon Marinatos?" she asked him early the next morning as they flew high over the Aegean on their way to the island of Santoríni.

"I wish I could," Andreas told her. "Marinatos is dead; he was killed in an accident at Akrotíri in 1974."

"Oh!" She had never thought of archaeology as a dangerous occupation before. "How was he killed?"

"He fell off a wall and hit his head; he died almost immediately. He's buried on the site, as was his wish, in one of the houses. You can see his grave there. I'll be talking to his successor. You should take a tour of the site; Marinatos believed that there was equality between the sexes in this society."

Kate smiled. "Is that a way of telling me I can't listen in on your conversation?"

"Listen if you like." He shrugged. "But you will find

the tour more interesting. We shall be speaking Greek."

She didn't look at him; it was her way of refusing to acknowledge that he had won a point. "Do you believe that it was the destruction of Santoríni that caused the destruction of the Minoan civilisation on Crete, as Marinatos said?" she asked.

"Of course," he said. "It is hardly a question of belief any longer."

"The book I read said some archaeologists still dispute it."

"Some archaeologists still dispute whether Schliemann found Troy. It is a question of what it is reasonable to believe. There is no other explanation that can account so well for the overnight destruction of a powerful civilisation. Other civilisations show traces of decline, or being overrun by invaders. The great palaces show no such signs. When an island blows up and sinks into the ocean, it must cause a great tidal wave. One that would travel very fast, be very high. It would cause enormous devastation. If it was not the cause of the destruction of the palaces, when did it strike? That two such events happened so closely in time, and are not related, is to me much more difficult to believe than that the one caused the other.

"There is a saying, in English I believe, 'When you hear the sound of hooves, think first of horses.' In my profession, too often we imagine giraffes and heffalumps."

One thing about Greece was that no matter where you were going, you were almost never in the air longer than forty minutes. Kate found the contrast to Canada enormous. Already, looking out the window beside her, she could see the spectacular sight of Santorini: a circular island with its centre and bits of its western rim missing.

From the north around to the southwest curved a rough horseshoe shape that comprised the largest island in the group. In the northeast gap, between the two tips of the horseshoe, lay the island second in size; and in the centre of the sea that these two islands now enclosed was a pair of dark grey mounds made of lava that marked the epicentre of the actual volcano.

"How many people live on Santoríni?" asked Andreas bemusedly.

"About eight thousand."

"But the volcano is still active, isn't it? It could erupt again any time? Didn't it just erupt recently?"

Andreas laughed aloud. "How many people live in San Francisco?" he countered.

"But— Oh, I see." She laughed. "Just another indication of the human condition, I suppose."

The island was small; they landed and caught a taxi straight to the site. Santoríni was unlike any other island in the Aegean, Kate soon realized. It had been covered with so much pumice during the volcanic eruption 3500 years ago that it was still barren. There were few trees; nothing seemed to grow very readily in the dry climate.

At the archaeological dig, that was even more obvious. The ancient city had been buried under several metres of volcanic ash, which was being painstakingly scraped away by the archaeologists to show a city still coated in the grey-white powder, from which all colour seemed to have been burnt away. Everything was the same barren grey-white as the pumice that had preserved the city for three millennia.

There were several different groups being led around the finds; Kate heard French and German being spoken by the guides. Andreas introduced her to a couple of the archaeologists, but when he settled down with the project director, Kate wandered off on her own. After a few minutes an English group arrived on another bus, and Kate attached herself to the back of the crowd.

It was certainly fascinating. The guide knew her subject well, and she spoke excellent English, unlike several guides Kate had suffered through on various sites over the past few weeks. None of the remarkable wall paintings were in situ, but Kate had already examined them all in the Archaeological Museum in Athens a couple of weeks ago, and the pictures the guide held up were sufficient to remind her of their beauty. Without a doubt, the Bronze Age inhabitants of Thera had been highly advanced culturally, architecturally and in their use of metals and tools.

The discussion of the role of women was just what she was looking for: women had been very important in ancient Thera. There had been a goddess associated with nature and fertility worship, and so far, no evidence of any male god at all. Flowers and animals had played a large part in the worship of the goddess, the animals guarding, the flowers decorating the small shrines where she was worshipped.

Kate was thrilled. Although the guide said that scholars differed in their opinions, it appeared that the argument centred around whether women had been completely dominant or merely superior or equal in ancient Thera. No one was suggesting anything like masculine superiority. It would be quite marvellous for her theories and her book that the most advanced civilisations of the Bronze Age world had been run by women.

Kate wasn't forgetting, however, the intriguing mystery of Samothráki, and a part of her mind not devoted to her own research was always on the lookout for hints. Nothing that she had so far heard seemed a good enough reason for Andreas Constantinou to come here for a talk with the director in the middle of his own dig season, especially when he was so pressed for time. As far as she knew, nothing of great significance had yet been found on Samothráki, and it would certainly have been difficult to keep the existence of something exciting from her, she was so close to the project now.

So he could hardly be here, at so early a stage in his own dig, to compare notes. He could hardly be trying to establish a trade connection when his biggest find so far was a primitive, locally made jug and some walls.

Constantinou and the project director were walking through the ruins now; Kate had seen them from time to time, high up on the ramparts under the site's protected cover, or inside the ancient Akrotíri mill, examining the foundations or merely walking along the beautifully constructed streets of this ancient city, Andreas nodding while the other man pointed and spoke. Kate wished she could be a fly on the wall—a Greek-speaking fly on the wall—at the conversation between the two archaeologists. It became an effort for her to concentrate on what the guide was saying at the front of the group.

Until the guide said, "One of the things that makes Akrotíri different from Pompeii is that here, we think the inhabitants had warning of the disaster."

Kate was at the back of the crowd and could hardly hear; that was one of the things that made concentration difficult. Sometimes she heard Andreas's guide's voice more clearly than her own. But this caught her attention for some reason; perhaps it was spoken a little more loudly, or maybe the acoustics were better here. She had decided she shouldn't ask any questions, considering she hadn't paid to be part of this group, but this seemed interesting. Fortunately a woman at the front said, "What sort of warning?"

The guide indicated a beautifully cut stone staircase set between two grey, pumice-covered walls above them. Each step was broken down the middle, as though the walls had moved closer together, forcing them to buckle. "This did not happen during the final destruction of Théra. We know from the evidence that it happened some time before, during an earthquake. Possibly more than a year passed before the volcano erupted and the island sank. Seeds which were left in the ruins of the houses had begun to germinate when the first volcanic ash fell.

"More important, no bones have been found. In the ruins of Pompeii, it is obvious that people began to flee the city as Vesuvius erupted. They could not get away in time, so their bones were found: in their homes, gathering valuables; in the streets, running; and at the city gates, which were choked with traffic.

"Here in Akrotíri, no bones were found, and no valuables. These people had time not only to escape, but also to take with them their jewels and precious metals, and some food supplies. It was an orderly escape, well organized; no one remained behind to perish. The only bones that have been found are the bones of a young pig that had already been slaughtered. So you see that they had time even to take their animals with them. It was a very well organized mass evacuation."

"Where did they go?" asked the fascinated woman at the front.

The guide smiled engagingly. "We don't know. Maybe they went to Crete; maybe their ships went down when the tidal wave came." She shrugged. "Nobody knows."

At the back of the crowd Kate was standing immobile, staring at the woman, her mouth open. I know where they went, she could have told them. They didn't go to Crete, and they didn't go down at sea. They escaped; they made it. We found the walls of the new homes they built last week, and we're looking for the floors. They sailed north, the Akrotirians. They settled at a place we've named Neathera, which I've just realized is the Greek for New Théra. They sailed north, all the way to an island called Samothráki.

They wandered in the town of Fira that evening, waiting for the ferry that would take them to Crete. Kate was in a state of barely subdued excitement, and at every souvenir shop she purchased maps, postcards, catalogues and guidebooks—anything that might have further information on Akrotíri.

"Judy Chicago would love this," she joked with Andreas, showing him a postcard bearing a picture of a "breasted ewer" as they sat in a pretty outdoor restaurant that overlooked the precipitous cliff and the harbour entrance far below. "It's nice to know the human race hasn't always been totally devoted to phallic symbolism in art and manufacture."

The "breasted ewer" was a type of pottery unique to Santoríni, she had learned this afternoon, and she agreed with those scholars who thought it proved the high status of women in ancient Akrotíri. They were jugs decorated like a woman's body, with earrings and necklaces, and two cones of clay for breasts set high on the curve of the ewer's belly. To Kate they were incredibly beautiful, not least because they assuaged some deep need in her, a need she would never have recognized except, as now, in its fulfillment—the need to be *valued* as a woman. The need to find in art a reflection of herself. And although she had heard it said many times in the last ten years, she only recognized the deep truth of it now, seeing for the first time what *she* needed to see in art: that most of the Western world's art, literature and artifacts reflected the masculine. And nearly anything in the modern world that reflected the feminine reflected it from the masculine point of view, and a degrading point of view at that: a point of view that allowed women to be nothing much more than sex objects.

In the breasted ewers Kate knew, by the response of something deep within her, that she was seeing woman from the point of view of women; women who had had a self-esteem so deep and so basic that as a product of today's culture she could barely relate to it. Yet she felt that if she looked at the pictures of the breasted ewers for long enough, she might be taught something; she might begin to learn a sense of her own value as a woman that had been denied her since birth.

Her smile faded; she felt a sense of loss so profound it was almost tangible, and tears started in her eyes. She looked at the postcard and then away, out over the blue of the caldera under which the civilisation of these women had sunk so long ago. "I wish I could go back," she said, almost to herself. "I'd drop this world in a minute and go forever, if time travel were possible."

Andreas said, "It must be very difficult to live in a world where the battle for a sense of self-worth is so arduous. I always think that so much of women's imagination is being diverted to that battle, it is no wonder they no longer rule the world."

She looked at him, unaware of the pleading that was in her eyes. "They survived, didn't they?" she asked urgently. "These people survived and went to Samothráki? They escaped the destruction?" She was willing him to tell her the truth now, to trust her with the knowledge she suddenly needed.

He took a sip of his drink. "They survived; at least, I believe they did. I believe they went to other places as well as to Samothráki: I am certain that a group either from Crete or from Santoríni landed in Israel, for example, and there was probably a Cretan settlement near Brindisi in Italy, if we are to believe Herodotus."

She was gazing at him, but it was not Andreas Constantinou she was seeing. "You have to tell me," she said softly. "You have to trust me, because I've got to know, Andrea. You've got to tell me all about it."

Andreas was gravely returning her gaze. "Of course," was all he said.

Chapter 9

CRETE

THEY SAILED OUT OF THE CALDERA JUST AT DUSK, PAST the threatening black mountain of the volcano's cone, heading into a sunset that painted the water thickly with gold. Kate had gone to the stern of the big ferryboat, to watch the huge cliffs of Santorini recede. Far below, four hundred metres under the water, a civilisation lay buried, and she felt the tragedy of it as an immediate thing.

Andreas had followed her, without a word, as though he understood her need to mourn. At last, as the cliffs receded further, till even the lights of Fira high up on top were no more than a bracelet of brilliants hanging in the near darkness, she said, "This was the end of women as a power in the world, wasn't it? After this, men took over?"

"So I think," he agreed quietly. "No one has ever suggested it before, to my knowledge."

What he knew from observation and deduction, presumably, she felt as a direct, inner certainty: In the aftermath of this terrible catastrophe, which had affected people as far away as Egypt, Israel, Africa and Turkey, women had gone into decline. Men had taken over, and their grip on the world had never slackened in the two and a half thousand years that had passed since.

"Of course, there were societies with male/female equality as late as Herodotus's day; he mentions the fact. But I believe these were isolated remnants of a system that received the death blow here."

Herodotus, the "father of history," who had travelled the known world in antiquity and written down his findings. She had been reading him a lot in her research. "Why?" she asked. "Why would women suddenly lose status?"

"I don't know. There was almost certainly a large part of the ancient world placing greater emphasis on the male, even at this time. Perhaps there was already a struggle between the matriarchal and the patriarchal going on. If Théra had been the stronghold of female power, perhaps this destruction was seen as a sign that the Sky God was more powerful than the Earth Goddess. Or perhaps the women were blamed for the catastrophe, as any government in power often gets blame or credit for circumstances it does not control."

"Yes, of course," Kate agreed. "When you say it I can almost see it happening." She was silent for a moment, considering. Then, "It must have been an extraordinary, devastating thing, mustn't it? It must have destroyed everything. . . . We're so used to the possibility of nuclear destruction, it wouldn't affect us the same way, now. But then, it must have seemed like the worst destruction possible. It would have seemed like divine punishment." Though of course even now such a catastrophe would cause havoc over a large area. It would grip the whole world's attention.

"We can imagine so, in any case."

"And they were driven into exile, weren't they? They had to settle in places like Israel, becoming neighbours of a people who were very male-dominated. And there were all those Sky God tribes in the north, too, weren't there?"

Andreas was watching her. "You are extremely intelligent," he said, as though he appreciated the discovery. But she hardly heard him. Kate was centuries away.

She went on, "If there were a nuclear war, do you think in the aftermath we might blame it on men? Do you think we might need a scapegoat so badly that we'd turn on men as the cause of it all?"

Andreas smiled faintly. "I have already heard it said that nuclear silos are no more than another form of phallic worship designed to symbolically represent men's power and desire to rape and plunder Mother Earth."

Yes, she'd heard it, too, though she wouldn't have thought it had come as far as male chauvinist Greece. "Men rule the world," she thought aloud. "But not all men."

"The establishment rules the world," he countered. "In a world where men are the dominant sex, the establishment will be composed of men. But not all men will be part of the establishment."

"Aristotle again." She grinned. "Where has he come up recently?" Certainly not in connection with "all p are s, but not all s are p."

"Has he? I don't know," said Andreas.

She said, "What made you decide to dig on Samothráki?"

"Samothráki was my second choice," replied Andreas. "Although it promised to be extremely exciting if my theory was correct, there was much more evidence for a settlement of Cretan or Theran refugees in Israel. Any archaeologist prefers the backup of written history, and there is textual evidence that they went to Israel. But I could not get permission to excavate in Israel."

"There *is*?"

Darkness was complete now, and it was getting chilly on deck, but neither of them moved to follow the last straggle of passengers indoors. Overhead the stars glittered against a black heaven. Andreas laughed, and his teeth flashed in the glow from a faint reflected light on the deck below.

"'It was Caphtorites from Caphtor who destroyed the Avvim near Gaza, and settled in the land there instead of them.'"

"It was?" she said. "I mean, what are you talking about?"

"'Did I not bring the Philistines from Caphtor?'" he said for answer. "'For Jehovah will despoil the Philistines, that remnant of the isle of Caphtor.'"

"Are you . . . is that from the Bible?"

"It is, yes."

"These people are mentioned in the Bible?"

"Why not? The Bible is an historical record of a people who also lived in the Bronze Age. Would you expect a history book of Canada to leave out any mention of the United States?"

"But how do you know they were called—what is it?—Caphtorites?"

"Because Egyptian paintings and records of the time make it almost certain that the local name for the Cretans, if not the Therans, was *Keftiu*. And Assyro-Babylonian texts refer to them as *Kaptara*."

"So the ancient Hebrews recorded the existence of a people who were 'brought out of' a country called

Caphtor by the Lord, and who were the remnant of an isle?"

"That's about it."

"But . . . but that's amazing! How exciting! Does anybody else know this?"

He laughed. "Quite a number of people have made the connection."

"And the descendents of those people were called Philistines?"

"It seems like it."

She said, "And the Philistines were always held up as an example of a corrupt, overly sensual people, weren't they? You can imagine that a Greek people would appear that way to the austere Hebrews, can't you? Especially if the women wore bare breasts." She laughed. "It would certainly tally with the attraction-repulsion that the Bible says was always going on between the Hebrews and the worshippers of Baal, wouldn't it? What else did the Hebrews say about them?"

"The Bible mentions that they were uncircumcised and worshipped a god called Dagon as well as Baal-zebub, that they consulted their priests and diviners in making decisions, and that they carried idols into battle. They were considered pretty barbarous, but as you say, between the Philistines and the Canaanites, the Hebrews were under constant temptation. It is possible they got a bad press because they were usually fighting against the Hebrews. The Bible also mentions that the Philistines had no king as such, but a confederation of city-states, the rulers of which cooperated whenever the need for joint action arose."

"Very Greek. And were the rulers women?"

"That's difficult to say; it seems not. But we have to remember that they are being reported through the eyes of a male-dominated society. Delilah may have been a Philistine, and certainly the rulers of Philistia appealed for her help to destroy Samson. Again, the Hebrew accounts say that she was bribed to do so. But it is at least possible that she was a power among the Philistines, perhaps the originator, even, of the plot. Wiser men than Samson have fallen in love with beautiful spies. And, incidentally, when Samson brought down the temple, it was filled with both men and women, and they were evidently not segregated, but mingling freely together."

She was so excited she could hardly breathe. "So you would have preferred to excavate a Philistine city? Why didn't you?"

"The site I wanted to excavate is in the Gaza strip. The Israelis wouldn't give me permission to dig, though of course there's always a possibility in the future."

"Why wouldn't they give you permission?"

He shrugged. "There are many reasons why a country might refuse permission to a foreigner. Greece, for example, gives out only five permits a year to foreign archaeological projects: to the Italians, French, Germans, Americans and British. That is why my own project receives American funding. Officially mine is a Greek-run project, and there is no problem getting permission. But there is not enough Greek money put up to finance all these digs, so some Americans have put up the money; and in return for this, I have American archaeologists on the project. In effect, though the government is turning a blind eye, this is a joint Greek-American project."

He was answering every question she asked, without a moment's hesitation. She could not understand what had made him decide to take her into his confidence. Did he trust her, or had she found the critical clue on

Santorini that made further attempts at secrecy academic? Or perhaps she just hadn't asked the right questions.

"Why did you choose Samothráki, then?"

"The evidence was all circumstantial, but I felt it was compelling enough. Right from the time I was a student, I have been fascinated by the Religion of the Great Gods, as they call it. I spent a season on the site when I was at the university. I also worked two seasons with Marinatos in Akrotíri; I was very lucky. Even then I was fascinated by the possibility that if these people had escaped, we could find traces of them elsewhere. . . .

"I saw parallels between the great civilisations of Crete and Théra, which certainly were connected somehow, and the remains of a forgotten religion on Samothráki. There were finds in the temple on Samothráki that I believed reflected finds at Akrotíri, and at Knossus. At first I thought only that the influence of the great Minoan civilisation had extended farther to the north than is generally accepted. This is still a possibility. But when Marinatos began to postulate a religion dominated by a female divinity, a society in which women and men were equal, it began to find resonance in my experiences on Samothráki." He paused and stared into the night. "If I am right, Neathera could be a crucial link between the Bronze Age and the classical period of Greece."

"Then why are you so pressed for time?"

"Not many people are as convinced of the possibility of a connection as I am, and even I wake in the night with doubts." He smiled, and though she could barely see his face in the dark she felt compelled to smile back. It was dark now, and the silence around them was very intimate, and in her new, mellow mood she found herself thinking that she would like to be there to comfort him when he woke with doubts in the night. "We have been given a time limit: two months to prove a connection with Théra before what limited funding we have dries up."

"That could make you rush the top layers all right," she said absently. Her mind was reeling with the excitement of what she had learned. Everything she had hoped to discover for her book had just been handed to her on a platter.

Andreas rubbed his head. "Yes," he said. "People with money so often are fools. They think that it will buy them anything, that it gives them the right to do anything. But if my theory is right, it is important not to rush the top layers, as you put it. We have a chance to watch the shift from female to male domination in society, or to observe a female-dominated bastion in a male-dominated world throughout the centuries. The Religion of the Great Gods was not abandoned until it was driven out by Christianity in the fourth century."

"So what are you going to do?"

"When we have found the floor, I will know better what we are up against. If we have a multiple-occupation site, we must dig what we find, of course, even at the risk of our money running out. Any archaeologist would do the same."

Kate wondered if that were true. At times the temptation must be very great, but perhaps a respect for all the evidence was inculcated during training.

At that moment Andreas put out a hand and drew her gently against him, so that she was standing between his arms at the rail, both of them looking out over the black water, her back protected by his chest.

For a while, neither spoke. Andreas put his hand, and then his face, lightly against her hair, and she shivered in the warm night air. At last he whispered, "Why do you fight me when you want me, Kate?"

She closed her eyes as her heart gave a terrific kick in her breast. Then she drew away from him. It was no good; she knew that.

"Why do you want me when I fight you?" she countered simply.

He turned his head to look at her; she could not see his expression, but she heard the quizzical note in his voice. "Do you think I would stop wanting you because you fight me?"

Her laughter tinkled out over the water. "Andrea," she said, "I think you *only* want me because I fight you. It brings out the conqueror in you."

"It's not true," he protested, his voice dark and throaty. "I don't care how you come to me. I lie in my bed at night and I dream of you coming into my bedroom, and I am hard under the sheet, and you put your hand on me, and you want me."

The note in his voice was melting her where she stood. Hadn't she imagined the same scene, lying in her lonely hotel bed? That his wanting would be so strong that he would just come to her, and she wouldn't be able to refuse him?

She croaked, "Is that how you want me?" and Andreas pulled her against him.

"I want you fighting; I want you willing; I want you in every way there is, Kate. It doesn't matter to me. I just want to hear you say the word to me."

His mouth was against her neck, and she was fainting with desire. "I've said it," she keened helplessly as his hands gripped her and his mouth burned against her skin. "Whatever word you've wanted to hear from me I've said a hundred times. I say it every time I look out and see you bending over your work in the sun; I say it when you're at your desk and you don't even remember I'm in the room. . . ."

His mouth covered hers with a passion that wiped out reason, and her body seemed to melt into his. She felt his touch, but she did not feel her own body. She was the night sky, and his hands stirred through the stars, making them shoot and spark and sing. When he lifted his mouth the sparks on the blackness of her lips stopped, and she knew that the night made soft noises, but that they came from her she did not know.

She did not know, either, how she was clinging to him, till she felt him grip her arms and pull out of her hold. Then his voice said, "We are docking," and people began to appear on deck around them, and Kate came to with a little shiver and stood away from him. She had no idea how long he had kissed her, how long they had stood wrapped in each other like that. She only knew that when he had pushed her away she felt empty, and that standing apart from him now was an effort of will. It chilled her a little to think that Andreas had been in such control of himself. She was not. There had been a moment when *she* would not have cared if all the world saw them clinging together. Then she noticed a few smiling glances in her direction and realized that much of the world *had*. Andreas had been as oblivious as she to what was going on around them. Kate dropped her eyes and tried to control both the bubble of laughter and the blush she could feel warming her cheeks, as she and Andreas held hands tightly and tried to concentrate on the docking procedure at Iráklion, capital city of Crete.

There were taxis waiting at the dock, and they caught one quickly, because Andreas shouted something in Greek to the driver at the end of the line and threw their bags in before the tourists in the lineup realized what was happening. He practically lifted Kate into the backseat, and got in with her, and the taxi quietly backed away from the line and drove off.

Kate giggled and snuggled into his shoulder. "You jumped the line," she accused.

Andreas shrugged. "Tourists are crazy—Americans, English, Germans—they are always lining up like sheep. Here in Greece we don't have lines. Only in summer, when the tourists are here."

"What did you say to the driver?" she asked. There seemed to be a kind of kinship among the locals in any country that had a large tourism industry, and aside from language, she had never known what that brotherhood consisted of. Had he bad-mouthed the foreigners? Had he called the equivalent of, Hey, brother, I'm one of us?

"I promised to pay his fine if he gets caught by the tourist police," Andreas said. "They aren't allowed to leave the line like that."

She didn't try to explain why that made her laugh so hard.

When Andreas had settled with the driver where they wanted to go, she put her arm up around his neck. "Do you mind what the driver thinks?" she whispered, and he lifted his hand and gripped her upper arm with a possessiveness that melted her. He did not answer; he simply bent and covered her mouth with a kiss of such sudden passion she knew it had been leashed in ever since the moment he had let go of her on the ferry. He had not been as cool as he'd seemed in the past ten minutes. And that knowledge and his passion now excited her beyond measure. She kissed him with an ardency that shook her. She had never felt such passion in her life. It was more than a need for sexual union; it was a deep, primal need to merge with him, to become one, not to be separate anymore.

"I need you," she whispered desperately. "Oh, God, Andrea, I've never needed anybody like this!"

She broke off abruptly as she heard her own words. Mother of God, what was the matter with her? She had spent all her energy during the past few days trying to convince him that she wasn't interested. She had almost managed to convince herself. Where was this coming from? Right now she was sounding as though she was desperate for him, and she wasn't. She wasn't! She was physically attracted to him, all right, she was adult enough to admit that, but she was also woman enough to know that an attraction like this was dangerous to her health.

That was a code phrase she had invented long ago to mean anything that threatened her independence. And she had learned that the biggest threat to her independence came when a secret inner voice urged her to pass her troubles and, incidentally, control of her life into someone else's nice, strong hands. Agents, publishers, lovers—there was no end to the number of Big Daddys out there who would have taken all the worry out of her life—and self-determination was the only price.

And now here was Andreas Constantinou, and she knew instinctively that he was a bigger threat than all the others. Because now her inner urgings were prompting her to give up not only her independence, but her entire personality, to the keeping of this man. And this was doubly dangerous, because he was so obviously *capable*, and because she was sure he didn't accept even intellectually a woman's need for or right to independence. Up till now, since Peter, she had chosen men who had grasped, intellectually if not emotionally, what the women's movement was all about. When they started making those masculine noises about her failure to live up to their image of a "little woman," at least Kate could call them on it, and at least they had tried to control their unconscious expectations.

Andreas Constantinou would try to control *her*. She knew that. Just as Peter had. And just as Peter had, he would have one powerful weapon against her: sex. It had taken her a long time to recognize what Peter was doing to her, because of what he had made her feel in bed. In the first year of her marriage, every little loving battle over her independence had ended up in bed, and somehow afterwards she had always smilingly, lovingly given in, because how could such a little thing matter more to her than his happiness?

In the second year, when Peter was interning, he had been too tired for either potent sex or battling her independence. Kate had gained back some of the ground she had lost; she remained at university and Peter had agreed that pregnancy could wait.

The third year Peter had been determined to regain his control over his wife. And that was the first time Kate realized that he was using sex consciously, deliberately, to get his own way. He had known the softening effect that lovemaking had on her, and he had been ruthless in using it. He would stroke her flank as she lay trembling in the aftermath and ask in an appealing, tender voice, "Are you *really* going to . . . ?" Do you *really* want . . . ?"

And somehow the answer was always no.

When it had finally occurred to her, with a little help from her friends, that if it shouldn't matter to her, surely neither should it matter so much to him, Peter had been furious. Now, when, in the aftermath of their loving, he asked her to give in, she had steeled herself to say no; she had forced the rational woman to take control from the loving, helpless child he had somehow drawn from deep inside her. And that was when the real battles began.

Well, she had come through it, thank God, but there was one thing no one knew but Kate: how difficult it had been to stand up for herself after their lovemaking. Through sex, Peter had touched some deeper part of her, someone who wanted union at any price, someone quite prepared to sacrifice self for that wonderful, soothing sense of togetherness—and wresting control from that self had been an anguish she did not want to go through again.

Andreas Constantinou had the kind of potent sexuality that would give him a power over her she might never break.

Unless she did it now.

The taxi drew up at the curb, and Andreas let her go. She got out and stood on the pavement in front of the hotel. In spite of the warmth of the Mediterranean night she was shivering. She stood there, trying to regain control, trying not to be afraid of what he might say when she told him.

When the taxi had pulled away and he bent to pick up the bags, she forestalled him by picking up her own. Then she put her hand on his arm and he looked at her. "Andrea," she said breathlessly. "Please, would you . . ." She took a deep breath to steady herself. She didn't have to beg for any favours. "I want to book separate rooms, please."

He nodded without speaking, as though he had expected it, and they walked together into the hotel. Kate could hardly believe it. What did it mean? She had given every sign of wanting to go to bed with him. How had he known she had changed her mind?

When they had booked the rooms and she had extended her credit card to pay for her own and been given her key, and Andreas had done the same, they got into the elevator together, and he set down his bag and reached for her. And then she understood: He thought she had booked the room to save her good name in front of the hotel employees. He had no idea that she had changed her mind.

He kissed her lightly, and the elevator doors opened almost immediately, and without a word she led the way down the hall. They had been given rooms on the same floor, but at least they were one number apart. Kate was nearly shivering with the combined effects of the need she felt to touch him, her determination not to and the buildup of the tension of knowing she must tell him so.

The door to 321 was immediately beside 323. The rooms were connecting ones. Damn all hotel receptionists and their assumptions. Kate bit her lip and bent to slide the key in the lock. She took a deep breath, but just as she opened her mouth to speak, Andreas got his own door opened and was inside. With a sinking heart, she stepped into her own room, closed the door and turned to where he was already tapping on the connecting door.

She would have to open it. She couldn't shout to him though the door like an outraged virgin. She owed him that: to tell him face to face in a civilised way.

Kate set down her bag and moved slowly to the door and unlocked it. He was not waiting on the other side; he had merely tapped and then moved to set his bag on the bed. When she opened the door he looked up from his unpacking and tossed his toiletries bag onto the bed, and walked over and took her in his arms without a word.

She let him kiss her because it was so hard not to want the kiss, but then she gently pushed him away. "Andrea," she said, and her voice was a cracking whisper. She licked her lips and tried again. "Andrea, I—" Oh, God, he wasn't going to believe this! How had she let herself get into this situation, a woman of thirty-two turning a man down at the eleventh hour? It would be forgivable in an eighteen-year-old—you didn't know what it meant yet, at eighteen—but she wasn't eighteen, and a man might reasonably expect that she would have put a stop to things much earlier in the proceedings if she had no intention of carrying through.

Especially a male chauvinist man.

He was waiting for her to continue. At the last moment her feminism bolstered her. What right did he have to her body? None at all. However impolite it was, this wasn't pizza and a movie she was backing out of. This was a giving and receiving of deep intimacy, and she had a right to change her mind. Any woman did. At no point in the proceedings did ownership of her body get transferred to a man.

"I'm sorry," she said calmly. "I know I've made you think otherwise, but I want to sleep alone tonight."

Whatever he had been waiting for, it wasn't this. His hands were on her arms, and she felt them tighten involuntarily. "Sleep alone?" he repeated. "What do you mean, sleep alone?" It was as though he did not want to believe it, as though the words had no meaning. "You will make love to me, and then you will come back here to a cold bed for the rest of the night? Why?"

"Andrea," she said, turning just in time to evade his kiss, but feeling the heat tremble through her nonetheless. "I don't want to make love to you at all."

This time his hands clenched almost painfully. "You do," he informed her. "That is a lie. You do." His eyes were black, and he was staring at her with a gaze as dark as the night sky she had been part of half an hour ago, and he was seeing her the way he had always seen her—the way she would look while he made passionate love to her.

She couldn't look at him if he was going to look at

her like that. Kate dropped her eyes. "No," she said flatly. "I made a mistake. I'm sorry."

He said roughly, "There has never been a woman who wanted to make love so much as you." His hands on her arms shook her a little, as though he wanted to shake her awake. "I know it."

"No," she said again.

Andreas let his hand fall and stood back from her an inch or two. Almost she followed; almost she reached out for him. "You are shaking," he pointed out softly. "If we are not touching, you don't know what to do."

She did not reply.

"Come here, Kate," he commanded softly, in a voice that caressed her like animal fur. She swayed towards him, towards the voice, without knowing till she felt the movement in her own back. Then she went rigid.

"Andrea," she said hoarsely, in a voice she could scarcely control.

"You want to make love to me," he said. "Your body tells me." He put a hand on her shoulder, and her eyes slitted and her head fell helplessly back. "Say it. Say it once, just once, and then you can say whatever you want. I won't listen; I will take you even if you scream no and kick and claw, Kate. You can fight all you want with me."

She almost fainted with the thrill of desire that went through her at his words. Oh, God, what a lover he would have been!

"Don't," she nearly sobbed, struggling for control of her voice. "Please."

"Please," he repeated, and he didn't even try to control his voice. It was raw with need. "Kate, touch me. Kiss me. I will make you forget whatever it is. I can do it."

He could; she knew he could. That was the danger. He would make her forget every hard lesson she had learned in life; he could reduce her to nothing. He was too dangerous; he was a dozen, a hundred times more dangerous than Peter. She had never in her life felt what she was feeling now, and he wasn't even *touching* her. If she let him love her, if she felt his body inside her, she might just go mad.

At the thought of her husband's name, she had felt a little trickle of cold penetrate the heat of desire that was fogging her brain. She reached for it, desperately, because she must save herself from this. Peter, she said to herself. Peter, Peter, Peter. And each syllable was like a drop of icy water dripping down from an icicle sword that hung over her head, threading her desire with cold fear.

Peter. *Your degree isn't really more important to you than I am, is it, baby?* "No, darling, of course not, but—" *Didn't you empty the wastepaper baskets today, sweetheart?* "I'll do it now, Peter." *Honey, you're my wife. Isn't that more important than being a 'human being'?* "No, it's not, Peter. No, it's not. *It's not!*"

Kate stepped back. "Andrea," she said. "I'm sorry. I'm really sorry."

"Kate," he said urgently. "I can change your mind, eh? You know it." She did know it. If he carried her to the bed and began to make love to her, she would give in, even now.

"Yes," she said. "Please don't."

"This is the first time for us," he said. "We will make love many times after this. But if I take you now—as maybe you want me to, but you can't say it—if I take you now, maybe you will like it, but then, afterwards, you will blame me. And then, always, you will remember that the first time was not good. Whenever you are angry, you will remember that. When you are angry with me, Kate, I want you to remember the first time and smile, you understand? And I want to remember, too. On the nights in the future when I want you and you don't want me, I want to remember how much you wanted me the first time, so I know it's only this one night you don't want me, that other nights will be like our first night. You understand? It's important."

She understood all right, but he didn't. "Yes, but Andrea, why—"

He bent and kissed her. "Because maybe you really don't mean no. So I have to explain to you why I don't make love to you, when I know I can. To tell you if that is what you want, tonight you have to tell me. You have to say yes."

She laughed shakily. Was he trying to turn the tables on her? "Andrea," she began, and then she thought, Well, if this is his way of saving face, I don't mind. It was about the most civilised—and the most gentle— way of any man in her experience. She thought suddenly, If that *was* what was in my mind, if I'd just been playing hard to get, that would be the right technique all right. I'd be falling into your arms right now.

She stepped back. "Thanks, Andrea," she said. "Good night now."

Before she could close the door, he stepped up against her and pulled her into his arms, letting her feel his strength, wrapping her so that she could not move. "But I am going to go crazy tonight with thinking. You think, too. You think what I could be doing to you while you are lying in your bed." Her head fell back over his arm, and his mouth teased hers till her lips parted hungrily, and then he kissed her till all her cooled-down passion came flaming back, and then he let her go.

Only just. He was breathing heavily, and he looked as though he wished he hadn't done what he had just done. "Now," he said hoarsely. "I won't sleep, and maybe you won't, either." He stepped back into his own room. "Lock your door," he said. "In the night I will want to come to you. If your door is open, you will not have to say yes."

She was trembling so uncontrollably she could hardly press the lock. It made an audible click as she did so, and she leaned against the door then, shaking helplessly, fighting not to let herself unlock it again.

From Andreas's side she heard no sound. The door did not close, the lock did not click. Kate shut her eyes. He would be waiting for her to come to him. The thought would drive her mad all night.

Everything that touched her drove her mad, too. The warm shower made her skin shiver into goose bumps. The rasp of the towel made her burn. When she brushed her hair she thought of his face against it, his breath on her neck. The fabric of her pyjamas was like his hands on her, and the touch of the sheet was torment.

Kate lay in the dark, aching, listening for any sound from his room, but she heard nothing. Was he lying there, waiting for her, as he had said he would? Desire was so strong in her now, she had to believe it was coming from him, too. It was almost a physical thing in the air; it could not be all her own. It was radiating at her from the next room, as hers must be communicating itself to him.

Her door was locked, but his was not. And he would not knock. She knew he would not knock. But he would hear, if she unbolted the door.

Kate turned restlessly under the sheet. Damn these hotels with no air conditioning, anyway. Didn't anybody realize it was *hot* in Greece?

There was a little breeze blowing, but though the window was open, the shutters were closed. Kate flung back the sheet and crossed the room to open the shutters. On the way back to bed she threw off her pyjama bottoms and then lay down without covering herself with the sheet.

Oh, great. Now she could stare at the full moon, as well. And watch the stars twinkle. And wonder what the sky would look like from Andreas's bed, and how the moon would affect her senses when she saw his head silhouetted against its light and his body moved in her. . . .

Oh, God. She began to cry, with the simple urgency of need. She needed him, she needed his touch, and how was she going to do without it? Not just tonight, but all the nights?

Because it would go on, this. It wouldn't stop just because she'd conquered it this one night. *If* she'd conquered it this one night.

He was waiting for her; she could feel it. He was willing her to come to him. What was it he'd said? "I lie in my bed and dream of you coming into my room, and I'm hard under the sheet, and you put your hand on me and want me."

Her stomach melted at the thought. Oh, God, was that how he was lying there now? Was it?

"Andrea, Andrea," she whispered, "please come to me."

He had said he would, hadn't he? He had said that in the night he would want to come to her. Would he try the door? If she undid the lock . . .

If she undid the lock, she would not have to say yes.

If she undid the lock on her heart, could she put it back on again? Because that's what she would have to do, wasn't it? If she let him get close, she'd have to make sure she pushed him away again afterwards. She'd have to be very careful about her independence. He'd have to know that just because he'd had her body didn't mean he had her life.

I'm making a bargain with the devil, she thought with sudden clarity. I'm playing with fire and pretending I won't get burned.

Well, she was burning now. It could hardly get worse than this. One night, she pleaded, not knowing with whom she pleaded. Just one night, and that's all, I promise.

It couldn't be dangerous, just one night.

She sat up in bed and looked at the door, bathed in silvery moonlight, and the little brass centre of the brass handle that she needed to twist only once to invite him in.

She wasn't twenty anymore. This fear of a sexually potent male being able to rob her of her independence was a foolish paranoia, a hangover from the days when she had not understood how to defend herself against it. There was no reason to fear that Andreas would even want to use her sexuality against her as Peter had done. He didn't want a wife, anyway; all he wanted was exactly what she wanted.

She could feel the force of his wanting through the wall, like a psychic heat. And she was a being, attracted to heat. Every time she moved, her muscles drew her towards the door.

Kate stumbled up off the bed and paced to the window again. She stood staring out over the hotel courtyard to the sea, listening to the distant roar. It had a sexual rhythm, an ebb and flow that stroked her senses and matched and thereby heightened the internal rhythm of her need.

He was a male chauvinist. He wasn't the type to treat sex as a meeting of equals at all. Yet he could have overcome her resistance, and he had known it as well as she. If he had gone on kissing her, if he had simply picked her up and carried her to the bed, she could not have resisted any longer. He hadn't done so. He had even told her to lock the door. He had insisted that *she* make the choice.

No man, not even the intellectual professor, had ever done that before.

As though a magnet drew her, Kate crossed to the connecting door and stood in front of it, fear and anticipation coursing through her. Was she making the most complete fool of herself?

No. He wanted her. He would be waiting. He had said he would wait all night. She could feel him waiting now.

Kate soundlessly turned the lock to let the little brass button pop up, and put her hand on the handle. Then she stopped. She could go back to bed now; she could leave it up to him. If he wanted her enough to try the door, he would find it unlocked, and if not . . .

But what about what *she* wanted? She was standing here burning up with her need for the man, and was she really prepared to go back to bed and passively wait to see if he wanted her? She wanted him. She had a right to say so, didn't she? And if he had changed his mind, he was capable of saying so.

Kate found herself smiling in the darkness with a complex mixture of fear, anticipation and unfamiliar joy that had something to do with being the aggressor. She opened the door almost soundlessly and looked across the room to Andreas's bed. He was lying in a patch of moonlight, his eyes open, black, his gaze burning into her as though his will alone had brought her here.

He slid up onto his elbows and fixed his gaze on her, as though he wasn't sure whether she was real or an image created by his own desire. For one long moment they were motionless, while the air of the room seemed to shimmer before her eyes. Then, just as he lifted an arm convulsively to the sheet that covered him, Kate moved across the carpet on soundless bare feet to the bed.

He was hard under the sheet, and she wanted him. She put out her hand to touch him, and said his name.

Chapter 10

CRETE

HE REACHED UP TO CUP HER FACE IN HIS UNSTEADY HANDS
with a touch so tender her heart turned over. She had
not expected tenderness, nor the look she saw in his
eyes as he drew her down into his arms and held her
there without speaking for a long, long moment.

Then, at last, he turned and kissed her, and the hard
knot of yearning melted into a slow sweetness that
flowed into every nerve and brain cell like a river of
forgetfulness.

It was not at all what she expected, and when he
lifted his head she looked at him from under eyelids
that felt too heavy and smiled.

"You are beautiful," he said softly as one slim finger
stroked her frόm eyebrow to chin. "You are a very
beautiful woman." He smiled, and his finger gently
brushed her lips, and she felt the touch like a small
dancing flame.

She did not speak, but in the moonlight he was
amazingly beautiful himself, and she wondered lazily
why she had pretended to herself that he was not. The
flesh on his face was firm, and it would be when he was

an old man; she had seen them on the docks—the fishermen, the labourers, those old men, still virile, their faces scored by the years, baked by the sun, lined, wrinkled, but still firmly fleshed. And his black hair, crinkled and thick, curling over his forehead and neck, feeling so coarse and male under her fingers— that was beautiful, too, and when he was an old man it would be white, but it would still feel like rough silk to her touch. Those thick brows would become grizzled and thicken with the years, and his black gaze would become more piercing. But when he looked at a woman, his woman, it would be with the same intensity of need in his eyes as the look that was growing there now, as he lay over her and smiled down into her eyes until the smile faded. It was replaced by the look that said he wanted to drive her mad with sex, the look that stirred her on a deeply sexual level, where she learned that until this moment she had known nothing about her own needs, and that this man would teach her everything.

Involuntarily, she raised her hand to his lips, because the promise she felt was almost frightening; but instead of holding him away, she stroked his lips with her fingers in the most sensual way imaginable, and he kissed her hand and slipped his tongue between two fingers, and the small shock of his touch shivered all the way down her arm and burst through her body.

"Oh!" she gasped on an indrawn breath, and Andreas smiled again, as though he took pleasure in her pleasure. His lips were cool, their full sensuality turning into a sweet softness when they touched hers, and she wondered how many times she could melt under his touch, how many times she could feel that sweetness travel through her body to her centre, with the same erotic impact, as though it were the first time she had ever been kissed.

His kiss trailed down her neck and came to rest at her pyjama collar, against the thudding pulse in her throat. He stopped there, his face against her skin, as though he drank in her scent and texture like a wine.

"Unbutton your shirt for me," he begged softly, and she realized that it didn't matter what happened now, because everything he said or did had the power to move her. Shaking, she lifted her hands to her pyjama front, and Andreas raised his head and watched intently as she unbuttoned the buttons, one by one.

There was something about the action that was profoundly stirring as she lifted both sides of the jacket and pulled the cloth away from her body while he watched. It gave her a sense of the enormous power of her sexuality, as though she were the embodiment of a great life force that matched his masculine power with an equal and opposite intensity that was not merely receptive, but powerfully active.

He said, "Tomorrow I will take you to see a statue who bares her breasts in just the same way as you have done. You will like her, I am sure." His hand cupped her breast, and he closed his eyes for a moment, as though sight were too powerful a stimulus.

"Who is she?" Kate asked, arching her back slightly to push her breast up against the pressure of his hand.

"A priestess of the Mother Goddess," said Andreas. He slipped his arm under her neck and gripped her shoulder as her head fell back. Then he began to kiss her again, and this time he meant it; and her flesh stirred at his touch, and she gripped him and caressed him and moved against him as he stroked and kissed her. . . .

She felt pagan and powerful, and not at all passive, as though he was here for her pleasure as much as she for his; she felt, for the first time, as though she had a right to demand what she needed from a man. She was of the race of priestesses of the Mother Goddess. She was not a vessel merely; she was a woman, and therefore significant. When he kissed and suckled her breasts, sending a high electricity through her, it was as though he took potent nutriment from her that only Woman could give. When he stroked her curving abdomen she felt her powerful fertility, and her great connection with the primal force of nature. When he tasted her flesh, she felt it as an act of worship of the feminine, expressing the male desire to understand the deep, abiding mysteries of her sex.

And when, suddenly, his passion became uncontrollable, and his hands burned and pressed her, she felt the unlocking of her own deep sexual nature, and his passion caught fire in her brain, and she had no thought anymore for masculine or feminine, but only union. She began to strain and whimper, losing track of time and of her self, only wanting what he could give her. At last he entered her body, and she felt the full force of the ritual, felt in a deep, primitive way how this coupling made the world more fertile, and understood for a moment exactly why the ancients had considered this act a sacred rite, dedicated to the appeasement of the goddess and the god.

He felt powerful inside her, and she could accept his power, welcome it, because her own deep power, secret and hidden from him in all save its effect, more than matched it. She could accept the pleasure he gave her as hers by right, in exchange for the pleasure she gave him.

Kate opened her eyes and smiled up at her lover, keeping them open against the thrust of pleasure his body made in her, in order to see and be seen. He was Andreas, and she was Kate; and she was Woman and he was Man; and in them was embodied in this moment the great struggle of the divided Soul to reunite.

For one long, short, shattering moment the Soul found its way, and the power of the reunion of its two great halves coursed through the bodies through which it met, and they shuddered, and cried out, and gloried in the hot, sweet melting of the Soul's fusion.

And then, too soon, his arm became his arm again, defined against the boundary of her flesh which was her flesh, and they drew apart and then, feeling this new/old separation, pressed together again, and wished that the union had been forever.

"So this is me, is it?" Kate laughed a little, standing in front of the tiny snake goddess that stood enclosed in glass. "She looks pretty angry, or is that a trance state?"

The statue, her arms outstretched, her white breasts prominently exposed, had wide, staring eyes and wasn't quite Kate's vision of herself; but she was certainly compelling.

"Who knows?" Andreas asked. "Maybe to control snakes like that you have to be in an altered state. Or maybe she was a sacrifice to the goddess; maybe the snakes killed her."

"That could make you stare all right," Kate agreed. She was fascinated by the little figure. What secrets lay behind this tiny remnant of the ancient religion? "Why did you say she reminded you of me?"

Andreas said slowly, "She has naked breasts, but she does not present them passively. She is not anybody's plaything, you see it? She wears her breasts bare as a sign of her power. She is not self-conscious about her body in the way that women of today are trained to be."

Kate said, "And this is the way I presented myself to you last night?"

"You were more self-conscious than this, of course.

But when you looked at me, you were aware of your power—not your power as a temptress or an object of desire, as so many women are, but your power as a woman, as a force of nature."

"Yes," she said, remembering. Marvelling that it had been so. "Yes."

It was odd, the effect that last night had had on her. She had never felt anything quite like that mixture of passion and strength in herself before. Andreas had been right not to try to seduce her, though certainly he could have, and certainly there had been something in her that had wanted him to do just that, to take the responsibility for what she did from her.

This morning, when she had opened her eyes, she had felt no regret, as she might easily have done if he had simply tormented her with her own desire till she could no longer say no. She had made up her own mind about how strong her desire was; she had known the possible consequences, and she had made her choice. And she had gone to him on her own two feet, in a kind of brazenness that she had never had the courage for before. She had gone to him knowing that he wanted her, gone without shame, full of the sense of her power and value as a woman. She had made an active, not a passive, choice to be in his bed, and the knowledge had fueled her sexuality and her response till at last they had felt an almost transcendental pleasure in what they did.

"It is the naked breasts in Minoan fashion that convince me, more than anything else, of the tremendous power of women in Bronze Age society," Andreas was saying. "They bare their breasts not as pinup girls, to excite men, but as a display of power. This, I think, is what you are looking for for your book."

Yes, it was, and what was more, last night he had given her a very powerful parallel experience, so that on some deep level she seemed to have an understanding of the powerful statue in front of her. Although the priestess/goddess's breasts were certainly not bared for sexual reasons, as Kate's had been last night, still she could communicate with this woman on a deep, female level.

And it was exactly what she was looking for for her book: a deep, intuitive, *female* understanding of the past.

"Yes," she said, hardly able to take her eyes from the small statue separated from her by glass. "Yes, thank you, Andrea."

"I shall be finished in about three hours. Shall I find you here in the museum?"

"Oh, yes. Yes, I'll need at least three hours. And then, are we going to Knossos?"

"Then my work is finished, and we go to Knossos."

He left her then and went to find the museum curator and look at some recently found and still unpublished artifacts from a new site in Crete. Kate went back to the beginning, to the artifacts from the prepalatial period, and walked through the rooms, following the history of Crete and the Minoan Empire, and the fate of women in prehistory.

The Neolithic inhabitants of Crete had apparently been peacefully invaded by foreigners, possibly from Asia Minor, in about 2700 B.C., who brought with them the knowledge of bronze. After this, there had been a sudden rapid development in arts and crafts: pottery, metal work, gold work, stone carving, and seal engraving.

In 1900 B.C., the first of the great palaces were built, at Knossos, Phaistos, Malia, Kato Zakros and perhaps elsewhere. This simultaneous development was significant because of what it indicated about the society: that they lived in peaceful coexistence without warlike antagonism. Was that a sign of a woman-controlled society? Perhaps not in itself, Kate thought, but there were other indications that it had been so, in spite of the name given to the civilisation by Sir Arthur Evans, the archaeologist who had discovered the great palace of Knossos. "Minoan," he had called it, after the semimythical King Minos, and Minoan it remained to this day.

In this period, too, the art of writing had arisen, in the form of hieroglyphics, to be followed in later periods by Linear A and then Linear B writings.

Between 1900 and 1700 B.C., earthquakes racked the island. Finally, in about 1700, there came an earthquake so severe it destroyed the palaces. Yet the civilisation was not destroyed. It seemed as though the inhabitants had managed to maintain the structure of their society and to continue to flourish, and they had immediately rebuilt the palaces. The period from this destruction of the old palaces to the later destruction of the new palaces was the richest and most creative in Minoan history. It was from this period that the myth of Theseus and the Minotaur had apparently arisen, the myth of children being sacrificed to the Bull. It was in the palace of Knossos that Theseus had wandered through the labyrinth holding the thread given him by Ariadne. It was at Knossos that the great double-headed axe, the *labrys,* symbol of the ruling power, of which Kate saw countless reproductions now in gold and other metals, had given the labyrinth its name. It was in Knossos that the famous wall painting of child gymnasts dancing with bulls had finally given credence to the ancient Greek myth of the Mycenaean Greeks under Theseus overthrowing the mighty Minoan Empire.

These two periods were called the old palace and the new palace periods by archaeologists, but it was the time of the destruction of the new palaces that fascinated Kate.

In 1450 B.C., catastrophe struck Crete, catastrophe so great that every palace was totally destroyed, except for Knossos. At Malia, Kato Zakros, Phaistos and at smaller sites like Agia Triada, life stopped. Only at Knossos was there any remnant left of palace life. It was this great disaster that Spyridon Marinatos had attributed to the destruction of the island of Santoríni/Théra and the subsequent great tidal wave.

The end of the new palace period had also marked the end of the Minoan civilisation as a power. The Mycenaean Greeks, a growing power, had subsequently invaded the island of Crete.

Kate found ample and heartbreaking evidence for her belief that the sinking of Santoríni had also meant the end of women as a power in ancient Greece. The pottery of both palace periods was filled with examples of feminine symbolism. Although there were no breasted ewers of the type that had been in use on Santoríni, she could marvel over the many jugs that seemed to have been designed in the exact shape of a woman's breast: a fluid, curving shape that she had seen countless times on the beach at Kérkyra, the shape of the breast of a woman lying supine, and in the centre, the opening, surrounded by a painted aureole. The female symbols seemed endless to her starved need to see the feminine truly glorified in art, and she wandered awestruck back and forth between the cases housing the new palace period finds. All the statues of women with naked breasts had that one marvelous subtext in common: As Andreas had pointed out, there was no self-consciousness about them. They were not on display for the gratification of men, but because their breasts marked them as women, and women were a force in the world.

Kate remembered the sense of power she herself had felt on the beach at Kérkyra, the sense of her seminudity being not a sexual but a political act. She laughed. It had been done before. No wonder women's public nudity inflamed religious moralists—the first rule of keeping women subservient must be to give them a sense of shame in their own bodies.

The heartbreak came in the postpalatial period, after the final destruction of the palaces. Now the statues of the goddess's hierophants, though still wearing the same flounced skirts and crowns, and still with the same bared chests, were obviously men in women's clothing. Now the chests were flat, the faces square and hard, and the quality of the art had sunk back into the primitive style of the prepalatial period of hundreds of years before. Men had taken over the worship of the Goddess—and was she already in transition to becoming overshadowed by Zeus?

It was obvious that men were beginning to assert their rights, and they had done it in exactly the same way as women were doing it now, three millennia later: by adopting the garb and probably the attitudes of the ruling caste. There was something both sad and amusing, to a woman who had grown up in a century where women had finally asserted their right to wear trousers, in the thought that there had been a time in history when *men* had asserted their right to wear flounced skirts. *Plus ça change*, Kate was thinking, *plus c'est la même chose*.

And phallic symbolism in pottery, which she had seen in a few artifacts from the palace periods, became more and more evident as she moved along the museum cases and through the years and centuries, while the breast and female symbolism became less and less.

Until, at one case, Kate felt her heart stop. There stood a woman again, a tiny statue with naked breasts. Only this time, there was a difference. This time, the little statue held her breasts cupped in her own hands, and she held them for approval. She was the embodiment of self-conscious female sexuality, the embodiment of the woman as sex object, and Kate knew with a sinking heart that this little goddess had been the conscious or unconscious role model of every woman born into the Western world since the moment she had been shaped, because after this there had been no other acceptable female sexuality.

She was looking at the very first Playmate of the Month.

Her first visit to the palace of Knossos could not possibly be her last. She would have to come back, Kate realized, because it would take a person days to get a proper view of the whole. The ruins were huge and extensive, and somehow compelling.

"Where next?" asked Andreas as she finished the guidebook commentary on the giant *pithoi* in the Western magazines and turned away. The sun was boiling hot; she could not understand how so many of the tourists were managing without hats. Crete was closer to an African climate than a Mediterranean one.

"Where did they find the little snake priestess? Was this really a palace?" she asked Andreas as they picked their way through the remains of what might have been the famous labyrinth underneath the palace.

"In the Temple Repositories," he said, guiding her along a stone walkway. "As far as I know it was a palace," he said. "What else?"

"I just remembered reading a book, when I was researching the Bronze Age, that suggested the whole thing was some kind of mortuary, a place of the dead."

"That's Wunderlich's theory. The Temple Repositories are down here." She followed him down a few steps, but the Temple Repositories were jammed with a German tour group. "Others ascribe to it, I believe."

"Well, which was it?" she asked. She had worked her way through the crowd a little and was craning her neck for a view of the cist where the little statue had been found.

Andreas laughed at her. "Are you asking me because I am a man and somehow know more than you? How can I know the truth?"

She blinked. "You're an archaeologist, after all."

"And Wunderlich was a geologist. And you are a writer. And we all have one disadvantage in common."

"Which is?" The German group was leaving at last, and an English group seemed about to crowd in. Kate jockeyed for position and stood at last over a rectangular hole sunk into the stone floor of the Temple Repositories, and wondered how and why the little statue had found her way here.

"We live in the second half of the twentieth century, at a time when conclusive answers to many of our questions of the past have either been lost or are not yet discovered. And in spite of all our theories, it is not possible to know many things that we would like to know."

"This is the antechamber to the Pillar Crypts," said a lightly accented Greek voice behind them. "Here is what Sir Arthur Evans called the Lobby of the Stone Seat. . . ."

Whatever the room had been, nothing spoke to her in the Temple Repositories. "Can we find the Queen's

Megaron?" Kate asked, wondering distantly when was
the last time she had interviewed, or even spoken to, a
man who refused the chance to debunk a colleague's
theories and insist on his own. Her husband, a medical
doctor who sneered at any and every form of alterna-
tive health care from chiropractic and acupuncture to
herbal medicine and natural birth, had seemed to her a
prototype of the scientific male. His favourite form of
argument had been sneering, mocking laughter accompanied by a put-down such as "Who told you *that*?" or
"Where'd you get *that* from?"

"We are crossing the so-called Central Court," Andreas said as they followed their shadows across a huge,
paved, open area. "Perhaps the bull jumping took
place here." Kate stopped in the bright sunshine to
stare about her. Lord, you'd need a week to cover this
place properly.

Long after Peter, as a woman interviewing men,
many of them in the sciences, about women's role
versus women's potential in modern society, Kate had
run into the same attitude, over and over. She had
come to consider it a disease of the scientific male, and
she had learned to play on it in order to get the
information she wanted.

Andreas Constantinou was one of a very few who
had not taken the bait. Even scientific women, having
forced themselves into the male mould in order to
succeed, had been victims of the disease, but at least
they had not been able to sneer at her for being a
woman.

"What's your opinion, then?" she asked. "Surely
you must have some conviction? You say this could
have been the place where the bull jumping took place.
Is that what you believe yourself?"

"I accept as a scientific working hypothesis that this

was a palace in a functioning and thriving society. I believe emotionally, as a man, that this was the factual basis of the Theseus myth," Andreas said. "As an archaeologist I am aware that there are other possible explanations. But whether it was a palace or a monument to the dead like the pyramids is not important to my theories right now. Whatever the ancient Cretans believed about the afterlife, we know that they had some sort of warning and got into their ships and fled in about 1450 B.C. And that is the part of their history that at the moment interests me."

"How do we know that? That they had a warning and left?"

"Herodotus reports it. 'All the Cretans except the people of Polichna and Praesus, in obedience to some sort of warning from heaven, undertook a mass expedition to Sicania.' But they could not conquer Sicania, which is now called Sicily, and so they gave up and went away. In the course of their voyage they were caught by a violent storm and driven ashore near Brindisi. And since all their ships were destroyed, they remained there, 'losing their name and *status* as Cretan islanders,' Herodotus says. And after that, according to the Praesus, who were left behind, various nationalities, mainly Greeks, came to settle on the island."

"Do you think the violent storm that destroyed their ships was the Santoríni disaster?"

"It is possible."

"And that would be why life stopped at the palaces, wouldn't it? The people had already deserted the island. Because I've been wondering why, except at Knossos, they didn't go back in and rebuild. The San Franciscans did, didn't they, after 1906?"

"You are right. Archaeology proves, time and time again, that after a disaster people return to their homes, no matter how badly damaged, and try to rebuild. By the way, this was, according to Herodotus, in the time of King Minos of Crete."

She smiled her wonder. "It really does all fit in, doesn't it? Why has no one else thought of it?"

"There has long been a tendency to discount ancient historians in archaeology. Partly, of course, because most of them did not write in the detached scientific manner we consider appropriate today. The Bible is not generally respected as history because, I think, Jehovah is so thoroughly woven into the fabric. Homer wrote poetry, which not many scientists can deal with. Before Schliemann, no one believed that poetry could be elucidating fact. That is why Herodotus is known as 'the father of history'—for the first time we have someone writing in a detached way that is closer to what scientists of today can recognize. Yet still, our arrogant belief in our age as the crowning achievement of man, I believe, prevents us from respecting the ancients. We respect Herodotus as the first historian, but we still do not believe what he reports. We consider him a child. Even when over and over again it is proved that the ancients had a great respect for their history and did not lie about the essentials."

"Everybody thought Schliemann was a fool for looking for Troy first in Homer, didn't they?" she remembered. "And no one believed in the labyrinth until Evans dug up Knossos."

"It is we who are the children," Andreas said as they began to descend a huge stone staircase. "Like children, we think we know it all."

They stopped to admire some restored paintings of shields on an ancient wall.

"What do you think of the restoration of Knossos?" Kate asked, because the extensive restoration of the palace was somewhat controversial. Arthur Evans, the turn-of-the-century archaeologist who had excavated the site, had arbitrarily "restored" many walls and pillars and painted them in the deep reds and blues he felt the originals had been. But she had heard and read that many people felt he had done his restorations rather randomly and not in accordance with acceptable archaeological practice.

"I don't mind what he did as much as some of my colleagues, because his reconstruction of the upper stories allowed him to excavate properly the deeper levels. And his guesses are as valid—though of course he made a few archaeological 'mistakes'—as anybody else's. What do you think of it?"

"The restoration? As a layperson, you mean?" She liked it and said so. Even if Evans's reconstruction was wrong, it gave an idea of the sheer immensity of the palace; it allowed your imagination somehow to encompass the possibilities. Yet, even so, it was just this sort of interpretation that she had wanted so desperately to avoid in her examination of the ancient world. "You know," she said, "even though other archaeologists don't physically stamp their finds with their own visions as Evans has done, in my opinion, they've built exactly this kind of structure, and on just as shaky a foundation, with their interpretations. I don't know why there's such a hullabaloo about what Evans did. They're all doing the same thing intellectually as he did physically. It's nearly as impossible to have a different opinion of a site once an archaeologist has decided what it is on paper as it is here."

"We have a tendency to find what we are looking for all right," Andreas agreed quietly.

Now, on their way to the rooms called the Queen's Megaron by the imaginative archaeologist, they were descending several flights of stairs, past heavy, impressive pillars painted red or black, past more reconstructed wall paintings, past stepped balustrades and double axes and lustral basins. "What romantic names he gave everything!" she exclaimed, her eyes moving between her guidebook and the treasures in front of her eyes.

"There is that to be said for it," remarked Andreas dryly.

But in the Hall of the Double Axes, she baulked. "'The *King's* throne'?" she read aloud in disgust. "How did he know this was the King's throne, and not the Queen's? That's pretty chauvinist, isn't it?"

"He lived in a chauvinist age," Andreas said apologetically, with only a hint of amusement in his eyes.

Kate only snorted. "And we don't, I suppose! Look at that throne! Does that look as though it was built for a man, just for a start? Pretty small man, if you ask me! Besides—"

She heard a choke of laughter and realized that she was entertaining several tourists who had entered behind them, and who evidently spoke English. But it was true. It was obvious. There was nothing whatsoever to indicate that the monarch had been a man, nothing to show that the "King's Hall" had housed a man, or the "Queen's Megaron" a woman, as far as she could see. Only the conditioned response of the viewer, a man, had dictated that the more important-looking rooms must belong to a man, and that likewise the ruler could only be male.

She turned to Andreas. "You see why it was so important that I get on a site as it was being dug, before anybody had glued their own ideas to the finds so thoroughly that it would be nearly impossible to shake them? We come from a male-dominated society, and we're bound to see other societies through that filter unless we deliberately work to see past our own conditioning. And I didn't think I could count on you or any archaeologist to be as willing to be aware of our conditioning as I am."

Andreas only nodded, but they returned to the subject later, as they lay on a beach and idled away a couple of hours before they had to catch their flight back to Athens. "I've been reading that book on Santoríni," she said. "I came across a very interesting little comment." She riffled quickly through the pages. "Here it is— 'It is hardly imaginable that male gods are completely absent in any religion.'" Kate snapped the book shut. "How do you like that?"

"A little fatuous, considering how little we know of the history of civilisation beyond a few thousand years ago. None of us knows how many civilisations totally unknown to us flourished and died in prehistory."

The Egyptians had said as much to Solon, according to Plato, she remembered. "And there's not only that," she pointed out. "How is it this writer didn't stop to consider the complete absence of *female* deities in most of *today's* religions? And if we can have the one, how can the other be 'unimaginable'?"

"A very unimaginative writer," Andreas agreed, idly flipping through the books she had piled beside her on the towel. "What is this? Ah—*The End of Atlantis*. Have you read this yet?"

"Some of it," she said. "Most of it, really. It's interesting, isn't it?"

"I haven't read it in a long time. Is this the one which gave you your ideas about Atlantis?"

"My— Oh! Yes, partly. I mean, at least he gives a good reason for believing that Atlantis wasn't outside the Pillars of Hercules, as Plato said."

He looked at her oddly. "Is that all? What made you suspect that Samothráki had a connection with Atlantis?"

She wondered if he was trying to make her feel a

fool. "Look, I'm sorry about that. I really am sorry. I would never have published that article as it was. Until you told me I had no idea that it could have such a devastating effect."

"But how did you find out? Was it only a guess?"

"For heaven's sake, how did I find out what?"

"So it was a stab in the dark?" Andreas lay back and squinted up at the sun. "You knew nothing about my theory, the suspected origin of my Samothrákian incomers? Nothing at all?"

"Not until you told me yesterday."

The sun glinted golden on his eyelashes as Andreas laughed softly. "Why?" she said. "What's so funny?"

"You bluffed me," he said. "I told you I have a sense of the ridiculous. It amuses me to have been made a fool of by you, to observe how quickly I jumped to conclusions."

Kate looked down at the book she held. She knew that the author believed that the island of Crete had been the Atlantis of the Platonic legend, and he had certainly accepted Marinatos's theory that it was Santorini that had caused its downfall. But Samothráki was hardly mentioned in the book.

"Wait a minute . . ." Kate said, staring into space, while the gentle laughter of Andreas continued like a musical accompaniment under her thoughts. *What are you protecting—the lost treasure of Atlantis?* she heard herself say, meaning nothing by it until he had made it clear by his reaction that she had touched a sore spot. But after her research, in spite of the article she had written, she had come to accept that he had been angry for the reasons he said—that any such rumour would bring sensation-seekers with it. Especially when she discovered that he was looking not for an established society, but for signs of immigrants. Especially when the pottery they found had been so primitive.

But now she had learned where he thought those immigrants had come from, and if Crete was Atlantis, and Santoríni had had strong links with Crete, and if the inhabitants of Santoríni had also had time to escape, then—

"Good God!" Kate said faintly, looking at him with amazed, wide open eyes. "I was right all along! You really are looking for the lost treasure of Atlantis!"

Andreas was lying there, shaking with amused laughter. "Yes," he said simply. "Yes, I really am."

Chapter 11

SAMOTHRÁKI

"NOT TREASURE IN TERMS OF GOLD AND JEWELS, OF course," he explained later that evening, as, having made a quick connection in Athens, they flew on towards Alexandroúpolis. "The treasure of information."

"But how can Crete or Santoríni be Atlantis?" she was protesting. "The whole premise was that the history of the civilisation of Atlantis was totally lost to the Greeks, and they certainly hadn't forgotten Crete."

"First of all," Andreas told her, smiling lazily into her eyes in a way that made her melt, "whether or not Thera was Atlantis is unimportant to any archaeological findings we make on Samothráki. It is incidental. I will not be concerned to prove that these people were refugees from Atlantis, only from Santoríni. Nevertheless, it is a curiosity.

"Now, what is important in the Atlantis legend is its source. It did not come down through Homer or Herodotus or any Greek memory, as far as we know. It came from the Egyptians, and if Atlantis does refer to

Santoríni, then it came with significant errors in chronology and geography which would have made it unintelligible to the Greek people."

"I think I'm following this."

"Yes. Supposing that the only connection the Egyptians had in the ancient Mediterranean world was with the highly advanced Cretans and Therans. The other 'Greek' races would have been backward, compared to them—the Athenians only seen as a source of supply of young boys and girls for human sacrifice, according to Homer. So it is not farfetched to imagine that the Egyptians did not have much contact with them.

"Now, all the people leave, and Théra blows up. Overnight, this wonderful civilisation in the Great Green, as the Egyptians called the Mediterranean, has disappeared. It has sunk into the sea. That information goes into Egyptian historical records; they have it on pillars.

"When Solon visits Egypt, nine hundred years later, the world has shrunk somewhat. The middle of the Great Green is no longer as far away as it used to be a millennium ago. So perhaps they interpret the great distance sailed by the Keftiu as extending beyond the Pillars of Hercules. And perhaps in their historical hubris, or perhaps not perfectly understanding the ancient writings of their forebears, they extended the nine hundred years and made it nine thousand.

"And from Solon's point of view, what would make him connect such a tale with the old Cretan civilisation, of which, in any case, little had come down to him? Who had been left to pass on the history of the Cretan civilisation to the race that subsequently conquered the island? There was almost no one left. And there was nothing at all remaining of the civilisation of Théra. How could it have passed into history, except peripherally, by way of the Bible and other such distant sources? They were no longer the superior civilisation. It is the winners who write history. Furthermore, whatever they did write is unfortunately indecipherable, for the most part."

All the little bits of history she had picked up in her researches began to fall into the pattern he laid out. The mysterious Eteocretans, or "true Cretans," who had maintained their own language and a sense of their superiority deep in the hills of Crete long after the Mycenaean invasion. The fact that there had been no Egyptian artifacts found on Crete that dated from later than about 1450 B.C., as though trade had abruptly been cut off. And then what had happened? An Egyptian sea captain had weathered a terrible storm in which clouds of lava had blackened the sun for days, and then had discovered the one island sunk into the sea, and the other deserted?

"It must have seemed a terrible calamity when they saw it go," she mused. "That great city, in one day." Then, hearing her own words, she sat up straight. "Mother of God!" she exclaimed. "It's in Revelations!"

Andreas looked enquiringly at her. "It's all there," she said excitedly. "Everything we've been saying, don't you see? It's in Revelations. 'Alas, alas, the great city Babylon. In one hour your time has come.' I've read it over and over. I know it almost by heart. It's God punishing this great city, and it was a sea power, and it was characterized as a woman—the whore of Babylon! Don't you see?"

"Not yet," Andreas apologized.

"Perhaps it was a legend among the Hebrews, how an ancient civilisation dominated by women whom they considered too sexually free was destroyed by Jehovah —the Sky God we were talking about before. I mean, the ancient Greeks had temple prostitutes, didn't they? Maybe the Therans did, too. The ancient Hebrews were always being tempted by the free sex of the Philistines and Canaanites, weren't they?

"Revelations talks about how the sea captains stood at a distance and cried out as they 'saw the smoke of her burning.' 'Alas for the great city, where all who had ships at sea grew rich on her wealth. In one hour she was destroyed.' Things like that."

"But wasn't Revelations a prediction of the future?" Andreas protested mildly.

"Yes, but don't you see? He might have been making the point that what has happened once can happen again. Hebrew history is full of repetition—the diasporas, for example. Couldn't the story of Thera have been part of legend, exploited to keep the Hebrews away from the Philistines? Couldn't John have been saying, 'You better watch out, because you all know what God did once, and he can do the same thing again'? Or he might even have seen a vision of the past and believed it was the future."

"I suppose so."

"And it would be just what you said—they saw the destruction of the great city as the triumph of the male god over the female one."

He laughed. "And shall you put this in your book?"

"Yes, yes, why not? It's a theory worth looking at, isn't it?"

"Oh, yes," he said. "But perhaps it will not be very popular in North America just at present."

She dismissed that with a gesture. "Oh, to hell with that! If I wanted my ideas to be popular, I'd never have become a feminist!"

"You like to fight, then?" he said, and she couldn't prevent that from reminding her of a hundred different things as she looked into his eyes. She smiled at him, and then, because they were in a plane, she said, "Tell me what you hope to find from Samothráki."

Andreas lifted her hand and kissed it with a firm and unmistakable pressure. "If I am right about the origins of the Neatherans, we have á chance of finding out more information about the people of Thera and Crete than we have had before. Perhaps most importantly, there is a chance of deciphering Linear A."

Linear A, Kate knew, was one of the languages discovered on tablets found on Crete, a language which had never been deciphered. Linear B was another, possibly later, language. Even it had been partially deciphered only recently, a couple of decades ago; and if the exhibits at the Iráklion museum were anything to go by, there hadn't been much to translate except lists of supplies. "Ten cows and twenty goats and twelve men" had been about the most exciting communication Linear B had had to offer.

Nevertheless, she knew quite well that any light cast on Linear A would be considered a major discovery by archaeologists, and even by the rest of the world. And it was at least possible that Linear B had been the language of the Mycenaean conquerors, while Linear A had been that of the original, preevacuation Cretans. In which case what was on the Linear A tablets might be very different in content from the Linear B ones.

"Are you serious?" she demanded, because it was truly exciting. Who knew what information about the ancient world lay hidden on the Linear A tablets?

Andreas said slowly, "Have you been to visit the museum at the Sanctuary of the Great Gods?"

"Yes," she said.

"Did you notice some small bits of pottery with Greek letters inscribed on them? What the label describes as a 'non-Greek language'?

She remembered having seen them; she had noticed them particularly. Undeciphered writings seemed, to her, a terrible waste. All that knowledge locked up in what amounted to a code.

"What did you notice about the writing?"

"I didn't notice anything, except I was surprised because it looked like Greek to me." She laughed. " 'It was all Greek to me,' " she quoted. "What I mean is, it was written just like the ancient Greek inscriptions I've seen in Athens and other museums."

"Yes," said Andreas. "Whatever the language was, there is reason to believe that that language was the religious language on Samothráki for centuries after Greek became the spoken language, somewhat as Latin is the religious language in the Roman Catholic church today. It appears to have been *transliterated* into the Greek alphabet at some time. And it is the transliteration which we see on the inscriptions."

"Sorry," Kate said, momentarily lost. "Why would they have done that?"

"For the same reason that languages with different alphabets are transliterated into English today. So that English speakers can pronounce the words, even if we do not understand the meaning. So we can pronounce the name *Koran,* even if we do not know that the meaning in Arabic is *something to be read.* So that we can read the name *Adam* whether or not we know that in Hebrew it means *man,* and can pronounce the names of cities like Moscow and Athens and Hyderabad without having to learn the alphabet of the language of origin."

"Yes, of course." She thought a moment. "So whoever brought the religion to Samothráki, you think they transliterated the holy words of their language so that a Greek-speaking people could pronounce them?"

"That's right."

"And if the people of the religion came from Santoríni, then—"

"Then perhaps the language has also been recorded as Linear A."

Kate felt the excitement he must have felt when he formulated the theory. "What are you doing to prove it?"

"I have someone working on the theory, of course, trying to find similarities between the two."

Kate wrinkled her brow. "But even if you do find a correlation, you still won't have a translation of Linear A, will you?"

"At the least we may find out what sort of language it was. We may find correlations with other languages. But certainly it would prove a Minoan influence on Samothráki; it would tell us more about the Minoan religion."

"Minoan," she said. "That's from Crete. Do you think the Cretans also influenced the Therans, and that they carried the Cretan religion to Samothráki?"

"Most people believe that the Cretans were the dominant power, and that their domination extended to Santoríni. I am going to look at it from another perspective: that it was the Therans on the island of Santoríni who were the first great power, and its influence went out to Crete, which then flowered into a power itself. Plato tells us that Atlantis was already somewhat in decline when it sank into the sea."

"So you think Santoríni itself was Atlantis?"

"I think it is possible. The dates which Plato gives are quite remarkable and consistent, if you subtract that one zero from each of the dates."

"Is there any other justification for doing that? I thought the Egyptians had pretty accurate historical records."

"Yes, we think so. But it is very interesting to note that, while they told Solon about this nine-thousand-year-old civilisation, and said that their records of their own civilisation went back eight thousand years, the actual King lists of Egypt and Mesopotamia which we know today extend back only three thousand years."

"So perhaps some error got into the system between the time of the Keftiu and the time of Solon?"

"It's worth thinking about."

"But everybody I've read who believed the Atlantis theory has only suggested that Crete was Atlantis."

"Perhaps because until Marinatos started digging in 1967, Crete was the only civilisation we knew to have been destroyed in that catastrophe. But there are two things noteworthy in the Atlantis legend: Plato seems to indicate that Atlantis was *circular*, and says quite clearly that it *sank*. Neither of those two criteria fits Crete. Both fit Théra. He also says that Atlantis had conquered many of the neighbouring islands, and had political influence as far away as Libya. This means that whether Crete or Théra was Atlantis, the other island fell under its dominion. It is also possible that Atlantis was composed of two islands. And whether it was Cretans or Therans who escaped to Samothráki, more light will be cast on the entire Minoan civilisation."

She was riveted. This was the most fascinating conversation she had ever had in her entire life. She kept him talking all the way to Alexandroúpolis, and into the taxi, and through the dark streets, and didn't come to herself again till they were on the pavement in front of the hotel in the summer darkness, and he was asking, "One room or two tonight, Kate?"

Ever afterwards she would be surprised by the instinct that made her say "two." She was more than half in love with Andreas, and she wasn't in the least concerned with what the hotel receptionist would think, if indeed he would bother thinking anything. So what was it that had caused her to make the choice she had?

Perhaps it was *because* she knew she was half in love with him, and some instinct prompted her to cling to an independence she felt was slipping. Perhaps her response to Andreas's lovemaking last night had frightened her with its intensity—the intensity that had always spelled danger to her.

Or perhaps it was, as the smile in Andreas's eyes told her, because she wanted to fight him. Perhaps she was testing him already. Perhaps that was it.

The facts were these, as she reminded herself later: When they got out of the taxi she had every intention of making love with Andreas that night. And even though they booked two rooms, she saw that Andreas made sure they were adjoining, and she was glad of it. And as they walked side by side across the long expanse of grass and gravel to their doors on the far end of the hotel, she felt the thud of anticipation building into a pattern of sexual need in her, a need that was directed only at Andreas, a need she knew he understood. She could hardly wait to hold him, to touch him, to experience her own passion at his hands.

Yet when they got to their rooms, she unlocked hers first, and then, unbelievably, she turned to him in the moonlight and said softly, "Good night, Andrea. See you in the morning."

He whirled. "What?" he demanded, but she merely nodded in his direction and slipped through her doorway, closing the door behind her.

She heard him come into the room next door, heard the barely controlled tension as he threw his bag onto a chair or something else that stood against the wall. She stood motionless, listening, as he unlocked the connecting door, and froze as the handle on her side of the door turned. Here there was only one connecting door, with two locks.

The lock on her side held. Kate let out her breath slowly, and then sucked it in again as his knock sounded. "Kate," he called, and knocked again. She made no answer, only stood frozen, staring at the door.

But Andreas did not call again, and after a moment or two she heard movement in the other room. With a slightly let down feeling, Kate turned and began to get ready for bed. The water was only lukewarm, as usual, but she showered off the travel dust and felt better for it. She slid into her pyjama top and opened the windows of the balcony door for air, but left the wooden shutters closed and locked. For all she knew, she and Andrea had a joint balcony out there, but in any case they were on the ground floor and she would prefer it if he did not come climbing over the balcony wall and into her room tonight.

For a few minutes Kate busied herself laying out clean clothes for tomorrow, then repacked everything else. She would leave out a book to read, because in spite of a long and tiring day, she knew she would not fall asleep for hours.

Her duffel bag was on the wooden luggage stand that stood right beside the connecting door to Andreas's room, and as she pulled out *The End of Atlantis* Andreas's voice was suddenly right beside her through the door.

"Kate," he said, his voice deep and carrying, "are you going to open this door, or do you want me to break it down?"

Kate gave a jump far beyond what would have been a

normal startled response, which showed her what unconscious tension she was acting under. She felt a shiver of something that was not quite fear thrill through her. She said nothing, staring at the door. She was locked now in her own contradictions. She was acting in a way even she did not understand.

"I know you are there, Kate, I know you are listening to me. I want you to listen well. If you really want to sleep alone tonight, if you do not want me to break down this door and come in and take what I want, you must say so. You must say to me now, No. That is all. You understand? So, I am listening."

She stared at the door, as incapable tonight of saying no as she had been last night of saying yes. What strange rules the man played by. And yet . . .

The phone rang, ripping her out of her nervous inaction, and she crossed gratefully to the bed and picked up the receiver. "Yes?" she said. There was a silence at the other end, and suddenly she understood, and her breathing stopped in her throat. She closed her eyes helplessly as her blood seemed to swell in all her veins, and stood there, waiting for whatever would happen now.

"No answer?" Andreas's voice said softly then, and he laughed a laugh that challenged and thrilled her all at once. Then there was the sound of the receiver being replaced, and Kate hung up her own phone and turned to look at the connecting door as if it might suddenly come alive.

It did. The first thump galvanized her, and she turned and flung herself towards the balcony door, grappling with the unfamiliar lock as though her life depended upon her escape from this room.

She heard the crack of the door lock and the tiny snap of hers at the same time, and then she was pushing the shutter aside and stumbling out into the dark of an unfamiliar balcony, and Andreas was right behind her. Ahead of her were the dark moon shadows of trees and scrub, and beyond them, only a few yards from where she stood, moonlight on the sea.

Bare-legged, she flung herself over the low balcony wall and ran for the shadows, hearing his silent pursuit as loud as thunder in her bones. A wide, barren path ran through the trees and bracken, and she tore along it, her bare feet slapping lightly on the earth, his echoing behind. She had no idea where she was going, what she was doing; she only knew that the exhilaration was in her blood, the exhilaration of being the fastest, the toughest, the best. When she reached the beach, she made a hard right and ran along the edge of the grove between the beach and the trees.

There was no one about; it was midnight, and save for the broad face of the full moon they were alone. Further along the coast behind her were the lights of the city, but just here, on the hotel property and beyond, they were encased in darkness.

Over her shoulder, the moonlight glinted on Andreas's face as he closed the distance between them. As he reached for her, Kate dodged, her feet sinking into sand as she left the hard-packed earth for the beach. She recovered quickly, and then, as he followed her onto the sand, he stumbled, and she caught him a blow on the chest that overbalanced him.

She whirled, but Andreas caught her wrist, and as he fell, she was pulled down on top of him, and as soon as that his arms were around her. His chest was bare, and as she had noted before, it was well muscled. So were his arms, so firmly locked around her, making her feel his strength and power.

Male strength and power, so very different from the

female strength and power she had shown him last night; and for one unbelievable, cosmic moment she understood the vast differences and similarities between man and woman, and why they must be equally balanced in the world for the world to survive.

She was still for a moment, looking into his eyes, and then she began to struggle. He rolled over with her locked in his hold and, as though her struggles inflamed him, began to kiss her. Passionate kisses that burned her brain to blackness, so that her mouth and her body hungered in a tearing response, and yet she was part of some deeper ritual, and without knowing why she tore her mouth away.

Andreas lifted a hand to her chin, and she broke out of his grasp in a lightning response, rolled away from him and stumbled to her feet.

It was incredible. It was like a mating dance, which only her subconscious understood, and perhaps only his. She was torn with desire for his lovemaking, and yet she was fighting him with all her energy. Or perhaps she fought him because of her desire, desire stronger than anything she had ever felt in her life. She didn't know. All she knew was that she fought him, and that the battle raised her desire to fever pitch, so that she wanted to fight him even more.

He knew it; he seemed to understand everything. Or perhaps it was his own desire that he understood; that, and knowing that she wanted to fight, and lose. As she stumbled to her feet he flung himself forward and caught her ankle so that she fell again. She kicked her ankle free and began to scramble away on hands and knees, panting with exertion now, but otherwise silent, as silent as they had both been from the beginning.

Andreas was behind her; she could hear his breathing, too, and she stumbled to her feet and ran forward, and was suddenly splashing into the water.

It was cool, if not cold, and its touch shocked her. In spite of the glinting moon, she had had no idea where she was; and Kate altered course to run along the beach through the shallows instead of deeper into the sea. There was splashing as he caught her wrist from behind and swung her around, and now every wild emotion she had was in turbulent motion, and she began to swing wildly at him, backing away, all her clawing passion in that flailing fist that sought for contact with his flesh, and yet beat him off.

She kicked at him, she clawed, she splattered water over them both, but still no word passed between them, and at last he closed in, powerful, deliberate, fierce in his passion. He caught her other wrist and locked both of them behind her back in one hand, then bent to slide his arm under her knees.

He picked her up high out of the water, locking her arms against her sides, with a need that was like fury, and she looked up into his shadowed face and saw her own tearing desire mirrored there, then dropped her head back over his arm in mute surrender.

He laid her down under the trees amid the grass and bracken and entered her with a sudden, hard thrust that made her cry out. She began to shake and tremble uncontrollably, as though that one thrust of his body was enough to give her release from the unbearable sexual tension that had built up in her. Andreas caught his breath against the groan of desire that was torn from him, and began to thrust faster and harder, driven to fury by her need, and his.

She was already at the peak, and he drove her over it into pleasure that exploded all around her, a wild, black, bursting pleasure that was like nothing she had ever felt in her life before; a pleasure that made her cry out over and over until his hand smothered the sound as he pushed and writhed against her and stifled the sounds of too much pleasure that came from his own throat.

Chapter 12

SAMOTHRÁKI

REBECCA SEIGEL WAS WAITING AT THE DOCK IN the battered Jeep with a broad smile of welcome on her face. "You're back just in time," she told Andreas, gunning the motor into life as soon as they had climbed aboard and roaring out of the dock area at speed. "We've been turning up lots of interesting pottery, and yesterday we found the floor."

Kate, sitting in the backseat, sat forward, leaning one elbow on the back of Andreas's seat, casually resting against his shoulder blades and resisting the impulse to stroke his black hair as she listened to his questions and Rebecca's quick answers. It seemed that Rebecca thought Neathera had been abandoned about two hundred years after the original settlement, perhaps at the time of the mysterious collapse of the Mycenaean civilisation. Bill's wall had been thoroughly dug, and several others found, and what they had was probably a thriving, if primitive, little village built by Bronze Age incomers.

"Not exactly single occupation, Andrea, but by the

197

look of it, not much happened except a peaceful integration, if that's what it was, with the locals.''

Rebecca lit a cigarette and threw the dead match onto the floor of the Jeep with all the other rubbish accumulated there. She took a deep drag, and then said, "That pottery that Sarah found before you left? Agapi's been working on it constantly. Andrea, she thinks what she's got—'' She flicked a quick glance in the direction of Kate, and said, "But I'm not going to tell you what she thinks. You'll be seeing it for yourself in a few minutes. How was your trip?''

If he was impatient to know what Agapi thought, Andreas showed no sign of it. He began to tell Rebecca the technical details of his meeting with the director of Akrotíri, and it was a strain for Kate to listen over the roar of the ancient motor, so she leaned back in her seat and turned her face up to the sun, soothed by its morning warmth and the rocking motion of the Jeep. She had had very little sleep, and the memory of last night was like wine in her blood.

They had lain exhausted under the trees in the aftermath of their passion, while the full moon overhead became entangled in the black and silver leaves, and the soft sighing of the sea flowed over them. Andreas's arm was across her stomach, his hand clasping her ribs just below her breast, and his face was against her hair.

Her brain had been empty of everything save the memory of passion, and even that seemed oddly blank, as though the ghost of a tiger raged through empty rooms.

They had not lain there long. And when they got up, and walked hand in hand back across the short distance to their balcony, she knew that it was more than a handclasp that linked them now. Now there was a thread between them, as real to her senses as if she could see it, touch it, and she knew that whenever Andreas pulled on that thread, she must come to him.

It wasn't till this morning that she realized that he was pulling on the thread just by being there. And what that meant, she was afraid to face.

The Jeep bounced over the hill track, and then there was the familiar sight of the dig spread out in front of them. Not much had changed, except that two of the baulks outlining Bill's team's square had disappeared, the square now joining up with its neighbours on the south and the west to make a huge L-shaped trench.

Andreas didn't bother going into the admin hut. Accompanied by the two women, he headed straight out to the dig, to Bill's trench, where half of the Neathera team seemed to be clustered, either watching or working.

Diagonally across the bottom of the trench was the exposed wall, not quite two feet high at the highest point, less than a foot at the lowest. At the southern end it was met by another wall, partially exposed, and in the angle formed by these two there was a broken jug, still in situ, which someone was busily photographing.

The broken jug was resting on the hard-packed earth and stone which was the floor of the house.

While Andreas and Rebecca and Bill examined and conferred, Kate stood on the edge of the trench and gazed down at the evidence of long-ago human habitation. With the addition of the second wall, and especially with the jug, it was easier to imagine that people really had lived here, and died here, and tried to make the best of their lives.

She stared at what they had left behind, trying to conjure up an image of what they had been and believed, wishing, as so many had before her, that the stones would speak.

If they did, she did not hear them. But she waited there in the sun, watching the archaeologists look for signs and interpret them, and then finally Andreas said, "I want to see Agapi's pottery now." Somebody gave him a hand out of the trench, and Kate walked by his side towards the lab tent.

Agapi met them at the doorway. *"Ya su, ya su, ti kaneis?"* she greeted Andreas, and then to Kate, "How are you? You had a good trip?" And while they exchanged meaningless pleasantries she led them towards a table in the corner where a solitary jug sat, surrounded by several tiny bits of itself that had not been matched up yet.

The jug was incomplete, at best. The handle was there, and most of the spout, but large parts of its belly were missing. Still, there were lines very faintly visible that might have once been a kind of painted decoration. It was a jug not much different from the vast array Kate had seen during the past few days: a container made for a purpose and painted to soften the purpose with decoration.

It was pretty, too, with a high-bellied shape that reminded Kate of something, but she could not quite see what had caused the excitement in Rebecca's voice earlier, until Agapi turned the little platform on which the jug sat, and the other side of it came into view.

This side was a little more complete. And high on this side, towards the front, a lump of clay had been rolled into a tiny ball and attached to the body of the jug. And then it had been painted in a darker colour that was still faintly visible after the passage of time, and a circular decoration had been daubed around it on the pale-painted body.

There was only one. Where the second would have been, there was only a broken hole where a large piece of the jug had not survived. But even to Kate's untutored gaze, the significance was unmistakable. There was only one place where she had ever seen that sort of decoration on a jug: on the island of Santoríni, at the ancient site of Akrotíri.

Almost without a doubt, she was looking at someone's attempt to reproduce, with inferior tools, a Theran breasted ewer.

"What does it mean?" she asked Andreas later, as they worked together in the admin hut. "Does it mean you can be absolutely certain now that your incomers were from Thera?"

"There aren't many certainties in archaeology," Andreas answered, looking up from his work to gaze, first at her, and then out the window to the site. "It might mean that, or it might mean that these people had trade with the Therans and tried to copy their ceramics, after or even before Théra's destruction."

"So it's really not that important?"

"It is tremendously important. We have at the very least established a connection between Samothráki and Santoríni, a connection which no one has known about until now. For all the reasons I gave you yesterday, this is vitally important."

Lucky Sarah. She had made a very significant find, just as she had hoped. "Is this going to weigh with your money-men, at least?"

He smiled. "If this does not satisfy them, I am not sure what we could find that would. At least they must extend the season for another month or two."

He looked down at the paper he was working on, playing with his pencil, and she asked, "Are you telling them now?"

He sighed, and seemed to make up his mind about something. "I want to keep it quiet a little longer. Until we know more. The moment we tell them, we shall have them here, poking around and feeling proud of themselves, and wanting the press to know all about it." He looked at her and laughed. "You know how I feel about publicity."

"But it's already nearly August," she pointed out. "Your funding runs out at the end of August, doesn't it?"

Andreas nodded and shrugged at the same time. "Well, that is four weeks without interference, isn't it?"

She hesitated. "Well, excuse me if I'm missing something, but when you're dealing with money-men, isn't it wise to pipe a little of the tune they want on a regular basis, to keep them happy, rather than making them wait for a concert?"

Andreas smiled a bemused smile at her. "Do you know, until I met you, I always thought I was perfectly fluent in English?"

She laughed, and marvelled at the warmth and liking that were between them. "I'm saying they'll be happier and more likely to cough up the money if you tantalize them with your finds as you make them."

He nodded reluctantly. "That's the conventional wisdom all right. But there has never been a convention since the dawn of time that hasn't got in someone's way."

He threw down his pencil and leaned back, and she asked suddenly, "How old are you, Andrea?"

"Thirty-four."

"And you grew up on Kérkyra?" She wasn't sure why she was suddenly asking these questions, but it had something to do with last night, with knowing him and not knowing him at the same time.

"Sometimes. When one parent is an archaeologist and the other doesn't want to stay home, your home is wherever there is an archaeological dig. A lot of the time I travelled with my parents, and lived near archaeological sites all over the world. It was pretty interesting."

It sounded fascinating. She'd never realized his father was an archaeologist, too. "You must have experienced a lot of different cultures. I suppose that helps you in your work, not being brought up in a particular culture."

She knew what that was like, a little. As a child she had seen two sides of the economic coin, and it would prevent her ever totally identifying with either the well-to-do or the poor. She told him about that, now, though there weren't many people she told about that awful transition from poor to rich.

"But you were very fortunate," Andreas pointed out. "Weren't you? Even if they were not good people, you got good things from them—food and an education are only two. How would you have gone to the university from such a situation as you were in?"

Well, he had a point. Now, looking back on it, she could see that her situation before she went to live with Aunt Pet and Uncle Sid had been as horrible, in a different way, as the life she lived with them. As a child, of course, she had romanticised it, that old life-style, but it certainly would have given her no start on life at all.

Remembering suddenly, she giggled. "You know, I was a pretty accomplished little thief by the time I was ten. I'd probably have been in juvenile court before I was much older."

Andreas grinned admiringly at her. "You are a survivor, you see. You think they killed your spirit, your uncle and aunt, but it isn't so. Maybe you were already too wild when you went to them, and they were too cold and narrow. There was a great distance between you, and probably you were made to travel most of the distance. But if this is so, you only have to travel back again, to where you want to be. Because, and I know this, they did not kill your spirit. You are not a dead person."

Kate blinked to keep the tears at bay, and tried to laugh. Maybe he was right after all. Certainly in the last few weeks she had felt very much alive, like the old self she remembered from so long ago.

She had felt alive like this in her first year of university, too, she remembered suddenly. All she had needed was to get away from the claustrophobic influence of Uncle Sid and Aunt Pet, and she had begun to blossom.

And then she had met Peter, and the whole stifling process had begun again. Well, it was ten years since she'd left Peter, but better late than never. And this time she'd make damn sure she didn't get stifled again.

She looked at Andreas Constantinou, and deep in the recesses of her mind, a tiny, distant warning rang, one that she hardly heard at all. She didn't notice it, because she was too busy basking in his warm, approving smile.

Work at the dig seemed to Kate to move much more quickly after that. The other squares, reaching the settlement level, turned up walls that were similar to the one in Bill's square, and gradually the extent of the town became evident. Pottery finds became more numerous, and Sarah joined Agapi's team in the lab hut full-time. Kate, typing up endless reports, began to see the thankless, unexciting part of archaeology that went along with the thrilling, more visible side: for every find such as the incredible breasted ewer, there were countless small artifacts that would have no meaning until they were all viewed together, and perhaps not even then.

Everybody knew that she and Andreas were having

an affair, except perhaps for Sarah, who had eyes only for archaeology and Andreas, and saw nothing else. And it seemed that no one cared to enlighten her. How they knew, Kate wasn't sure, unless it was because in such a close society as a dig, nothing could remain secret.

Perhaps it was because she was being obvious about it. It was possible. Anything was possible. In their lovemaking, Andreas was showing her things about her body and herself that she hadn't discovered in thirty-two years. To him, it seemed, there was nothing forbidden between them, nothing about her body and its secrets that he did not love, nothing that need ever shame her in their search for their own and each other's pleasure. And because his body excited her, too—its shapes, its scent, its power and its vulnerability—the experience of being Andreas Constantinou's lover was becoming almost addictive; and perhaps that showed in the way she looked at him or in her movements when he was near.

Oddly enough, after that devastating night on the beach at Alexandroúpolis, she had been frightened, and the next night, in her room in Kamariotissa, she had been somehow withdrawn, and he'd noticed.

Under his gentle questioning, her feminism had come to her rescue, and she had said, "Look, I don't know what happened last night; I really don't understand myself and what I did. But if it made you think I—I like violence, or want to be hurt, Andrea, you got the wrong idea."

He looked surprised. "Did I hurt you?" he demanded. "How? Where did I hurt you? I didn't know."

She made herself hold his gaze. "No, you didn't hurt me, Andrea. At least . . . well, you were pretty forceful." Fierce was the word, but she did not say it, because it was the fierceness in him that had made her so wild. "What I'm trying to say, Andrea, is that a lot of men think that women have a rape fantasy, and it's just not true. And if last night gave you that idea about me, well, it shouldn't have."

"Ah," he said. "Yes, I understand. You do not know me yet. When a man and a woman make love before they know each other well, it is the woman who runs the risk. Last night, you were not hurt, yes? You enjoyed it; it was good for you, but today, in the sunshine, it changes. Perhaps you trusted me too much. You don't know what I will do to you, what I want to do to you, tonight."

"I'm sorry," she said. "Yes."

He had his hand in her hair, stroking a curl around his forefinger as he lay propped up over her on the bed. "Kate," he said, "I will try to tell you who I am, all right? And you try to trust me to tell you the truth."

He was waiting for an answer. "All right," she agreed.

"Kate, your body is very beautiful. I want to do many, many things to you. I want to give you pleasure no one ever gave to you before. When I make love with you, I lose myself. Last night, maybe what you are afraid of is that I lost myself. I never went as crazy as this over any woman. Last night, when you began the game, I thought I would come into your room and then I would kiss you and touch you until you begged for more. And when you ran I thought I would catch you and bring you back and it would be the same. And then, sometime out there, it changed for me. It wasn't a game; I needed you. I couldn't wait. I looked in your eyes, and I knew that you wanted it, too, but you would never stop fighting until I showed you that fighting me was useless."

The memory of it, called up by his voice, was melting her. When her eyelids started to droop, she forced them open. "Kate, what I did to you then, I never did to a woman in my life. Except when I was seventeen—like all boys I had no control—I never lost control of myself with a woman. Only with you, last night and the night before. I am sorry for this; I am sorry if I frightened you. But I tell you this, Kate, even if I lose control again with you, if for the rest of my life I have no control over myself with you, still I promise you one thing: Violence and sex never, *never* were connected in my mind. I will never deliberately hurt you; I will never take pleasure in hurting you. Only in giving you pleasure, in giving you what you want."

She believed him. She trusted him. She said, "And you would never think that I would want you to hurt me?"

He kissed her and shook his head. "Do you want me to hurt you?"

"No," she said, and couldn't repress a shudder for the memories of the battered wives she had seen in her neighbourhood as a child, and the horror stories she had heard in her women's group. "No, never. The thought of it makes me sick."

"We can be everything to each other, Kate; we can try every sexual and loving possibility with each other, and even if we live another sixty years, we don't need to scrape pain from the bottom of the barrel.

"But if you like me to chase you, if you like to feel that you fight and I win—and I am a fighter, too—please don't confuse this with rape, or pain. And when you want to be aggressive, when you want to conquer my body and do with it as you please, I will enjoy that, too. Yes? We will not think in stereotypes, you and I; we will not think what is right or wrong, or what feminists say, or male chauvinists say. We will think only of what we want, and pleasure. Because with you, I want to experience everything."

In the days that followed, she began to feel that she would truly experience everything with him. Under the onslaught of what he did to her, she began to open herself physically and mentally to him, and to herself, and to the incredible spectrum of their human needs. The first time that he lay against her breast, and took her nipple between his lips and closed his eyes, not in passion but in some other need, Kate looked down at his peaceful face and felt a fiercely maternal emotion sweep through her that was as devastating as anything she had ever felt. And it gave her a pleasure as deep as any sexual stroking of her breasts had ever done, and far more emotionally disturbing.

She remembered the women in her group, years ago, belittling any man who was attracted to a woman's breasts in this way, and understood that she had wordlessly prevented the intellectual, sensitive men she had known from ever expressing any such need to her.

And when he held her close to his powerful chest, crinkling with such very masculine hair, and she felt a catch in her throat and remembered her dreams of the father she had never known, she felt a love for him that went far beyond the deep sexual attraction and gratitude she had already given him, and the feeling this engendered in her had nothing in common with the sharply defined and criticized "Daddy's girl syndrome" that, through her consciousness-raising group, she had learned to condemn.

And only now, ten years later, could she begin to see that *any* dogma that prescribed what needs lovers should fulfill for each other, what people could be to each other, was stifling.

It was a hard lesson for her to accept, and yet in her heart she had known it for a long time: for all the real truths the women's movement had made society face, and there were many, much of what she had seen as liberation had been the mere exchanging of one set of conditioned responses for another.

One scorching Sunday afternoon in August, when the entire team had gone swimming, Kate mounted the little motorbike behind Andreas and they drove out to the Sanctuary site again. He took her into the cool museum, and this time, as she walked through, she saw the exhibits with fresh eyes.

"My God!" she exclaimed as they stood in front of the stone parapet block that had once formed part of the Rotunda of Arsinoë. "A bull! A decorated bull's head! That's interesting, isn't it?" Of course, by itself it wasn't conclusive. There had been bull worship in other places besides Crete in the ancient world.

But beside the carved bull's head there was a flower, and that flower, too, she had seen in the museum at Iráklion, carved into stone, and shaped in gold jewellery, and painted on pots—a circular flower, divided into eight perfect petals, that had seemed to be a regal or religious insignia.

"Is this what gave you the connection?" she asked Andreas, for perhaps they were even more significant than they seemed to her layman's gaze.

"They were additional curiosities," he said with a grin. "In here is the find that first made me start to think along these lines." He led her through another hall and into the last, large room, where she had first seen the pottery with the inscriptions in the "non-Greek language." Over in the corner, in front of one of the glass-fronted cases, he stopped. "The bottom shelf," he said. "What do you notice?"

The case was devoted to artifacts from later antiquity, from the time of the Roman Empire. Even in those days, the Sanctuary at Samothráki had continued in importance as a religious centre, and many important

Romans had come here to be initiated into the mysteries.

Perhaps the mysteries had continued unchanged down through time, too; there was no way of knowing. One of the problems of mystery cults for modern archaeologists was that only the initiates had learned the mystery, and they had kept it secret.

The origin of the mystery Religion of the Great Gods would probably remain forever lost to the world, but nothing could change the fact that in this particular museum case, what Kate was staring at now, on the bottom shelf, placed almost negligently at the back, was a fragment of white marble labelled first century A.D. on which, unmistakably to the eyes of anyone who had so recently been to Crete, was carved the famous *labrys*—the double axe insignia of the ruling house of Knossos.

The symbol that was supposed to have been wiped from history from the moment of the terrible destruction of the Cretan civilisation, until its fabulous discovery, three and a half millennia later, by Arthur Evans in the ruins of the labyrinth.

Kate crouched closer. "Is it really?" she demanded. "Is it certain that's what it is?"

"Nothing in archaeology is certain," Andreas said, as he had said before. "I thought it a remarkable coincidence, however. Enough to make me investigate."

She straightened up. "How do others explain it? I mean, what does the museum say it is?"

"They suggest that it is an early representation of a Christian cross," Andreas said. "This is dated first century A.D."

"Mm." Kate pursed her lips. "Doesn't look much like a cross to me. If they'd said a mast and sail, it would be closer. Was the cross even a Christian symbol as early as the first century A.D.? I thought the early Christians used a fish symbol."

Andreas shrugged. "The cross wasn't widely used by Christians till Constantine, in the fourth century A.D. It was certainly widely used by other religions before Christ; we saw it in some Minoan jewellery in Iráklion, if you remember. The cross in circle. It's also in one of the wall paintings from Akrotíri, as an earring."

"So even if it were a cross, the chances are it's not Christian?"

"Samothráki was a stronghold of the Great Gods mystery religion. It is hard to believe that Christianity got a foothold here as early as the first century, although Paul stayed here on his way to Kaválla. Lehmann, who excavated the Sanctuary site, was of the opinion that the Samothrákian mysteries were more like the Christian concept than any other model of ancient Greece."

"Do you think Paul was an initiate here?"

"I don't know. He certainly speaks in one of his letters—the one to the Corinthians, I believe—of a higher mystery that was shown only to those who exhibited an aptitude for it."

Kate looked at him. "You're very broad-minded," she observed. "Are you a Christian?"

Andreas smiled at her. "No one who has excavated the remains of as many of man's religions as I have could believe that mankind could be given the truth without corrupting it beyond recognition. Our instinct for ritual and symbol and idols is too strong for the message, whatever it was, to have passed down through so many centuries. The very fact that we worship Christ's death instead of trying to understand his life and teachings is enough to show how far from those teachings we have come. And in every society in the ancient Mediterranean world we uncover, there are religious artifacts which have echoes in today's Christianity. Mithraism, the Mother Goddess, the Tree Cults, Platonism—hell, resurrection, circumcision, baptism, forgiveness of sins, the Soul. Religion today, as in any era, is a cluster of traditions and rituals which are hung on the Truth like baubles on a Christmas tree, until it is so weighted down you can't see the tree at all.''

She was fascinated by his mind, and it was a rare enough experience in her life. Not many people she knew were so constantly stimulating. She could feel her mind stretching, reaching, working in areas that had had little exercise in the past. It gave her a kind of exhilaration, and she suddenly remembered his saying to her, "You are very intelligent," in a certain tone of voice, and thought that he had been feeling then exactly what she was feeling now: the joy of meeting another curious mind, the happy recognition of a fellow seeker.

She said suddenly, "The thing about you is that you have no sacred cows. It makes you such a joy to talk to.''

She was thinking, suddenly and unexpectedly, that it made him a joy to make love with, too, but she didn't say it. It was something new, a discovery of significance that she had just made about him, but she wasn't sure yet what it meant. But it all fitted together somehow.

The one thing she was sure of was that Andreas was different from any man she had ever met before. Different, and better.

That's what she thought, all through one glorious week when, whether they worked together, or argued together, or made love, everything they did seemed like an embrace on the deepest levels of her being. That's what she thought when she began to imagine herself deeply, unalterably in love with him. That's what she thought when he told her she was beautiful, and with the impact of a blow over the heart she remembered him saying, "I find beautiful what I love."

That's what she thought, until the afternoon when she came out of the back room of the admin hut one day during siesta, when the whole dig was smothered in heat and silence, to find Andreas standing there with Sarah.

Sarah, wrapped in his arms, and literally swooning under his kiss.

Chapter 13

ATHENS

IF THEY EVER WANTED TO KNOW HOW THE PALACE of Knossos was destroyed, she could tell them. It had been attacked at the foundations, with one horrible blow that had brought down the whole beautiful edifice.

She had known that as she stood there in the admin hut and felt the dream castle she had built out of such solid-seeming rock crumble into dust all round her, leaving nothing for her comfort, nothing to give her any solace, save the naked fact that she had been a fool, and that she ought to have known.

Now, sitting at Sophia's kitchen table again, and feeling as though she had come home, she was trying to make light of the whole, stupid experience, both to Sophia and to herself, and wishing, as she watched Sophia draw cigarette smoke into her besieged lungs, that she could squash her feelings the same way.

She tried to laugh. "Sophia, I've never met anyone

who could make slow suicide seem as attractive as you do."

Sophia didn't smile. She was concentrating on her thoughts. "If I don't smoke, the pollution will kill me anyway. So, what did my cousin say when you saw him kissing this girl?"

He hadn't said anything, not then. He had lifted his lips from Sarah's and smiled quizzically at Kate, standing there with her mouth open and her heart going dead in her breast. Then he had turned away to speak to Sarah, who was looking at him with a face like a flower, smiling as though she were going to burst into tears.

She was as deeply, desperately in love with the man as Kate was, and Kate heard his voice say quite clearly, "A man loves a woman because she is young and pretty," though his lips weren't moving. If she was going mad, it was only her own fault. She'd had plenty of warning. She had smiled blindly in their general direction, lifted a hand to the couple as she walked past and then got out as fast as she could.

She had gone straight to her motorbike and driven hatless down to Kamariotissa, where within half an hour she had turned the bike in to the rental office, packed and checked out of the hotel. Then she had bought a ticket for the ferry and gone to a *cafenion* and sat down to wait till she was allowed to board.

Andreas had found her there, just before boarding time. She had heard the chair opposite scrape on the pavement and looked up from her coffee to see him standing over her, a god of wrath. "What are you doing?" he demanded furiously. "What the hell do you think you're doing?"

Kate gazed at him in mingled astonishment and rage. What was he coming after her for? Who did he think he was? She said, very precisely, "I am drinking a cup of coffee. I'd ask you to join me except that I prefer to be alone. Good-bye."

"Why have you checked out of your hotel? Why is your bag here? Where are you going?" he demanded, all at once.

"Because I don't intend to sleep there anymore, because I want it here, and none of your damned business!" she snapped back.

"Not my business? Of course it's my business! What the hell is going on? Where are you going?"

Heads were beginning to turn, but almost certainly no one understood enough English to follow this rapid-fire exchange. "I'm going back to Athens," she said, and then, in spite of herself, she broke. "What did you think I was going to do? Sit around and watch you make love to a child half your age? Thank you for the sex education course and go on my grateful way? For God's sake, Andrea, if *you* have no finesse—"

He interrupted harshly, "*Make love?* I was not making love to anyone! Do you tell me that this is why you have left like a crazy woman, because I was kissing Sarah?"

"What did you expect me to do? Give her your references? Give you my bless—"

"I expect you to understand that I have no real interest in Sarah and to trust me enough to wait for an explanation!"

"If there's anything I can't stand, it's a male chauvinist explanation for sexual promiscuity. If it's all the same to you, I think I'll pass on the 'man is not a monogamous animal' bit!"

"Don't put words and attitudes in my mouth!" he said harshly. "You are an intelligent woman. You know Sarah thinks she is in love with me! Everybody knows it! What do you expect me to do? Fire her?"

"I sure as hell don't expect you to make love to her!

And that's what you were doing, Andrea! And don't tell me that she flung herself at you, because the girl was being very thoroughly kissed! And don't—"

He was interrupting again. He had a knack for not letting her finish. "Will you stop putting words in my mouth? Damn it, Kate, she *asked* me to kiss her! She wanted—"

She let out a laugh that turned the heads of even those who were pretending not to be fascinated. "Well, fancy that!" she hooted. "She wanted you to! And you couldn't resist, right? How many other women want you to kiss them, Andrea? Am I supposed to stand by while you satisfy them all? Don't interrupt!" she stormed, flinging up a hand as he opened his mouth again. "I tell you here and I tell you now, Andrea, there is one thing in life that I will not do, and that is *share a man* with anybody! Do you understand me? I'm into serial monogamy, as the magazines say, okay? And this seems to be the time to move—"

"What the hell is serial monogamy?" he demanded.

"I didn't think you'd recognize the term," she shot back. "It means *one lover at a time*, Andrea!" She stood up and reached for her bag. "And it's time I moved on to the next! Have fun with Sarah; she looks like a *very* apt pupil!"

"Kate."

It stopped her; that tone in his voice would always stop her, wherever she was, for the rest of her life. She stood there, not looking back.

"Kate, I love you," Andreas said quietly.

"*Tyn agapá,*" translated a female voice a table or two distant, and the rest of the table made warmly approving noises.

If she stood there a second longer, she was going to burst into tears. Kate took a firmer grip on her heavy duffel bag and started to walk. "Kate!" he called, and she shut her eyes tightly and told herself it was her own fault for getting mixed up with a male chauvinist. *"Kate!"*

She turned, still moving away. "Thanks for the sex education course!" she called. "Sorry I couldn't stick around for my diploma!" And then she turned and strode across the street and down to the ferry at the dock, and he did not follow her.

Two hours later she was in Alexandroúpolis. The only hotel she knew was the one she had stayed in with Andreas, and it didn't help that they gave her a room on the water again, almost next door to the ones they had had that night they had come back from Crete.

Then, in spite of her efforts to tell herself she had had a lucky escape, Kate had cried into her pillow all night. She loved him. It was more than sex, and it was more than admiration for his mind. It was the feeling she had had with him, of sure and total belonging; it was the joy she had felt in togetherness, the slow, steady learning to trust. It was the coming home.

Now, not looking at Sophia, Kate shrugged. "He didn't say anything much. What was there to say? I suddenly remembered you and Takkis, what you told me about Greek men never marrying divorcées. He just— Oh, hell!" she burst out suddenly. "If there's one thing above all others that I can't stand about male chauvinists, it's their ability to separate sex from any feeling other than lust! That's the one thing in the women's movement that I think we were totally wrong about: the idea that women should learn to treat sex the way men do. We should have been teaching men to treat sex the way women do! My God, how can they do it? How can they be so cut off? How can they fake all that emotion without feeling even a glimmer of sincerity? It makes me sick! Men make me sick!"

She began to cry again, though it was the one thing

she had promised herself she wouldn't do in front of Sophia. Sophia was Andreas's cousin; she must be feeling a divided loyalty. And besides, she had her own love problems.

"That's all right," said Sophia, standing up to put a pot of water on the stove. "Women have to stick together, don't we? Now, let's have coffee, and then I'm going to phone some people and we'll go out tonight. Maybe we'll go to *bouzoukia*."

Greek men might be the world's worst chauvinists, but they were fantastic when they danced. There was something about seeing a man from the audience get up on stage and just dance, all by himself, leaping and twisting and posturing in a way that was totally masculine, glorying in the movement of his body in a way she had never seen a North American or Englishman do. Most of the men Kate had known had seemed to look on dancing as some sort of punishment, or purgatory, undertaken only for the pleasure of the female.

The audience danced on the same stage the singers inhabited, a state of affairs that should have meant chaos, considering the vast amounts of broken plates and flowers that also accumulated on the same tiny space. But everyone seemed to manage. As the night wore on, more and more plates smashed onto the stage, more and more flowers were shredded and strewn over the singers. And the air got so thick with smoke it seemed as if the whole of Athens had a death wish— including Kate, because she had the sudden feeling she could spend the rest of her life in this country, among this vibrant, wonderful race, male chauvinist or not.

"*Apo sena tha pao, apo sena tha pao.*" Ilias, beside her, was singing under his breath along with the singers. "*Apo sena p'agapo.*" He smiled at Kate and poured more wine into her glass. *"Apo sena tha pao . . ."*

Kate began to pick it up. It was a popular song just at the moment; she had heard it often. She leaned to Sophia on her other side and shouted into her ear, "I like this song. What does it mean?"

" 'I shall be hurt by you,' " Sophia obligingly translated. " 'By you whom I love.' "

Not surprisingly, it was a woman who sang it, and Kate had a sudden moment of real insight into the lives of these Greek women she admired so much: ignored, belittled, put down on every side, working harder than any man just to stay alive, fighting for their freedom against heavier odds than any Kate had known—still they put their heads up and went out to meet life with a kind of stubborn joy, a refusal to be broken. There was probably as much feminine courage sitting right here at this table—Kate looked into the faces of Sophia, and Veta, and another woman friend Sophia had introduced her to—as there was in the entire NOW movement of the eastern seaboard.

And they met heartbreak in the same way they met all the other blows life had to offer them. Kate had a sudden, certain understanding that Sophia had a kind of fatalistic acceptance of what Takkis had done to her. She had, perhaps, in spite of her own hopes, even known that he would do it, leave her to marry someone younger, a virgin. Yet she fought the battle she had to fight, the battle of her own self-esteem.

It was a way of meeting life that Kate Fenton recognized from long, long ago: the way of the warrior. Her way. She wasn't going to shed one more tear for that chauvinist, heartless cheat if she lived to be ninety.

She got progressively gayer and wilder as the night wore on. She sang, she danced, she drank and she laughed. And she enjoyed herself; she truly did. There was something beautiful, almost breathtaking, in being able to laugh so hard in heartbreak's face.

The next day was Sunday. Sophia staggered out of bed at eleven o'clock to cook brunch for the group of friends who would be coming around about one, a fact which Kate took in with some difficulty. They had left the *bouzoukia* only when it closed, at four, and from there had gone on to a seafood restaurant for fish soup and deep-fried squid. At six, when it began to look as if the end of the evening were approaching, and Kate was congratulating herself for having had the stamina to keep up with all these mad Athenians, they had piled into their cars and everybody had driven back to Sophia's for coffee.

There had actually followed a political discussion, at which no one seemed to have any less energy than they had started the evening with. Kate, in fact, had got her second wind herself by that time, but in order to take part in the discussion she would have had to ask Sophia for constant translation, so she had simply sat back and listened to the exchange of excited sounds.

At seven, the group had finally left, some of them making arrangements to return in a few hours for the brunch which Sophia was now cooking. Between seven and seven-thirty, Kate and Sophia had conducted their own postmortem on the evening, and at eight Kate had finally fallen asleep, accompanied as usual by the sounds from the neighbour's rooster, who did not take Sunday off, either.

And now it was scarcely eleven, and Sophia was deep-frying scallops. At this rate, Kate thought in some amusement, she would forget Andreas in a week.

She sat at the kitchen table in her bathrobe, peeling and slicing potatoes for the fries Sophia would make, and after a while, she asked, "Tell me about your cousin."

Sophia shrugged and looked very Greek. "*I* don't know." She smiled. "What can I tell you?"

"Well, what he was like as a boy, things like that. Have you met many of his women friends?"

She shrugged again. "I never met any of his women; I don't see him so much, you know. When he's at the university, sometimes he comes out with us to *bouzoukia* or for souvlaki, but he never brought a woman with him."

"Has he ever been married?"

"No, not yet. Men don't get married so young in Greece." Kate had noticed that. She had never in her life met so many single men in their thirties as she had in Athens. They all seemed to wait till they were thirty-five—and then they chose eighteen-year-old brides, as Takkis had done.

As perhaps Andreas was doing. The thought of that girl in his bed, that girl learning what she, Kate, had learned from his expert, loving hands, was suddenly clawing at her, ripping her apart. She couldn't remember ever having felt jealousy before, not for anyone, not for the nurses who got crushes on her husband, not for the students who had thrown themselves at the professor. Jealousy was supposed to be an unreal emotion, an invention of men, foisted on women to divide sister from sister. For the past ten years it had been a political no-no to feel jealousy, and Kate had gone along with that.

But this was no invention. This was real, as real as the table underneath her hands, as real and sharp and cutting as the knife she was holding, and if Sarah had been sitting opposite her right now, Kate might just have scratched her eyes out.

She tried to tell herself that she wouldn't want

Andreas now, knowing what she knew. She tried to tell herself that it was impossible to love a man who was a cheat. But it didn't feel that way. She loved him; she loved him so much that, even though she never saw him again, she might love him forever. And even though there were only those few days or weeks to remember, she might never want another man.

"I swear to God, the one thing I would never wish on any woman is to fall in love with a Greek man," Kate said suddenly, digging into a potato with a satisfying gouge. "Here you are, cooking yet again for a bunch of men who call themselves your friends, and what do they ever do? They don't even wash the damned dishes when they're through! Who'd want to be married to one of them? No wonder they have to choose eighteen-year-olds! Any woman over twenty would have too much sense!"

"You're right," agreed Sophia. "*I'm* never getting married again, if a king asks me!"

"I believe you. My God, I should be grateful to Andreas for what he did. The last thing I need is to be hooked on another male chauvinist!"

Sophia laughed. "But I told you, Andreas is not a male chauvinist. He's not even a real Greek."

Kate dropped the potato into the bowl with a splash that drenched her face with water. She ignored it. It was at least cooling, in an apartment that was already hot at eleven in the morning. "He's not what?"

"He had a Greek mother, that's all. But he was born in England, when his mother, my aunt, was at the university there. His father was at the university, too. His father was English. He was a poet. He's dead now."

Kate was shaking her head. "He told me his father was an archaeologist; he said he and his mother used to follow him all over the world."

Sophia raised her head and her eyebrows in the Greek signal for no. *"Ochi,"* she said. "His *mother* was an archaeologist. She is very famous in Greece for this. Andreas travelled all over with her; she worked in many parts of the world, not just Greece. Andreas learned six languages when he was a child."

"His *mother*?" Kate could only stare open-mouthed. "His mother? But he told me—he said—" She broke off. What exactly had he said? "When one parent travels and the other doesn't want to be left behind . . ."

Kate began to laugh. And *she,* she who was supposed to have had her consciousness raised years ago, had made the assumption that the one who travelled with a job was a man, and the one who didn't want to be left behind was a woman! And she was pointing the finger at someone else and calling him a male chauvinist!

Kate choked, "So Andreas Constantinou followed not in his father's, but in his mother's footsteps, is that what you're telling me?"

Sophia said, "He was always there, at the digs; he used to come home to Kérkyra in the winter and tell me what he had seen, what they had found. When he was ten or eleven he told me he was going to be an archaeologist, too. His father encouraged him. And his mother, of course."

"And his father was English? But Andreas's last name is Constantinou; it's Greek."

"His father's name was Constantine. Edward Constantine. Andreas changed his name when he decided to work in Greece—for political reasons, for the university, you know. He speaks Greek, he's got Greek citizenship, it's better if he has a Greek name. Anyway, it's difficult for Greek people. They would call him Constantinou anyway."

"And who was his mother?"

"His mother is still alive. She is very famous. Her name is Eleni Kazantsidis."

"Mother of God, I've read one of her books. She dug Jericho or someplace like that, in Israel, didn't she? She's brilliant. She's incredibly exact."

Sophia shrugged. "I told you, she's famous. Andreas told me once he'll always admire women who make a career. He saw that it was difficult for his mother; he said she had to be twice as good as a man to get where she was. He's not a chauvinist. You see all my friends, they're chauvinists, I know. Andreas, when he comes here, always he helps me. He cooks, he washes the dishes, something. Always. And when we go out to eat, always Andreas pays for me, because of the times he eats here."

Sophia shrugged. "Maybe he cheated you with this girl; I don't know. Maybe as a lover, he's a chauvinist. I can't ask my own cousin if he's good in bed!" Sophia laughed, and it turned, as usual, into a smoker's cough, even worse than usual because of last night's heavy smoking. Immediately she lit a cigarette.

Kate gazed into the middle distance. What justification had she ever had for her fixed assumption that Andreas was a chauvinist? Somewhere along the line, she had taken it as a given, and then she had never bothered to revise that given in the light of circumstance. Yet, of all the men she had ever met, Andreas was far and away the least chauvinist. He admired her brain; he respected her work. . . . Yet, because of his sexuality, she had labelled him in her mind. Just exactly the way men labelled beautiful blondes as dumb.

She had been guilty of an attitude in her private life that she castigated unmercifully in science: sticking to a theory in the teeth of the evidence, and looking only for the evidence that would support the theory. Well, after this, she would have a little more respect for the human failings that caused that scientific attitude.

"No, he's not a chauvinist in bed, either." Some women might call that aggressive masculinity chauvinist, she supposed, but then, it existed side by side with his enjoyment of her aggressive femininity. So what did that mean? She shook her head. "No, he's definitely not a chauvinist in bed, but he's—he can be very masculine."

"Mmm," interjected Sophia appreciatively. And Kate had a sudden memory of her professor, who had been gentle and understanding and sensitive, and probably, knowing who she was, too terrified of her feminist leanings, to ever be strong with her. Or perhaps he had been attracted to her because he knew that with her he would never have to be strong. And she had always intellectually approved of that gentleness.

Intellectually. Emotionally and sexually Andreas had shown her more sheer excitement in one night of running through a forest like a Dionysiac than she had ever felt in her life before. The only other man who had even come close to thrilling her sexually had been Peter. Peter was probably the only other man in her life who had actually been really *passionate* with her. At first he had, anyway.

And Peter *had* been a chauvinist bastard, and . . . and what did that mean? Kate thought of some of the men she had said no to in the years after Peter. Men she had said no to for various reasons, or so she'd thought at the time. "Because I don't know you very well," she had told one man who had truly excited her, "and if you can't say no to your own desires now and then, you aren't much of a human being."

Most of those men had had one thing in common: an

aura of passion that had threatened her independence. Because they might, like Peter, be chauvinist.

Somewhere along the line, Kate was thinking, we started dictating what could or should happen between a man and a woman in bed. No wonder men got frightened of us. It's the old damned if you do, damned if you don't soft-shoe. If a man got passionate, if he made an advance that was anything other than "low key" . . .

That was all right for some women. Women who had reason to be frightened of sex, or men, or life. Or women who weren't themselves very passionate. What about women like herself? I'm a fighter, Kate thought suddenly. Damn it, I've been fighting from the moment I was born, and if I'm not fighting, I forget I'm alive! Does that make a man who understands that, a man who likes a challenge, too, a chauvinist?

Poor old Peter, she thought suddenly. Why had she ever thought his passion was to blame? It was so obvious to her now what had been wrong with Peter. It wasn't his passion that made him a chauvinist—it was being a doctor! He learned to think of himself as God in *medical school*; it was entirely unconnected to the fact that he liked sex so much. In fact . . .

In fact, the farther along in med school Peter had progressed, the more chauvinist he had become—and the *less* passionate.

But Kate, with a little help from her friends, had equated that arrogant masculine superiority with his sexual passion. She had never forgotten that it was after making love to her that Peter won his greatest victories over her.

And so Andreas's incredible passion had worked against him when she had walked out of the little room behind the admin office and seen what she had seen. In

spite of all that he had said and done that indicated—
proved—the contrary, when it came to the crunch, she
had labelled him sexist. And sexist meant not to be
trusted in any way, shape or form. About anything at
all.

Because why? Because he had fought her when she'd
wanted to be fought? Because he had used the age-old
excitement of the male/female chase to excite them
both to a passion more blinding than anything she had
ever experienced? A passion whose memory even now
had the power to make her knees weak and her womb
sing?

She was out of her mind. She was out of her tiny
mind. She had walked out on a man she loved more
than she had ever loved anyone, a man more intelligent, lucid, *interesting* than any other man she had ever
been privileged to meet, a man whose mere glance
melted her to mud in her tracks, and for what? Because
she saw him kissing a child who had a crush on him a
mile wide. A child of eighteen, who was no more
competition for Kate with a man like Andreas than a
baby!

Perhaps he'd been attracted to Sarah; perhaps all
that hero worship had been too much for him. In spite
of what he'd said, perhaps he even thought he was
seriously attracted to her. But he wasn't. He was a
brilliant, demanding intellect. She'd pall on a brain like
his in a month. Give her ten years and she'd be a match
for anybody, but Sarah didn't have ten years. She was
eighteen, and very sweet, but it was Kate that Andreas
had called beautiful, though she wasn't. She was well
put-together and nicely attractive, but the man who
thought she was beautiful had to be blinded by love.

"You've peeled that potato down to nothing." Sophia's laughing voice broke in on her thoughts, and

Kate looked down at the potato she had "peeled" over and over until it was the size of a small egg. She choked on a laugh and looked up.

"I'm a fool," she said. "The world's worst fool."

"What are you going to do?" asked Sophia.

"You know, there was one rule of behaviour that both my reactionary aunt and my radical liberated friends, for all that they looked at life from opposite sides of the fence, always agreed upon, if for different reasons: Neither a 'lady' nor a liberated woman should ever chase after a man and try to take him from another woman." Kate was laughing, and Sophia had joined her. "A lady didn't do it because it was unladylike. A woman didn't do it because no man could ever be worth a divisive battle between two sisters." Kate was slicing potatoes as though they were all the rules of behaviour she had ever been taught. "Funny that they should agree about that one thing, isn't it? Funny, because both sides left one factor out of the equation. Love. We all forgot about love. My aunt thought love was undignified, and when our generation got liberated we decided that love was a male chauvinist fiction designed to keep 'em down on the farm. But it's no fiction, is it?"

"No," agreed Sophia softly. "Love is real. Sometimes it's too real."

Kate looked up. "I thought I was in love with Peter, once, and I was very fond of the man I called 'my professor.' But love is a lot more than what I felt for either of them. It's some kind of meeting of the souls, isn't it? It's like two halves getting together to make one."

"Don't," Sophia protested quietly, involuntarily, as though the word had been torn from her. Kate stared at her wordlessly, understanding for the first time why it was that Sophia was refusing Takkis, knowing she should have understood before. "I'm sorry," she whispered.

"That's all right," Sophia said. "Go ahead. You can talk about it; I'm all right."

But Kate did not need to say it aloud. She knew it deep inside herself, a knowledge that was crystal clear, once she got past the learned responses, her own conditioned thinking patterns. It was something she had known ever since that first night with Andreas, when for the first time she had felt the measure of her own soul, and love had been the yardstick.

She loved Andreas, and he had said he loved her. Whatever that meant to him, it was something to work with. Whatever his feelings were for Sarah, he had cared enough to come after Kate, to ask her to stay. Only she had been too tied up with her view of the universe to see what was in front of her.

"What are you going to do?" Sophia asked again.

If she lived to be ninety, there could never be another man for her. No matter how hard she tried to tell herself otherwise, she was dying a little every minute she was away from him, every minute during which he might be learning to do without her.

She came out of her reverie and smiled, and tried to condense all the knowledge that had flowed through her in the minutes just past into a few light words. "What I am going to do is—I am going to break every rule of good behaviour I ever learned, and do what *I want to do*." She laughed.

"I'm going to go after my man, that's what I'm going to do. And I'm going to fight for him, if I have to, with every weapon in my arsenal."

Chapter 14

SAMOTHRÁKI

"YOU MISSED ALL THE EXCITEMENT," REBECCA TOLD HER, heaving a huge box of supplies onto the backseat of the green Jeep. Kate had seen the Jeep from the deck as the ferry came into port, and her heart had thudded with the hope that it was Andreas's morning to come in to meet the boat. Then she had seen Rebecca's blond hair in the crowd.

"What happened?" asked Kate. She had spent three frustrating days in Athens, waiting for a seat on a flight to Alexandroúpolis. Anything could have happened in the meantime. One thing that hadn't happened was any phone call from Andreas.

"We found a shrine." Rebecca smiled, jumping in. "A stone table that would have been used as an altar, in one of the houses. There were rhytons around it, too—I guess you know rhytons were used for pouring libations of wine to the gods—but most importantly, we found a breasted ewer, the real thing, in the same room. Agapi dated it as contemporary with the

Akrotíri ceramics—it was even made there. So it was a pretty exciting day."

"So Andreas's theory is proven, then?"

The Jeep's suspension had gotten, if anything, worse. Kate clung as Rebecca bounced carelessly along the Kamariotissa street and then mercifully turned off onto the smooth Prophétes Elías highway.

"Well, it's not, because these people could have been trading with the Therans or the Cretans. But it makes it look very, very likely. Combined with the later attempt to reproduce the breasted ewer—well, none of us is in any doubt."

"Yet they could have been attempting to copy the jug they had imported after Santoríni was destroyed, surely?"

"They *could*. But, you know, we've found some Mycenaean artifacts on the site, too. That means that, when Samothráki lost its connection with Santoríni, if it had one, the blank was probably filled in by the Mycenaeans. From the point of view of human nature, I don't think the locals would have cared whether they traded with Santoríni or Mycenae. I think it's far more likely that the Therans, banished from their home forever, would have tried to reproduce some reminder of their former glory—especially if the ewer had some sort of religious significance. See what I mean?"

"Yes, of course," breathed Kate.

"Mind you, there'll be those who dispute the findings; there always are. But that comes later. Right now it's been a tremendously exciting week."

"I'm sorry I missed it all."

Negotiating a curve, Rebecca glanced curiously at her and nearly ran down a mule. After the evasive action and Greek recriminations were over, she said, "Well, you haven't missed it all, by any means. The money-men were out here being courted with that late breasted ewer and a few other choice exhibits when the shrine was found. They were tremendously impressed, and they've stayed on for a few days. The timing couldn't have been better if we'd planned it. The Mother Goddess may well be on our side."

Kate laughed. "Revived any of her rites lately?"

"If I knew what they were, I would. It may be that in her honour young couples used to go off in the spring and fornicate in the fields to fertilize them, a rite still practised in some areas of Europe right up into modern times, but if so, she's going to have to do without that one."

Kate dropped her eyes. Was that what had seized her that night in Alexandroúpolis? Some race memory of what the Goddess demanded as due to her honour? Perhaps all this digging at her old places of worship had awakened her from her long sleep? That would be nice. With a Goddess on their side, perhaps women could really give sexism a run for its money.

She laughed and shook herself out of the reverie. "Have the money-men made any commitment yet?"

"I haven't talked to Andreas about it, but it's pretty unlikely that, with all this evidence, they'd cut off the funding now. It's a very valuable site, wherever the inhabitants came from."

They were bouncing along the bad road through Lákoma now, and there was no time for Rebecca to ask what she clearly wanted to know: why Kate had left so suddenly a week ago. Kate kept up a light chatter in the final few minutes, just to be doubly sure, because she had no idea what to answer. She could hardly plead an urgent phone call when the site had no phone, and she had no idea what excuse Andreas had given for her absence.

But Rebecca was going to have her say after all, it seemed. Taking a deep breath, she abruptly braked the Jeep, turned off the noisy engine and cut through Kate's pointless chatter with, "Andreas has been like a dead man since you left, Kate, so I assume it's some sort of lover's quarrel that made you leave."

The suddenness of it robbed her of all coherent thought. "Oh. I—uh—" Kate babbled uselessly.

"You don't have to tell me. But I just want to say, if you're coming back to try and make it up with him, all right. If you're coming back in a spirit of scientific detachment, to finish the research you're doing, I don't think I want to be the one who drives you in there. So do you mind telling me which it is?"

She was astounded. "How do you know I'm doing research?"

Rebecca laughed mirthlessly. "Kate, I'm twenty-five. I took a women's studies course at the university, just like all the other women my age. Your book isn't exactly a classic of the revolution, but it's certainly required reading for any feminist, and it was required reading in my course. I recognized your name and your face the moment we were introduced. I thought you were pulling a fast one on Andreas, but he told me he knew you were a writer." She shrugged. "That was okay by me, but I'm an archaeologist first and a feminist second. We need Andreas functioning on all cylinders right now, which he's just barely managing to do. If your presence is going to stir things up, I'd rather you didn't come up to the site for a week or so. I'll drive you back to Kamariotissa, if you want. If you're determined to come up, you can rent a scooter there again. But I'm not going to be the bearer of bad tidings at a moment like this. Archaeology is a tough enough profession as it is. I'm real fond of Andreas, but he's got a rough temper on him. And I sure don't want him exercising it on me when it comes time for me to get a recommendation."

"Andreas would never do that," Kate protested. "He's too fair."

"Yes, all right. But in this profession we spend a lot of our time biting each other on the back. There are other people besides Andreas to worry about. Word might go round that I'd deliberately sabotaged Andreas by bringing you back just at the psychologically worst moment. And reputations have foundered on less, believe me. So please just tell me—is he going to be welcoming when he sees you, or not?"

What a question. Kate shook her head, laughing helplessly in a way that was perilously near tears. "If I knew that," she said. "If I only knew the answer to that."

"Well, then . . ." Rebecca said pointedly. So the battered green Jeep was turned around, and twenty minutes later Kate found herself at the hotel in Kamariotissa, asking for a room, not knowing whether to wait for the week that Rebecca had asked for or rent a scooter and go and see Andreas.

In the end, it was easier not to decide. Kate rented the scooter again, for something to do, and that afternoon explored some parts of the island she had had no time for during her weeks on the dig. She ate lunch in a village called Loutra, at a taverna where she discovered *melitsanesalata,* a delicious dip made from eggplant and garlic, which she ate with fries and pork souvlaki. Mentally she compared the food she was eating now with the fast-food of North America, and felt a sudden burst of pity for all Greeks who emigrated to Canada or the States. It must be a terrible shock to the taste buds. No wonder there were so many Greek-run restaurants in Toronto. They must feel like missionaries among savages, trying to spread the word: Food actually has flavour!

After the meal she drove down to the sea at the end of the road and lay in the sun for a little. Not in her monokini, not on this remote island. She could see what Andreas meant about the beaches. You'd never get the sun worshippers out here, not unless someone invested a few million in some white sand. Kate found it in her heart to be glad of that: tourists changed everything, and it would be nice if Samothráki didn't lose its character.

But she caught some sun, in spite of the discomfort of the beach, and came back late to her hotel, ready for a bath, a nap and a meal, in that order.

The bath was soothing, but she tossed and turned on the sheets afterwards, unable to get to sleep. Was Rebecca right? Would she be an unwelcome interruption to Andreas right now? Suppose Rebecca wasn't telling her the truth about why she wanted Kate to stay away from Neathera? Suppose she had another reason —like wanting Sarah to have a chance, or being in love with him herself?

Suppose she was right? Suppose Andreas screwed up with his money-men because she was there? Suppose—

But she didn't get the chance to suppose any more. There was a knock at the door just then, and when she called, "Who is it?" the answer, in a deep, urgent voice, was:

"Andreas."

She flung open the door, crying his name, and he stepped inside, pushed it shut again and caught her in a fierce, soundless embrace that threatened to break her bones. When he bent his head to find her lips she closed her eyes and clung, and the sweet burning of him flooded through her.

His hands held her so tightly it hurt, and he moved her to the bed and fell down on it with her, and then his mouth found hers again, and his tongue drove over and over again into its warmth, with a rhythm that moved her to frenzy.

There was a fury of passion in his hands as he stroked and gripped her, all the fury of his fear that he had lost her, all the passion of a need escaping tight reins. Each touch, each painful grip, dragged her own passion up from that dark nesting place inside her where he had found it before, where it had lain hidden for more years than she could remember, closer and closer to the surface, till at last she was shuddering under his hands, trembling under his kiss. A moan broke from her throat, the moan of a deep, primal need of him, and only when she heard it did she understand what a terrible fear had been locked up inside her, the fear that she had lost him forever, the fear that she had kept dammed up because it hurt too much to think of it.

There were tears on her cheeks; she was crying now as he pressed her body, pushing her robe aside to touch and caress each square inch of skin; and her flesh puffed into flame everywhere he touched her. She pushed against his hands, wherever they touched her, pushed against the exquisite pressure of his touch, moaning, crying with the pleasure of what he could do to her. And he watched her face with hooded, burning eyes, taking in the sight of her pleasure to build his own desire to fever pitch.

She couldn't bear those eyes, so full of love and need and passion. It was too much. Kate squeezed her eyes shut, and the pain that was too much pleasure fountained up inside her, and she knew that he watched her face and that this was what he had wanted to see. And when he bent and kissed her with a mouth more fierce. than she had ever felt before, she knew that the sight was too much even for him. She laced her fingers blindly in his hair, and held his head, and opened her mouth wider and wider under his, begging for every ounce of his passion, begging him to do to her everything that he wanted to do to her.

His khaki shirt and shorts were gritty with dust from the site, and the scent of his flesh was a man-smell of work and passion that went to her head like fierce wine. She wanted him to be a man; she wanted to feel her femininity defined against him, hard and relentless and demanding where she was soft and yielding and demanding.

Always demanding. As the flames that were her flesh burned higher, she pushed at the rough clothes that kept his flesh from hers, making him take them off, wanting only the roughness of his skin, now, the masculine roughness of hair-covered skin against her breasts and arms and legs . . . and stomach.

The touch of him against her stomach, hard as she could never be hard, was like fuel poured onto her flames, and as that hardness pressed into her, soft as he could never be soft, she sent up a small cry of worship to those gods who had made the word flesh.

Enclosed at last by the flames of her flesh, Andreas went still, looking down at her with eyes that blazed with his own passionate fire, letting her see in that look how desperately he had needed this touch, the touch of her softness enclosing him; showing her in the torment of his pleasure how much he had feared never to feel it again.

And now the fire blazed up into her brain, as he

moved in her and watched the reflection of it in her face, heard it in the wordless cry of protest that was a kind of disbelief that flames could burn so high, or flesh be so much pleasure. He moved in her, watching it in her face, again, and again, till she was gasping and crying in the heat of an unbearable passion, the burning of a need that was torment, and he himself was blind in the fire.

The fire and the heat enclosed her brain then, and burned her mind to blackness, and in the blackness there was nothing but the knowledge of Andreas; and she was Woman and he was Man; and then they were both, and neither; they were all things and nothing, and at last, they were One.

The oneness exploded simultaneously in her brain and her body, his brain and his body, the ecstasy of union bursting into a million splinters that travelled through the universe like the stars of a new constellation in a dimension that only they could ever know, or explore.

"Kate," breathed Andreas, in a voice that she would always love. "Kate." And there had never been anything as sweet as the sweetness that flooded them now.

"I prayed that you would come back to me," he told her softly, later, much later, when the room was in darkness lighted only by the warm glow of the bedside lamp. "I prayed to every god that ever was, the Mother Goddess, the Sky God, and all the gods of the earth and trees and water whose names I could remember. I didn't think you would come back, but I prayed all the same."

It was in his voice, the pain that he did not put into words. She said, "Why did you think I wouldn't come back?"

"I told you I loved you, and you walked away from me. If you did not want that, what could bring you back to me? There was nothing else I had to offer."

"I'm sorry," she said. "I would have been here sooner, but the planes were full."

"Oh," he said, as though it meant something, hearing that.

"I tried to come back the day after I arrived in Athens. Sunday. I couldn't get a seat till Wednesday. And then I had to spend the night in Alexandroúpolis, of course."

He said only, "I wish I had known."

"If I had known that you still wanted me, I'd have tried to phone, tried to get a message through somehow, but what could I have done? Called the hotel and asked the receptionist to tell you, if he happened to run into you? Anyway, I was scared."

"Scared of what?"

She propped herself up on one elbow. "Scared you'd forbid me to come or something. And what could I have done then? If I just came, I thought I'd have a better chance with you; I thought at least I'd have the chance to fight for you."

He laughed at that. "Fight? Fight whom?"

She curled a lock of his dark hair around her forefinger, marvelling at the rich texture of it. She said, "Do you—why did you kiss Sarah, Andrea? I mean—"

She broke off. He took a deep breath, and his eyes ran over her face as though searching for something. After a moment, he said, "Didn't you ever fall in love, when you were a teenager, with somebody who was unsuitable?"

She shook her head. "Not that I remember. Nothing painful, if that's what you mean."

"I did. I fell desperately in love with the wife of one of my mother's associates. She was very beautiful, very womanly. Everything she did seemed sexual to me. For six months I was crazy. I couldn't work; I couldn't study; I could only think about her. I knew it was hopeless. She must have been nearly twice my age; she was happily married. But I couldn't get her out of my mind.

"I used to think, If only I could kiss her, just kiss her once, tell her how I felt, it would leave me; it wouldn't be so awful. But I never could. She probably would have understood, but society wouldn't let her allow such a thing to happen. I knew it. I knew that even if she would let me kiss her, society wouldn't let her let me, if you know what I mean."

"Yes."

"It was hopeless. So all I could do was wait, try to live through it. Sometimes I was afraid it would never go away. It was terrible; it was wonderful and terrible at the same time." He reached up and touched her face. "Like loving you." He smiled briefly. "Wonderful and terrible at the same time.

"So I saw Sarah, what she felt for me. I knew it; everybody knew it. When it happens to you at that age, you don't have any way to hide it, it's so new to you. But this time, I was in control, and I don't care what society will let me do or not do." He moved his shoulder. "Anyway, it's different. A young girl and an older man, society doesn't mind this.

"Sarah came to me that afternoon, when I was working in the office. I didn't know you were there, but it wouldn't have changed anything if I had. It wasn't anything to make you jealous. She spoke to me; she said she knew I didn't love her, but if I would let her, she would just like to tell me how she felt, that she loved me. And I was looking at her and seeing myself, and I thought if I let her do this, she'll be free of this terrible crush; she'll be able to forget about it, the way I wanted to. And I said that I would listen to her, and that I understood.

"When she told me, she cried, and then she asked if she could ask one more thing, and the one more thing was a kiss, and she promised to read nothing into it and never to ask again. So I kissed her, because I understood, and I made it a good kiss, Kate, because a friendly kiss wasn't what she wanted. I kissed her the way I wanted that man's wife to kiss me when I was seventeen, and in a way, I even felt as though that woman had kissed me.

"And then you were suddenly standing there, and Sarah whispered something, thank you or something, and when I looked up again you were waving and walking out the door. I didn't think anything of it. I thought you were going somewhere, to the cooktent, the toilets, I didn't know; and then Sarah left and I heard your scooter start up. And that's the first moment I even thought of how it might have looked to you. Even then, I didn't believe it. But when you didn't come back, I came after you."

"I'm sorry," she said. "I'd been trying hard not to be in love with you, and when I saw you with Sarah there was no way to pretend anymore."

He stroked her arm. "Why didn't you want to be in love with me? You knew I was in love with you."

He had certainly told her so in every way except with words. "Well, that scared me, too; I guess I was running from that, too."

"Why? For God's sake, Kate, love is all there is in the world. And most people don't get it. We are the lucky ones."

"I know. I do know." She bent and kissed him, because of their incredible luck. "But you're so masculine, Andrea. You have so much passion."

He laughed. "That's funny, coming from you. I never met a woman of such passion as you."

She bent and kissed him. "Do you know about Takkis and your cousin Sophia?" she asked.

"Yes. Takkis is a fool. Like too many men."

She said, "But you said something to me once that made me think you might be like him. You said, 'A man loves a woman because she is young and beautiful.'"

"Never," said Andreas flatly. "I would never say this; it's ridiculous."

"Don't you remember? You were asking me why I left my husband, and you said—"

"I said that many men marry a woman for this reason," he said, remembering suddenly. "But not me! I told you that I find beautiful what I love. I remember this very clearly. Isn't this what I said?"

"Yes, but . . ."

"Anyway, you are beautiful, much more beautiful than Sarah, so why were you worried?" He kissed her and laughed. "And you will be a very beautiful old woman; your eyes will still flash with intelligence and anger and make me crazy to make love to you."

"I know how you'll look when you're old. You'll still be virile when you're ninety." She bent down and kissed him again, and closed her eyes as he held her head and trailed kisses across her eyelids and cheek and lips.

"And does that frighten you?" he asked as she lifted her chin and his mouth found her throat. "Is that why you were running away from me?"

It was, but it seemed foolish now. She said, "You aren't a male chauvinist, are you." And it wasn't a question, it was a statement of fact, because she was sure now.

"No," he said. "I don't think so. I always wanted a woman to be a partner, my equal. I wanted my marriage to be interesting, not just sex and nothing else. I always wanted someone with a brain like mine, not someone stupidly admiring, like the wives my friends chose, or worse still, pretending stupidity. I like women; I like to be with them. You are the most intelligent woman I ever knew. Like my mother. You and my mother will get on very well."

He bent and kissed her, and deliberately she traced her tongue over his lips. In retaliation, he slipped her little finger into his mouth and nipped the end of it. "You are also the sexiest, most passionate and most beautiful."

"Only with you," she said, bending to kiss him and feeling the sweetness start in her as his hand involuntarily closed over her breast. "Hold me," she whispered. "Love me."

He cupped her head and pulled it down to his gentle lips. "But you thought I was a male chauvinist?" he asked in surprise. "Why?" He was kissing her eyelids, her cheeks, the corner of her mouth, and his voice was lazy with passion when he said her name.

When he drew her down beside him and leaned on an elbow over her, she said, "There'll be time for explanations, won't there?"

"All the time in the world," agreed Andreas, and his lips brushed her throat, and then her mouth again, in a way that made her breath quiver and her womb sing, and he began to make love to her again. "All the time there is."

Two hours later, as they lay lazily entangled, talking a little, almost asleep, he said suddenly, "Good God, I'm picking up these people for dinner! What time is it?" He reached for his wristwatch, which had somehow found its way to the bedside table, with the arm that lay under her, and held it up for her to read.

"Nine o'clock," she read. "What people? Your money-men? Are they staying in the hotel?"

"My money-men, yes. And yes, they are." He was slowly disentangling himself from her, sitting up. "It's important; I think tonight they are going to tell me about the financing." He rubbed his head and reached for the phone. After a moment he spoke into it in Greek; then after another short wait, he began to speak in English.

"Harold?" he said. "Andreas here. Look, I'm a little late tonight. Can I pick you up in forty-five minutes? Yes, fine. No, no problem, Harold, my fiancée has finally arrived. I've been expecting her." He looked up and smiled. "No, only from Athens. Yes, of course, if you would like to meet her; I don't think she'll be too tired." He raised his brows enquiringly at her, and she nodded agreement. She wasn't missing the money-men, if she could help it. "Yes, she'll come. All right, then, yes, ten o'clock might be better."

"Do you want to shower here first?" Kate asked when he had stood up. Rudimentary showers had been set up at the dig, but from all reports they were temperamental, at best. "Then you'll only have to grab your clothes up there."

"Wait a minute!" Andreas said suddenly. "Didn't I leave some clothes in your closet before? I had some shorts, a couple of shirts, didn't I? What happened to them when you left?"

"I left them in a parcel for you at the reception desk," she said. "Didn't they tell you?"

"Maybe he said something to me when he told me you checked out, I wasn't listening very closely after he said you'd gone." He reached for the phone again and spoke in Greek, and a few minutes later the parcel she had packed with such cold hopelessness in her heart was delivered to the door.

"There," said Andreas with satisfaction, pulling her down against him on the bed. "Now we have half an hour to make love and twenty minutes to get dressed."

"I hope you aren't expecting to get the shower first, then," she told him.

"Twenty minutes to make love," Andreas amended. "Half an hour to get dressed."

Harold Cadbury was the director of a fund that had been set up under the terms of the will of a wealthy businessman who had come to culture late in life. Gerald Towne was his assistant. They were well aware of the power the dead man's money gave them, but otherwise pleasant, and they started the evening by recognizing Kate's name.

"Yes, I read a review of your latest book not too many months ago," Harold said. "Unfortunately for me, the fund gives grants to authors, and I have to read so many books in my job that I do very little reading for my own pleasure. Now that I've met you, of course, I'll make a point of reading it."

"Thank you," said Kate. "I hope you find it interesting."

Harold laughed. "You're being modest. It was a very angry review that I read, if I recall. So I'm sure 'interesting' will be the least of it. Are you working on another book at the moment?"

They discussed the theme of her new book, and Harold and Gerald were both duly impressed by the information that there had been a time in the world when there had been equality between women and men. "So you're here at Neathera in a professional capacity as well as a personal one," Harold said. "Well, I'm sure you'll be very interested in what I have to say to your fiancé." He smiled. "I wanted to let you know, Andrea, that I'm placing a very strong recommendation before my board that we extend your financing for the remainder of the current season and commit for a full season next year. Then an ongoing commitment, to be reviewed annually with regard to need and progress."

Andreas and Harold went on to discuss the details of this season's funding, while Gerald informed Kate quietly that the committee's vote would be a mere rubber-stamping of Harold's recommendation.

"I see," said Kate, sending a smile across the table to Andreas, because a no vote tonight would have meant packing up in a little over two weeks and beginning the harrowing process of finding funding for next year all over again. And nobody knew what might happen to the site once it was abandoned without a guard. The archaeological black market was a going concern in Greece, and even if robbers found nothing of value, they might have left the site ruined for any archaeological purposes.

He smiled back, and she wondered if he would always have the power to make the world disappear. She had opened her mouth to say "I love you" when Gerald's voice sounded in her ears. "It's rather pleasant here, isn't it?" he said.

They were sitting outdoors at a restaurant just across the road from the sea, not far from the ferry dock. There was a small, cooling breeze, and the stars were bright. The food was very Greek, and very good.

"Yes," Kate agreed. "It's a lovely island."

"Backward, of course, very backward," said Gerald.

"Lovely to know there's still somewhere on earth with no hamburger stands and no Coca-Cola signs, isn't it?" She smiled.

"The service is poor, though," said Gerald, just as

though she hadn't spoken. "We've run out of hot water at the hotel several times. Well"—in a tolerant voice—"we're a long way from New York, that's for sure."

Kate felt her eyes glazing over. "You must have been quite thrilled by Neathera. I understand there was an important find while I was away."

"Oh, yes. Yes, it was very exciting," he said, in the tone of voice of a man who has been intolerably bored and thinks he is hiding it well. "Your fiancé is a very astute man. Very intelligent."

"Yes, he'll be very glad to be able to go on excavating. It's a very interesting site, isn't it?"

"I don't know much about the ancient world, myself," said Gerald unapologetically. "I prefer this century. Nobody's ever progressed the way we have this century."

She looked at him, wondering whether to bother.

"This is the century that matters. Give me flush toilets and hot baths any day over some old temple or piece of pottery. That's the kind of stuff that matters. Anybody can make a bowl."

"You are aware, I suppose, that the Cretan civilisation had flush toilets and hot baths and an extremely advanced drainage system three thousand five hundred years ago? And all that without industrial pollution."

He looked at her. "Really?" She nodded. He shrugged. "Yeah, well, where are they today?" Gerald laughed at his own joke.

"They did last several hundred years at their peak. Their civilisation was destroyed by a natural disaster—earthquake and tidal waves when a neighbouring island sank. That's the island which Andreas believes—"

"So if they were so great, how come they couldn't plan for that? Take precautions?"

Kate shook her head. "And what will they

say about America when she is destroyed by atom bombs?" she wondered, half to herself.

He sobered a little. "Well, that's not going to happen."

"If it doesn't, will it be luck, or planning?"

"Say," he said suspiciously, "are you—"

At that moment, to her relief, they were interrupted by the arrival of the meal, which came in the Greek manner, all at once—salad, bread, main course, side dishes and wine. Harold and Andreas had finished their discussion, and the conversation became general and much more pleasant. Harold was a great deal less insular than Gerald, and more interesting, and Kate could not for the life of her imagine why he had Gerald as his assistant.

"It's a good thing the food came when it did," she told Andreas later as they walked home under the stars. "You might have lost your financing after all. I was about ready to clout that man."

Andreas laughed. "You are very impatient with people who are not as intelligent as you."

"Is that what it is? Intelligence?" she asked. "I would have said imagination. He seemed totally lacking in imagination. And that does make me impatient."

"I suppose it depends on whether imagination is a function of intelligence."

"I suppose it does. What do you do, to keep your patience, I mean? He said just as many fatuous things to you, and you didn't even raise your eyebrows. I was watching."

"When I looked at you, you made me want to laugh. So I had to be very strict with myself. It's something you learn in a profession like mine, where you deal with fools often. Patience. Probably you don't need it so much as a writer."

He had a point there. She said, "I won't be much of an asset to your career, will I? You'll be much more of an asset to mine, really. Half my book is going to be stuff you put me on to."

He smiled down at her in the soft light of the distant streetlamp and the stars. "Do you know that 'asset' is a term for property? Perhaps we should not use it with regard to each other, eh? You will make me happy, Kate. My career can take care of itself."

She wrapped both arms around his arm and stopped him where he stood. "Then will you marry me, Andrea?"

He laughed as though something delighted him, but it was too dark to read his face. "Do you love me, Kate?" he asked, as though he really did not know.

"Yes, I love you, I'll always love you. There'll never be another man for me."

He looked into her eyes with a warm and lazy look that pierced her with sweetness. "I have been waiting for you to ask me this question since the day I came to see you at my cousin's apartment," he said, with a tiny lift to the corner of his mouth. "You were a long time, eh?"

"That day? You were screaming mad that day, and don't try to deny it." She kissed him. "You haven't answered my question."

"I was angry, yes, but when I said to you, what's your price, what do you want, I had a sudden crazy feeling that even if you said, I want you to marry me, I would agree to it."

"I see," she said disbelievingly. "Do you think you might put me out of my misery with an ans—"

"I am an instinctive archaeologist," he said. "Do you know what that means?"

"No."

"It means, I sometimes know where is the best place

to dig without any reason. I just feel, dig here. That is how we found the altar. I knew somehow that one of the squares we were not digging had to be dug. And there it was."

"This is a fascinating digression. I'm about to withdraw my proposal, however."

"Later I knew I had had it that day with you. The feeling, I mean. I was just too mad to understand it at the time. You can't withdraw your proposal till I have answered it. It's against the rules."

"Ten . . . nine . . . eight . . . sev—"

"You see, that's women for you. Always changing the rules to suit themselves."

"Five . . . four . . ."

"Yes, of course I'm going to marry you. What do you think?" He wrapped his arms around her and kissed her long and thoroughly. "Now, I have a question to ask you. Will you marry me, Kate?"

"Yes, I will. You see? I don't make you suffer at all."

He looked at her. "Yes, you make me suffer," he said softly. "Every minute I look at you when I can't touch you, I suffer. Every time you smile at me like this and I'm not inside you, my heart aches." She gasped with the sudden hollowness in her stomach, and his hold tightened. "I love you, Kate. I know it's hard for women in marriage. I know what can happen. I promise you, I'll never ask you to be what you don't want to be. I want you always the way you are—free and equal, the way I saw you the first night we had together—as proud as a priestess of the Mother Goddess."

She felt tears of happiness in her eyes as he bent and kissed her, and as they turned for home again, she sent up a silent prayer, and a vow that tomorrow she would take some wine to the ancient shrine, and pour a libation of thanks to the Mother.

READERS' COMMENTS ON SILHOUETTE INTIMATE MOMENTS:

"About a month ago a friend loaned me my first Silhouette. I was thoroughly surprised as well as totally addicted. Last week I read a Silhouette Intimate Moments and I was even more pleased. They are the best romance series novels I have ever read. They give much more depth to the plot, characters, and the story is fundamentally realistic. They incorporate tasteful sex scenes, which is a must, especially in the 1980's. I only hope you can publish them fast enough."

S.B.*, Lees Summit, MO

"After noticing the attractive covers on the new line of Silhouette Intimate Moments, I decided to read the inside and discovered that this new line was more in the line of books that I like to read. I do want to say I enjoyed the books because they are so realistic and a lot more truthful than so many romance books today."

J.C., Onekama, MI

"I would like to compliment you on your books. I will continue to purchase all of the Silhouette Intimate Moments. They are your best line of books that I have had the pleasure of reading."

S.M., Billings, MT

*names available on request

READERS' COMMENTS ON SILHOUETTE SPECIAL EDITIONS:

"I just finished reading the first six Silhouette Special Edition Books and I had to take the opportunity to write you and tell you how much I enjoyed them. I enjoyed all the authors in this series. Best wishes on your Silhouette Special Editions line and many thanks."

—B.H.*, Jackson, OH

"The Special Editions are really special and I enjoyed them very much! I am looking forward to next month's books."

—R.M.W.*, Melbourne, FL

"I've just finished reading four of your first six Special Editions and I enjoyed them very much. I like the more sensual detail and longer stories. I will look forward each month to your new Special Editions."

—L.S.*, Visalia, CA

"Silhouette Special Editions are — 1.) Superb! 2.) Great! 3.) Delicious! 4.) Fantastic! . . . Did I leave anything out? These are books that an adult woman can read . . . I love them!"

—H.C.*, Monterey Park, CA

*names available on request

Silhouette Intimate Moments

COMING NEXT MONTH

MIDSUMMER MIDNIGHT
Parris Afton Bonds
Damon was a freedom fighter committed to a revolutionary ideal; Sigourney was a journalist who dreaded war. For Damon she would overcome that fear and stand by him...if only he would ask.

BOUNDARY LINES
Nora Roberts
Aaron was a Murdock. Jillian Baron had been taught never to trust a Murdock, but when rustlers began to endanger her family ranch, it looked like she would have no choice.

NINA'S SONG
Anna James
Ambition had driven Nina and Alex apart ten years before. Now fate was bringing them together again. He had the words, she the music; perhaps this time they could be united in perfect harmony.

STAR RISE
Pat Wallace
Dreams can be very fragile. Lt. Col. Mike Nesbitt held Lisa Heron's dream of the stars in the palm of his hand. What choice did she have but to trust him to handle her with care?

AVAILABLE NOW:

VALLEY OF THE SUN
Elizabeth Lowell

SOFT TOUCH
Möeth Allison

THE MALE CHAUVINIST
Alexandra Sellers

TIGER PRINCE
Erin St. Claire